THE TIME KEEPERS

PRAISE FOR THE WORKS OF ALYSON RICHMAN

THE TIME KEEPERS

"Once again, Alyson Richman entrances the reader with her signature lyrical prose and captivating storyline. Powerfully humanizing various perspectives of the Vietnam War, *The Time Keepers* interweaves the journeys of a wonderfully diverse cast." —Kristina McMorris, *New York Times* bestselling author of *Sold on a Monday*

"*The Time Keepers* holds so much power. It has the power to stop a bitter word on the very tip of your tongue.... And like any truly great book, it has the power to bridge divides, to remind readers of the redemptive power of love and forgiveness, and to heal." —Katherine J. Chen, author of *Mary B: An Untold Story of Pride and Prejudice*

"A powerful and emotional saga, woven with themes of love and compassion.... This novel will make your heart soar." —Sofia Lundberg, international bestselling author of *The Red Address Book*

"A powerful story of longing, the pain of war, and the transformative effects of friendship. The hands of time may always move forward but Richman deftly reveals how a constant pull between past and present can co-exist in our hearts." —Marjan Kamali, bestselling author of *The Stationery Shop*

"An astounding novel of unlikely friendships and true love gone awry.... Once again, Richman's brilliant storytelling doesn't just immerse us in the past, it tells us how to live with grace and bravery today." —Ariel Djanikian, author of Barnes & Noble Bookclub Pick *The Prospectors*

THE SECRET OF CLOUDS

"A riveting tale that explores the bond between an isolated student and his connection to the outside world: his tutor." —*InStyle*

"An exquisite story. . . . Richman's great strength in designing the emotional ebb and flow of her engaging narrative should win accolades and a heap of new readers." —*Washington Independent Review of Books*

"A story of family bonds, heartbreak, healing, and hope. . . . The tenderly written ending will bring you to tears, but in the best possible way." —Lisa Wingate, *New York Times* bestselling author of *Before We Were Yours*

"A tender, captivating, and ultimately satisfying story. . . . Thank you, Alyson Richman, for another heartrending tale." —Jamie Ford, *New York Times* bestselling author of *Hotel on the Corner of Bitter and Sweet*

THE VELVET HOURS

"Richman's writing sings. . . . A beautiful and compelling portrait of two women facing their unknown past and an unimaginable future as their world begins to crumble." —Kristin Hannah, *New York Times* bestselling author of *The Women*

"Richman fills her novel with vibrant details, much as Marthe decorated her apartment: always with care, craft, and a sharp eye." —*Publishers Weekly* (starred review)

"A love letter to the stories we tell and the stories we keep. . . . Imaginative, rich, and emotionally satisfying, *The Velvet Hours* is a treasure." —Jewish Book Council

THE LOST WIFE

"Staggeringly evocative, romantic, heart-rending, sensual, and beautifully written. . . . [It] may very well be the *Sophie's Choice* of this generation." —John Lescroart, *New York Times* bestselling author of *The Missing Piece*

"One of the best. The horrors of war serve as the backdrop to a love affair that spans a lifetime, and that love story stayed with me long after I put down the book." —Lauren Weisberger, *New York Times* bestselling author of *When Life Gives You Lululemons*

THE TIME KEEPERS

ALYSON RICHMAN

UNION SQUARE & CO.

NEW YORK

**UNION
SQUARE
& CO.**

NEW YORK

UNION SQUARE & CO. and the distinctive Union Square & Co. logo
are trademarks of Sterling Publishing Co., Inc.

Union Square & Co., LLC, is a subsidiary of Sterling Publishing Co., Inc.

ISBN 978-1-4549-5323-4
ISBN 978-1-4549-5324-1 (e-book)

Library of Congress Control Number: 2024012316
Library of Congress Cataloging-in-Publication Data is available upon request.

For information about custom editions, special sales, and premium purchases,
please contact specialsales@unionsquareandco.com.

Printed in Canada

2 4 6 8 10 9 7 5 3 1

unionsquareandco.com

Cover design by Jared Oriel
Cover art © Elisabeth Ansley/Trevillion Images (hands);
arteria.lab/Shutterstock.com (background)
Interior design by Kevin Ullrich

For Pete

THE TIME KEEPERS

PROLOGUE

Vietnam, 1978

THEY HAVE BEEN WAITING ALL NIGHT BY THE RIVER, THE DARK water smooth as glass. They carry nothing but a bundle filled with food and canteens of fresh water all tied in a square piece of cloth. A single tin pot. A sack of lemons and a box of sugar.

The boat is late. The children are hungry. The men and women who are with them are standing still as trees.

The moon cuts through the darkness like a scythe. As they wait, looking for the boat they were promised, the tide inches closer to their silhouettes. They walk backward, retreating into the marsh, tall spears of reeds behind them. The cicadas loud in the wet grass.

It is the youngest boy who first sees the flash of light. A small beacon from a torch pulsating atop the head of the fisherman.

They walk into the river. Treading past the water hyacinth, a mass of green leaves and singular pink flowers. First, ankle-deep. Then, knee-deep. Finally, waist-deep. The children are afraid. Seaweed wraps around their legs, pulling them down. Still, they inch toward the boat. The weight of the river slowing them with each step until there is no sand or silt beneath their feet.

They reach their arms up toward the boat. The current flows against them. In the shadow of the ship's hull, they see a woman extending her hand. A rope is thrown out to reach them, curling first on the surface of the water before sinking down.

PART I

CHAPTER 1

Long Island, 1979

GRACE GOLDEN WOULD NEVER KNOW WHY, ON THAT SUNNY afternoon in late May, she had chosen to walk down Gypsum Street after Mass instead of her usual route to the grocery store. Maple Avenue had always been the fastest way from Saint Bartholomew's to Kepler's Market.

Her husband, Tom, believed Grace picked Gypsum Street because the cherry blossoms there were at their peak. That was the thing about his wife, he explained. She'd always go out of her way to encounter something beautiful. But neither of them could have anticipated on that fine spring day, as Grace's heels rhythmically struck the sidewalk, her shopping list tucked inside her leather purse, that she would notice a little boy curled up against the side of a building. Sleeping on the hard cement, his body was tucked so tightly, he reminded Grace of a small whelk nestled into its shell.

She stopped and hovered over him. Then she leaned down to nudge him.

"Are you lost, love?" The lilt of her Irish accent, still detectable after years of living in New York, floated through the air. "Let me help you up," she offered her hand.

But the boy remained fixed in a fetal position, his arms locked even tighter around himself and his feet inched closer to his bottom. One of his tennis shoes had a hole in its rubber sole. The other was missing its laces.

She still could not see his face, only the tiny edge of his ear and the shock of straight black hair.

"Please."

His head rose slightly, revealing his dark eyes, heart-shaped lips, and small nose.

It was the face of a child, frightened and alone.

CHAPTER 2

"I'M GRACE." SHE OFFERED HER NAME, HOPING HE'D ALSO SHARE his. But he remained silent. His body fixed to the sidewalk, still as a stone.

She unlatched the clasp of her handbag and pulled out a candy wrapped in shiny silver foil.

He studied her, then cautiously accepted the sweet. Grace took another piece from her purse and unwrapped it, placing the small chocolate in her mouth.

She looked around to see if she could spot anyone searching for a lost child or if a policeman was patrolling nearby. But Grace saw no one.

"Are you lost? Why don't you come with me," she said as she reached her hand out and guided the boy up from the ground.

He found his footing and now stood before Grace, but his eyes still avoided hers. His pants were too short, exposing his thin ankles, and the Incredible Hulk decal on his T-shirt was peeling. But Grace's hand remained open, and eventually his fingers found their way into her own.

The warm touch of a child's hand was instantly familiar to her. But through his grasp, she also felt his fear. The skin was clammy. The fingers were slippery.

He walked beside her, his hand fidgeting against her own. Every few minutes, she turned to catch a glimpse of him sideways: the bony limbs, the long lashes, the angular eyes. She estimated he might be around ten years old, close to the age of her younger daughter, Molly.

She did not stop at Kepler's to pick up the eggs and milk and the various other provisions on her shopping list. Instead, she gripped his hand tighter, not even noticing the cherry blossom petals falling on their shoulders and hair.

A few blocks from home, she saw Adele Flynn walking toward her car.

"Grace?" Adele paused for a moment, her keys in one hand. "Is everything all right?" Her eyes scanned the boy with the worn clothes, the foreign face, and the averted gaze walking next to her friend.

Grace did not stop to chat. "Everything's fine!" she hollered over her shoulder, ignoring Adele's look of confusion as she led the boy toward her home.

Once there, she opened the front gate and walked past the rose-bushes that grew exuberantly along the short path to her house. The child hesitated when they reached the front steps. He let go of her hand.

"Don't worry," she reassured him. "I'm going to make a call." She pretended with her fingers to make a telephone to her ear. "We'll get you home."

She turned the doorknob and walked inside, the boy silent beside her.

"I'm back," she announced, laying her bag on the sideboard. Her eyes fell upon Molly's shoes by the stairwell and the girls' coats on the floor, their sleeves carelessly inverted. Then to Katie's backpack spilling out papers and brightly colored folders. The house bloomed with children.

For a split second, Grace tried to reconcile the reality of her household with the fact that she had brought a complete stranger into it.

"You're home?" She heard Molly's voice ring through the air before the girl bounded down the stairs, and her face immediately revealed her bewilderment.

"Mommy?" Her eyes were fixed on the strange boy next to her mother. "I thought you were going to Kepler's. . . ."

Before Grace could answer, she turned and caught the reflection of her and the child in the large oval mirror beside the door.

He was shaking.

Tom was down in the basement with his ear pressed to an old wall clock that needed tuning when his wife returned. He stopped the pendulum with his finger and went to greet her.

Walking up the basement stairs, he pushed through the stiffness in his bad leg, gripping the banister tightly with each step. In the vestibule, he found Molly at the base of the stairwell, staring wide-eyed at a little boy standing beside his wife.

"Gracie?" Tom stepped closer. The faded image of the Hulk on the boy's orange T-shirt seemed ironic; the boy's arms were the width of a pine sapling.

"I found him curled up sleeping in a corner near Maple Avenue. I didn't know what to do."

Tom crouched down. "What's your name, little fella?"

The boy shifted his weight from one foot to the other but still didn't answer.

"We'll have to call the police, Grace. Somebody out there has to be looking for him."

"I know. I just thought it would be better to make the call from home. Not at Kepler's, with everyone staring at us."

"Want to wash up?" Grace made a simple pantomime of rubbing her hands together, then pointed toward the powder room.

He lifted his arm to move the hair out of his eyes, and that's when she observed the scar on his left wrist. The shape of an open mouth, like someone had bitten him.

The boy noticed Grace staring at the old wound and covered it with his hand.

She opened the door to the bathroom and then went into the kitchen to call the police.

CHAPTER 3

THE POLICEMAN ON THE OTHER END OF THE LINE PRESSED Grace for more details.

"Can we have a physical description? We'll need to look into if the child's been reported missing."

"He's maybe four foot three . . . and he's quite skinny with dark eyes and straight black hair. Asian. He's wearing an Incredible Hulk T-shirt and tennis shoes . . . if anyone's reported a boy missing who's wearing that . . ."

"You'll have to bring him down to the precinct," the officer instructed, his voice was flat and detached.

"I'd like to feed him before I bring him to you. I don't know when he last ate, and I'd hate to him to go so long without a meal."

"Fine. But bring him in as soon as you can."

Tom rubbed her back as they waited for him to emerge from the washroom. "I bet his mother is worried sick."

But something struck Grace as not being quite right. The scar on the boy's wrist was still troubling her.

"He's so little, Tom. He looks the same age as Molly—can you imagine her all alone out there like that?"

"No, I can't."

After a few minutes, the door unlocked, and the boy came out. The smudges on his face erased, his hair pushed out of his eyes.

"Are you hungry?" Grace tapped her belly.

He nodded and followed her toward the kitchen.

* * *

She made him scrambled eggs and a cup of warm black tea. It was something her own mother would have made her back in Ireland when she wasn't feeling well or needed something mild to fill her stomach.

"This might be easier." She reached into the drawer, replacing the fork she'd given him with a spoon. He took it and began shoveling the eggs into his mouth.

Grace glanced at her watch. Katie would be home from her friend's house any minute now, and then she could leave the girls alone and go with Tom to the police station.

She was just putting the dishes away when Katie walked through the side door and went straight to the fridge, grabbing a Tupperware of cantaloupe from the shelf. Only when Katie turned around did she see the boy sitting at the table. "Who's that, Mom?" she asked, raising a single downy eyebrow.

"A little boy . . ."

"I get that, but . . ."

"I found him alone this morning. . . ." She tried to find the right words to explain the situation. It seemed incredible to Grace that she could discover what looked to be a homeless child on the streets of Bellegrove. "Katie, we don't know all the facts yet, but I think he's lost."

"Lost? He looks like he's a long way from home, Mom."

Grace gave her daughter a disapproving look, then untied the strings of her apron and called out to Tom.

"Honey, get your keys. We're ready to go to the station now."

The Goldens' station wagon sagged from years of good use. It had shuttled Grace to her doctor appointments each time she was pregnant. It had withstood constant abuse from the girls eating crackers in their car seats, the windows smeared with drawings by sticky fingers, and the occasional bout of car sickness. Its trunk had been filled with countless suitcases and overnight bags for family vacations and sleepovers and brown paper grocery bags that over time could have sustained an army. Grace liked to think of the old Pontiac Catalina as their own little boat that could ferry the family anywhere, always ensuring their safety. It wasn't fancy like some of their neighbors' Oldsmobiles or Lincolns, but it was dependable and trustworthy, something Grace valued not just in her choice of cars, but the people she surrounded herself with, too.

When Grace opened the door so the little boy could get inside, he hesitated. The back seat, which never felt big enough for her two girls who were prone to pinching each other and bickering, seemed like it could swallow him whole.

"Would you like me to sit in the back with you?"

The boy stood quiet. So Grace slid in first, moving toward the window on the other side, one hand smoothing down the front of her dress and the other extending to draw him in.

Tom opened the front door and settled into the front seat, checking on both of them in his rearview mirror before he pulled out of the driveway.

"How 'bout some music?"

"Not now, Tom."

She glanced over at the child, who was now staring out the window as they passed by a row of houses with white picket fences and manicured lawns before his eyes focused on a swath of dark clouds forming in the distance. He wore an expression that was all too familiar for her. One that could take over her as well—most often when the sky turned gray and the rain came down in heavy sheets. The bright flowers outside her front door could evaporate in an instant, and her mind pulled her back to her village across the ocean.

CHAPTER 4

IN THE BACK SEAT OF THE CAR, THE LEATHER UPHOLSTERY sticky beneath her, Grace tried to push thoughts from her own childhood away.

Everyone had hidden pain. At least that was what Grace told herself on those particularly rainy days when she drove past the river near her daughters' school and water spilled over the embankment and flooded the roads. The river's flooding always stirred a deep melancholy inside her, its strong current drawing her back to her village on Ireland's western shore. Even after nearly twenty years in America, she still felt the dark pull of the water. Like a ghost that lived deep within her bones.

Her father had been a fisherman, just as her grandfather and his father before him had been. On the nights when he left home to take his boat out into the ocean, he would cup Grace's face in his large palms and bring his lips to her forehead, kissing her and her younger sister, Bridey, as though each time might be the last.

Even after all these years on Long Island, there were nights when Grace lay in bed and she could still conjure up the sensation of her father's hands against her cheeks, their texture rough from a lifetime of pulling up ropes and casting nets into the sea. She had charted those lines on his palms time and again, her father telling her they were a map that would always bring him back home.

She had held her sister's hand that day in early June, when the sun sparkled over the glen, pulling sheets of golden light over the grass.

They were happy to leave behind their crowded home, attached to a row of others, and escape the mothers pinning clothes on laundry lines and chastising them for being too loud.

Her four-year-old sister had raced beside Grace to go meet the bakery van as it drove through the streets. Bridey was laughing with her head thrown back, the skirt of her cotton dress dancing in the wind. At her ankles, the family's new puppy, with its soft coat, trailed beside her.

Grace had just paid for two iced buns when she noticed her sister was no longer next to her. Neither was the puppy. Grace assumed her sister had just lost herself in the familiar grounds of the village center. Children all roamed freely back then. The streets were full of boys playing with balls and girls jumping on hopscotch squares.

Eager to finish her sweet, Grace found some shade under one of the willow trees near the old church. She licked her fingers clean from the sugary glaze. She took off her shoes and wiggled her toe out of the hole in her white sock.

When Carol O'Reilly asked her if she wanted to come play with her, she followed happily into the meadow, where she and three other girls climbed trees and pretended to be fairies, weaving wild daisies and wisps of heather into garlands for their hair and using long sticks as magic wands.

Their fantasy world overtook them, and the girls soon retreated into the green terraced hills farther beyond the village. There, the flowers were even more bountiful, and the girls picked them by the fistful, stuffing them into their dress pockets and twirling until they fell breathless to the ground. Grace even discovered a long, narrow gull bone, bleached white from the sun, and lifted it toward her friend, like a queen.

It would be several hours later, after she wandered back toward her house, tired and with her imaginary scepter still clasped in her hand, that she ran into one of the men in the village.

"Hurry home," he bluntly informed her. "Your mother thinks she's lost two children in the river today. It'll be a blessing to learn it was only the one."

Grace hadn't gone home straight away. Instead, she went down to the river to prove what the man had told her wasn't true. There was even part of her that thought her white gull bone could resurrect her sister. But when she arrived, she saw a group of men standing over the rocks, her sister's body covered by her father's raincoat. Patrick McKinley's large arm was wrapped around her father, whose eyes were fixed on Bridey beneath his dark jacket. His head lowered, his expression melting beneath his tears.

Grace threw the useless bone to the ground and ran all the way home.

Because she had died by drowning, the neighbors all called Bridey's death a *pisough,* a bad omen. For several hours, not a single neighbor volunteered their home for the wake. Afraid of bringing tragedy upon their own families, people would only express how sorry they were for the family's terrible loss.

As the sun began to set, her father had stayed by the river, refusing to leave Bridey's side until someone offered their home for his baby girl's wake. She later heard that he cradled Bridey's body in his arms, rocking her like a newborn, howling as he held her to his chest.

It was the childless Delilah, nearly eighty years old, who eventually extended her house for the wake. She was far too old to fear bad omens, unlike the other women in the village who feared their husbands or sons might drown if they brought bad luck into their homes. "I'd be honored to have an angel in my house," she said. And so little Bridey was washed and prepared for her burial by the ancient woman with the deepest respect. Delilah carefully bathed the girl's body and pulled the seaweed out from her hair. She cleaned the sand from between her toes and powdered her skin so the blue of death was obscured.

Another family provided an old communion dress, a pair of rosebud-trimmed socks to cover her feet. Then, with the help of one of the fishermen, Delilah laid the girl out on an old wooden table near the hearth and laced Bridey's fingers in front of her with a posy of forget-me-nots in her folded hands. A photograph of Saint Thérèse, known as "God's little flower," was placed by Bridey's side.

From that day on, Grace would always cover her ears when the river became too high and crashed over the stones. Every time she heard the rushing of the river, it brought back the pain of Bridey's death.

Years later, when she was eighteen and had won a lottery to emigrate to America, Grace went down to the river one last time and grabbed the ugliest stone she could find. She held it in her hand and marveled at its craggy shape, its mottled color, and she forced herself to still find beauty in it.

Then she cast it as far into the water as she could. Sinking all of her sorrow deep into the blue-green channel.

The melancholy still returned sometimes. Like now, when Grace looked at the little boy beside her. She wondered what lengths he had traveled to arrive at Bellegrove. The sorrows he had endured. She felt the pull of water stirring inside her again as they drove toward the police station.

"Tom, how about some music?" she asked, hoping to restore her sense of calm.

Her husband was kind. He didn't remind her that he'd been the one who had just suggested the radio, believing it would soothe everyone's nerves. He simply turned on the dial and let Karen Carpenter's voice fill the air.

CHAPTER 5

THEY EXITED THE CAR AND BEGAN WALKING TOWARD THE STA-
tion house, three shadows of varying sizes stretched across the asphalt
like string puppets on a dark stage.

Inside, the strong smell of stale coffee and disinfectant clung to the
air. A man at the desk wrote down their names, then motioned them
toward the waiting room and told them to sit down.

"We've got some good news," an officer soon informed them.
"There was a Vietnamese boy reported missing about twenty-four
hours ago who fits the description you gave us. The Hulk T-shirt gave
it away." He glanced down at his paperwork. On the top, attached by
a single paperclip, was a copy of a photograph that matched the child
in front of him. "Are you Bảo Phan?" He struggled to pronounce
the name.

Grace noticed the child's eyes flicker.

"Come with me," he said, waving them to follow him down the
corridor. "Looks like he's been living at Our Lady Queen of Martyrs. He arrived there several weeks ago, with a few other Vietnamese
refugees. . . ."

Grace recognized the name immediately. The sprawling brick
building with stained glass windows was only a few miles away from
Bellegrove. It was situated on the grounds of a large natural preserve
that, according to local lore, had been donated to the church by a childless widow back in the 1920s. A small group of Sisters still lived on the
property, but Grace had no idea they were now housing refugees there.

"And what about his parents?" she cut in.

"It seems he's under the guardianship of his aunt," the officer said. He pulled open a door.

"Her name is Anh Ho. She showed up about an hour before you and the boy did."

They stepped inside the sterile conference room, and Grace saw the boy's chin drop to his chest.

Across the long faux-wood table, a slender young woman, flanked by a social worker and translator, leapt up. She called out Bảo's name so loudly it sounded like a wail.

"Anh," the social worker said softly, guiding her back to her seat.

The woman fell back into the chair, but the words she now uttered were full of emotion and urgency. She tucked a few wisps of long black hair behind her ears and then reached for the small plastic container she'd brought. Inside, it contained five perfect slivers of mango and some cut strawberries. She pushed the container toward Bảo and again murmured something Grace didn't understand.

The translator interpreted for Grace and Tom. "She's brought him something to eat. She was worried he'd be hungry."

But Grace sensed it was more that. As Bảo took the slivers of fruit, Anh's eye wetted with emotion. The mango had been brought with love.

CHAPTER 6

Vietnam, 1976

ANH'S BELOVED OLDER SISTER, LINH, POSSESSED A SPECIAL talent for picking fruit off the vine that was perfectly ripe. Not one day too soon nor a day too late. *Let your eyes, your nose, your fingers all be your guide*, she reminded Anh. All of one's senses were needed to ensure that the fruit wasn't plucked too soon.

The girls grew up sleeping beside each other on woven mats and exchanging stories as moonlight crept through the cracks of their childhood home. Anh learned everything she knew from Linh, from how to braid her hair to how to wash grains of rice. But the greatest wisdom Linh had imparted was how to take the fruit from their orchard and transform it into money for their family. The sisters' fruit stand at the local market was a jewel box of vivid colors and assorted shapes and textures. Bell-shaped water apples, bright orange papayas, and cactus-green pomelos. Their baskets brimmed with crimson rambutans and golden longans, each bundle of tiny marble-sized fruit still attached to its stem and leaf.

During the war years, every piece of fruit from their family's orchard became infinitely more valuable. As much as the sisters missed the independence and financial rewards of their market stall, it was far too dangerous for them to journey outside their village, particularly with their husbands away for weeks at a time working as mechanics for the South Vietnamese army. But fruit and other goods were still exchanged between their neighbors through a trusted bartering system. Three mangoes for some cooking oil. Some pomelos for a new needle and mending thread.

When Bảo was born, her sister, Linh, wrapped him in a scarf and kept him close to her at all times. When he grew bigger, she placed him in a basket, giving him the morning fruit to touch and eventually hold. She called him her "little man," always running her fingers through his hair. At the end of the day, she'd retrieve one last mango, tucked away just for him. "I saved the sweetest one for you, *bé tí*," she'd remind him, using her special term of affection, before kissing him on the head.

Anh never tired of looking at her young nephew's savoring the fruit in his hands before bringing it to his nose to inhale its intense fragrance. It reminded her of watching her sister comb through their family's orchard in search of the morning's perfect bounty. Linh had taken to motherhood so naturally, and Anh craved that she, too, would be so blessed one day. She watched as Linh took the knife out of her apron and peeled the skin away from the mango's flesh and cut it into slices. As Bảo ate the succulent fruit, its juice running down his chin, he'd smile as though his mother had just plucked for him the most wonderful star from the sky.

Since their parents' death, Linh was the one who Anh looked to for guidance. She was desperate to conceive a child and clung to each word Linh uttered. *Drink this tea after your monthly cycle. . . . Eat this herb to strengthen your womb.*

"What did our mother used to say? 'Nurture the soil, and the flowers will come,'" she reminded Anh. "Steep the nettles I gave you. It will help with your fertility."

Anh hoped so. Just that morning, the first day of the lunar month, she'd placed a smooth and perfect custard apple on the family altar and put fresh flowers in the vase, praying to their ancestors that she would conceive.

The two sisters now sat on the edge of the wooden porch, watching as Bảo played outside the family home. A small black bird pecked at the ground nearby, searching for food. "Fear is not good for the spirit. We must have faith," Linh said. "Didn't I tell you our husbands would return safely from the war? And just as I promised, Minh came back to you."

What she said was true. While Anh had worried about her husband when he was away, her sister possessed a confidence that eluded her. Linh's fortitude only grew stronger after Bảo's birth. Motherhood had given her a sense of purpose and shielded her from despair in a way that Anh couldn't help but envy. She yearned for something similar of her own. Her days were spent cleaning and cooking for her father-in-law, who was so frail, he spent most afternoons drifting in and out of sleep.

When her husband, Minh, did return home, however, it was short-lived. Only a few weeks later, he and Linh's husband, Chung, were arrested by the new Communist regime for having supported the Americans rather than fighting for Vietnam's independence.

Yet, as devastated as they both were, Linh continued to reassure her. "They will come back to us, just like before. You'll see," she promised Anh.

The two men were sent to a reeducation camp. While the conditions had been harsh and the methods of indoctrination brutal, Linh had again been proven right. Their husbands did eventually come home to them. But she had not predicted that their family's suffering would continue as it did.

Under the new regime, the two couples were forced to give up their home, and the sisters' family orchard was confiscated. They were ordered to relocate to a patch of land on the outskirts of the village that their husbands were expected to cultivate, despite their lack of any farming experience.

While every family in the village was given a rations card for a certain amount of rice, those who were considered traitors received the smallest portion and grains that were almost always infested with bugs and larvae. Ignoring her own hunger, Anh's heart broke as she watched her sister struggle to feed Bảo, who no longer looked like a healthy seven-year-old boy, but one who was scrawny and malnourished. She helped Linh as they tried to stretch the meager rice portions with bits of boiled cassava root and water. But even that wasn't enough to fill their empty stomachs. Her father-in-law, who had somehow managed to stay alive through the war and the famine, soon grew weak and died.

Anh wondered how long they could exist on what felt like nothing more than boiled water and air. Hungry and weak, Bảo never complained there was no food for him. But sometimes, almost out of reflex, he would curl next to his mother, his small fingers searching for a mango hidden in her pocket. But there was never anything there.

"We must find a way to leave," Anh's brother-in-law, Chung, began to whisper in private. Despite Linh's concern for their safety, Chung kept a Japanese radio hidden in the shed. He'd found it discarded on the road and, with a little tinkering, was able to make it work again. Sometimes when they believed the village was deep in sleep, the two men would secretly turn the dial to search for the Voice of America broadcast and then usher their wives over to join them. It amazed Anh how close the voices sounded. As though America wasn't so far away at all.

CHAPTER 7

Long Island, 1979

GRACE WATCHED AS THE BOY QUICKLY DEVOURED THE FRUIT. As he ate, relief washed over his aunt's face.

Within seconds, Anh had walked over across the table and wrapped Bảo tightly into her arms and rubbed her cheek against the crown of his hair. The boy, stiff and withdrawn at first, soon softened against her body. The air in the room shifted and eased. It was a scene that Grace only wished her own mother had been afforded years before, her stomach now twisted at the memory.

"We'll just need to take a statement about where you found him. Then the two of you can be on your way and we can take it from there," the police officer cut in.

"Of course," she said quietly and followed him out the door.

In a separate room, the story of how Grace had found Bảo on the corner tumbled forth. "My only concern was making sure he was returned home safely." But she also felt compelled to mention the troubling scar on his arm.

The officer scribbled down his notes. "We'll make some inquiries. But if it's not a fresh wound, it could have happened a while ago."

Graced reached for Tom's hand. While she was grateful that Bảo had been reunited with his aunt, she still felt a lingering concern over why he'd run away in the first place.

As a mother, she was no stranger to the dramatics of children. Her eldest, Katie, had threatened to run away on several occasions when she was around the same age. Grace recalled one particular episode when Katie had stuffed her pillowcase with what she believed to be her necessities: her prized sticker album, a copy of *Teen Beat* magazine (given to her by the babysitter), and some chewing gum, but she'd never gotten farther than the driveway.

"You mentioned Bảo and his aunt were staying at Our Lady Queen of Martyrs," Grace said.

"Yes. At the motherhouse. The Sisters sponsored a group of boat people."

Grace flinched. She'd seen the photographs on the front page of the *New York Times* about the thousands of Vietnamese refugees who'd crowded onto tiny vessels trying to escape persecution after the fall of the South Vietnamese government. So many had perished at sea from starvation and capsized boats to even pirate attacks.

"It's a good thing the Sisters have tried to help, though it's not easy being new to a place as close-knit as Bellegrove," Grace said. "It can feel a little like a country club, with the new people not permitted entry."

Grace was pensive when she got into their old Pontiac wagon, and Tom started the engine. Outside, it began to rain.

"It's interesting," she said as she looked out the window, the melancholy returning to her as the pavement became speckled with drops. "When we came to the station, my only concern was about making sure the boy was okay. But now, I can't help thinking about both him *and* his aunt." She swallowed hard. "We don't know what happened to his parents, either."

"Anh seemed like a very compassionate young woman." Tom's voice was soothing. "You could see how worried she'd been."

"Yes. But can you imagine arriving here not knowing the language, the customs. . . . It's an entirely different world." Her head leaned against the glass. "It was hard enough for me coming from Ireland. People used to tell me they couldn't understand a word I said, with my accent."

"It was part of your charm, Gracie."

"You should have seen the way Adele looked at him. You'd think I was walking down the street with a criminal."

"You know better than to suggest Adele is like everyone else in town."

"I know." Grace straightened and shuffled through her handbag for a mint. "It just feels like we left the police station too soon."

"You worry too much," Tom said as he reached for an eight-track tape of a Beatles album that Grace loved. The sound of the familiar tunes laced the space between them as they headed home.

When they reached the house on Morris Avenue, Tom pulled slowly into the driveway. He switched the car's lights off and turned to Grace.

"I didn't realize how late it is. The girls are going to be hungry." His hands fell from the steering wheel to his lap. "Should I get us a pizza?"

Grace glanced at her watch. In the twilight, her face looked somber. "I completely forgot it's Sunday night. Jack's supposed to have dinner with us." A sinking feeling came over her. She had been on her way to get the groceries for a nice supper when she found Bảo, and the meal with Jack had completely slipped her mind.

"I'm sure the kids told him what happened," he reassured her. "He'll understand. How often do you find a runaway?"

"Yes. But I still feel bad." Her Irish guilt took over. She knew that Jack, who lived above their family store and kept mostly to himself, always looked forward to a home-cooked meal. "Please tell him I'm sorry when you see him."

"Of course, but we did the right thing. Bảo is back with his aunt. We can give Jack a rain check for another Sunday night." He reached for her in the passenger seat and ran his finger over her forearm. The softness of her skin never ceased to surprise him. Grace always felt new to him.

But had they really done as much as they could? Grace wasn't so sure. When she first arrived in Bellegrove, her experience had hardly been smooth. And Tom's parents—the only Jews in the town—had also been considered outsiders. Treated politely for the most part, but hardly fully embraced.

Her fingers now reached beneath her neckline to touch the tiny amulet of Saint Thérèse resting against her skin. Delilah had given it to her after her sister's funeral, and she still wore the necklace to this day.

Grace closed her eyes and remembered when Delilah shared how she was guided by the spirit of Saint Thérèse and her belief that small acts of empathy could change the world. The Irish in Grace sensed that Bảo had come into her life for a reason. And perhaps now Anh, too. Her late mother-in-law had called it *chesed*, the moral obligation to always be kind.

CHAPTER 8

THE FOREST GREEN–AND-BRONZE SIGN THAT READ "THE GOLDEN HOURS" had been in Bellegrove for as long as anyone could remember. Nestled on the ground floor of a white brick building on the corner of Main Street and Maple Avenue, the store had become a part of the village landscape, just like Butler's Shoes and Kepler's Market.

Its windows were filled with tall, graceful grandfather clocks of varying shapes and sizes. The walls displayed mounted clocks with different sized numbers and fonts. Antique tables upheld elegant mantel clocks positioned in the center, some in gilt bronze with florid details and others in ebony or rosewood. There was even the occasional clock made of hand-painted porcelain. Grace's favorite was a delft blue-tile clock that had sat in the shop for over a year, before Tom brought it home and surprised her with it for Mother's Day.

The shop had been a large part of her life almost from the moment she began dating Tom. Founded by Tom's father, Harry, Grace soon realized that the store was the very heart of the Golden family. And while over the years she envied that her husband could retreat to such a peaceful workspace when she was frazzled at home with two young children, Grace had come to see the Golden Hours as a place that restored not just watches and clocks, but also broken men.

Grace knew Tom had spent countless afternoons at the store as a little boy. Early in their courtship, he'd confided in her how his earliest memories were of sitting quietly next to his father and being surrounded by the unique rhythms there—the sound of a second hand

moving with each tick, the chime of bells on the hour, or the soothing pulse of a pendulum swaying in its window box. When he was ten
years old, his father gave him the task of winding each clock with its
own special turnkey. Harry imparted to his young son that turning the
clocks was one of the most important rituals of the day, for it kept them
powered up, pushing each minute, then hour, ahead.

Now, as her husband approached forty, Tom had become even
more self-reflective and soulful. Sometimes he would tell her that he
felt he was still sharing the space with his dad, despite the fact that
Harry had recently passed away in a nursing home for veterans fifteen
miles away.

Grace would always be grateful that her late father-in-law
changed the course of her husband's life for the better. The man
helped get Tom back on track just before they began dating, offering
him a job at the family store, not because he thought Tom had an
eye for clocks or a talent for repairs, but because he saw that his son
had lost his way.

While Tom had been a good student and even an Eagle Scout, by the
time he was eighteen, he hit a rebellious streak. His family's tight-knit
values felt provincial and insular. And while it had faintly amused him
as a kid to introduce his predominantly Irish-Catholic friends to the
tradition of Sunday bagels or matzo ball soup, as a teenager he just
wanted to be like everyone else. He grew his hair longer and combed
it back with Brylcreem. He played loud music his parents hated, like
Elvis and Little Stevie Wonder. He concentrated less on his senior-year
studies, finding more interest in extracurricular activities like smok-
ing cigarettes behind the A&P and riding the secondhand Triumph
Tiger motorcycle he had bought to impress girls. Even the toughest
punks who had called him "Jew boy" when he was in grade school were
impressed with his transformation.

After taking four years to graduate from a two-year community college, Tom contemplated joining the army. He was confident his father, who had been a World War II veteran, would be pleased that he'd decided to serve his country and finally shape up after spending years drifting away from his full potential.

But the conversation ended up quite differently from what Tom could have ever anticipated. On a warm Saturday evening in the spring of 1963, he and one of his buddies, Bobby O'Rourke, went down to the Ace Hardware Shopping Center to join a group of friends to race their motorcycles.

After he and Bobby struck their engines and barreled toward the finish line, Tom lost control and found himself wiping out on a turn. Thrown to the pavement, his leg was crushed beneath the Triumph's heavy metal frame.

Tom shattered his fibula in eight places, causing him to have a permanent limp and pain whenever it rained.

His parents had met the ambulance at the hospital. The doctor read the X-ray with a grave look on his face and informed them that Tom would need to stay in traction at the hospital for the next two months, and even if the bone did fully heal, he would probably always walk with a limp.

When he awoke from surgery, Tom was dreading how his father was sure to react. But Harry very much surprised his son. "This dumb accident just might have saved your life," he told Tom.

With the thunderclouds brewing in Vietnam, Harry had been nursing a concern that America might end up in a war there, like it had in Europe in the 1940s and Korea a few years later. Having himself experienced the horrors of war, the terror still sometimes returning to him at night when he found himself reliving the scene of him witnessing his best friend Jimmy getting blown up when he stepped on a land mine only a few yards away, Harry now felt more relief than anger over Tom's accident. Now his son would be medically exempt from any future fighting.

Tom's friend Bobby O'Rourke, who had bragged about his victory in the race that night as Tom was being lifted into the ambulance, would enlist a few years later.

Bobby passed his medical exam with flying colors, only to die a year later in a jungle outside Nha Trang.

CHAPTER 9

No one in Bellegrove ever forgot the afternoon Bobby's parents received the news. They all heard about it, even before his name was read aloud on the radio a few days later. The neighbors had all held their breath on that rainy day in March, when the military vehicle pulled up to the O'Rourkes' home and two soldiers dressed in uniforms solemnly walked toward the front door.

The ghost of Bobby O'Rourke still lingered in the small town's air. Adele, his older sister, lived two streets away and had named her son after him.

Grace knew her husband thought about his dead buddy often, for it was because of Bobby he had learned how life was shaped by random accidents. That one incident could alter the lives of several people forever. He confided in her that there were times, when he drove past that Ace parking lot, he contemplated how different things might have been had it been Bobby who had skidded out and busted his leg and not him.

"We wouldn't have met had you not gotten hurt," she reminded him. It was true. If he hadn't had been left with a limp that made him too self-conscious to dance at that mixer in Queens, she might not have sat down next to him that night.

Grace had left Ireland with a suitcase containing two good dresses, one skirt, three blouses, two pairs of nylons, one pair of black pumps, and a navy mohair coat. A family in Queens had sponsored her as a nanny to help with their three children, all of whom were under the age of five. She was terribly homesick when she arrived in the States. Not because she missed her family back home, as she had already been away from them at the Catholic school she'd boarded at since she was thirteen, but for Ireland itself. The lush green grass and meadows full of delicate red poppies and wild heather. The stretches of blue sky, the sunlight that peeked through the daily showers of rain. Her foreignness was only intensified by the unfamiliarity of the cement and asphalt of Sunnyside, Queens. The endless rows of apartment buildings. The parks that had playgrounds for children but no lawn in sight. Still, she found joy on the days she traveled into glamorous Manhattan, where she could lose herself in the museums she loved. The enormous Museum of Natural History on the Upper West Side was her favorite refuge. There, the collection of butterflies with their fragile wings and brightly colored markings reminded her that beauty could be both delicate and strong.

Her friend Fiona, another transplant from Ireland, told her about a social sponsored by the Irish Club of New York. Grace initially hadn't wanted to go, as she had no desire to stand around drinking warm punch while the men offered whiskey from metal flasks in their breast pockets.

But Grace loved to dance. So when Fiona mentioned they'd have a live band and the lead singer was from Galway, no less, she couldn't refuse.

She danced for hours. Her face flushed, her blue cotton dress clinging to her skin. While one of the boys went to get her a drink, she sat down to catch her breath and she found herself next to Tom. He hadn't gotten up once all night to dance, even though she had caught him staring at her on more than one occasion.

"Not much of a dancer, are you?" Grace asked, her voice sounding more confident than normal, as the exhilaration of the music seemed to give her more courage. She was drawn to his dark brown curls and hazel eyes. There was also something genuine about him. His sports jacket was rumpled, his shirt untucked, but when he lifted his head to smile at her, she felt her heart leap inside her chest.

"Can't dance. Busted leg," he said, pointing toward his left shoe. "My friend Lewis dragged me here. He's a senior at Fordham. It gave him a kick to bring his only Jewish friend to an Irish dance."

Grace smiled. She had never met anyone Jewish before she moved to New York, and she loved the exotic fabric of so many different ethnicities outside her doorstep in Queens. As Grace looked over at Tom, she thought he seemed sweet and handsome. Lewis, on the other hand, was sweating profusely over the punch bowl. "Looks like Lewis is finding the cooling system here more challenging than college."

Tom laughed. His friend might be smarter than he was, but at least Tom's shirt was dry.

"Does it hurt?" Grace eyed the khaki pant leg of his trousers.

"Not anymore, just makes me look clumsy. Doesn't quite work like it should."

Whenever people asked them how they met, it was one of the only things in their marriage that they remembered exactly the same way. She had taken his hand later that evening and gently led him to the dance floor. Grace didn't twirl or kick up her legs as she had earlier with the faster dances. Instead, as the band played a slow ballad, she guided Tom's hands around her waist and let him pull her close. And as he steadied himself to her rhythm, his self-consciousness fell away.

Weeks later, when he mentioned to his parents that he was dating Grace, their first instinct was that their son was rebelling, yet again, by bringing home a blond, blue-eyed Catholic girlfriend, straight from Ireland, no less.

They assumed his attraction to the girl would wear off and their relationship would eventually just run its course. But the young couple soon proved them wrong, as their connection only grew stronger.

"She came here for a new life, just like your own parents." Tom finally summoned up his nerve to confront his mother, who had yet to invite Grace for dinner. "She lost her sister at a young age, so maybe I'm drawn to her because she embodies the Golden family philosophy that you have to find a way to move forward."

His voice was strong and full of conviction. "So, Mom, please don't tell me that we come from two different worlds."

As the newspapers blazed with headlines of societal change, the space program's goal of putting a man on the moon, the confirmation of the first Black Supreme Court Justice, and rising anti-war protests, Tom's courtship with Grace was swept into a wave of progressive thinking that his parents couldn't ignore. And while his mother worried out loud about her future grandson having a baptism instead of a bris, and his father's heart was broken by the loss of nearly all Jewish life in Europe and hoped to somehow replenish the number, both of his parents eventually warmed to Grace despite her different religion. They came to recognize her good values and her deep appreciation of family. Harry loved her caring nature and the homemade shortbread in a recycled blue cookie tin that she brought to their house. And when Grace asked if she could learn how to make Rosie's brisket, it lifted his mother's spirits to know this young woman was interested in traditions other than her own.

His father mentioned he'd noticed that Grace never wore a watch. The only adornment he could find on her was the simple saint's medallion hanging from her neck.

One evening, after Grace helped clear the dishes, Harry gave Tom the keys to the shop. "Go pick out a watch for the pretty girl," he instructed, winking at his son. "She deserves something lovely to go along with that smile."

Grace blushed. "It's not necessary, Mr. Golden. You've already been so generous with having me over for so many Friday-night dinners." She patted the waistband of her skirt.

"Go on, now," Rosie said as she smiled and pushed them both toward the door.

Tom pulled Grace's wool coat from the closet and slid it over her shoulders. "It's a brisk walk or a short drive to the store. . . . Which do you prefer?"

"The brisk walk, of course!"

"Just no motorcycles!" Rosie called out from the kitchen.

"No, Mrs. Golden, I would never!" Grace's giggle filled the hall.

As he slid the key into the store's front door and ushered Grace inside, her face lit up when she saw all the antique clocks. "This one's from England," Tom said, pointing to a small brass carriage clock. "And this one is French Revival." Her eyes danced from one clock to the next. At the glass case he looked for a watch that would be just perfect for her and found one on a black grosgrain ribbon. "Is it too dressy?" he asked as he began to wrap it around her wrist.

"It's so elegant," she whispered. And when she lifted her head upward to him, he kissed her in the moonlight. His heart raced at the touch of her lips.

CHAPTER 10

As Grace cleaned up the kitchen, the phone rang.

"Grace?" Adele's voice sounded urgent. "Is now a good time? I tried to wait until after dinner to call. . . ."

Ever since she saw Adele in the street that morning, she knew she'd be hearing from her. Adele loved gossip.

"Yes . . . I'm just doing the dishes. . . ." Grace cradled the receiver against her shoulder and shook the water off her hands. It was nearly 9:00 p.m., and all she wanted to do was crawl into bed after such a long day.

"I just wanted to check up on you. I was a little worried when I saw you this afternoon with that . . . boy."

"Worried?"

"Oh, you know what I mean, Gracie. He clearly wasn't from around here. So I was concerned."

Grace kept her voice measured. A lot had happened over the years between the two women. Adele was one of the first to welcome Grace to Bellegrove after she married Tom. Those first few months in the town had been particularly hard for Grace, as so much of suburban East Coast life was unfamiliar to her. When she lived in Queens, she was surrounded by loads of girls just like her, from small Irish villages, who all still kept a little bottle of holy water and a prayer book tucked inside their handbags, along with the rosary from their first communions. None of those girls cared if someone's house hadn't had indoor plumbing back home.

But in Bellegrove, she had on occasion found herself being described as "progressive," a term she'd never heard before. When she inquired its meaning to Tom, he had laughed. "Gracie, it's their way of saying someone's broad-minded enough to marry a Jewish guy like me." He bent over and kissed her.

"I just feel like a country bumpkin...that's all...." she said. While Tom was smitten by her old-world innocence, she couldn't help but feel insecure about her lack of sophistication. She hardly felt like a trailblazer. Her cloth coat and sensible shoes looked dated, and her Irish accent only reaffirmed the notion that she was still very much a new immigrant.

When Tom and his mother suggested she might want to join the local branch of the City of Hope organization, a group of young women who raised money for that prestigious research hospital, she took their advice to heart, hoping she'd soon find a circle of friends willing to welcome her. While nearly all of the women had snubbed her, preferring to socialize with friends they'd known for years, Adele had come up and introduced herself to Grace at that first meeting.

"Are you the new Irish girl who married Tom Golden?" she asked with an enviable confidence that Grace found intimidating. She dazzled in her green angora sweater and strand of cultured pearls, her slim hips fitted in a wool pencil skirt and kitten heels.

"Welcome to Bellegrove!" Adele squeezed Grace's hand and then paraded her around the basement room, introducing her to the other women.

Grace had felt lucky when Adele first befriended her, as if some of her new friend's glamorous shine might rub off on her. She was elated when Adele offered to take her shopping to update her wardrobe or offered to share her "American" recipes. And when her brother Bobby died in Vietnam, Grace's heart broke for Adele, especially knowing the young man had been a childhood friend of Tom's. But as much as

Grace wanted to have compassion for the O'Rourke family tragedy, she soon saw another side of Adele that made her pause. There had been many times where she felt Adele was inappropriately relaying information that should have been kept private, like news of miscarriages or husband problems. It made Grace reconsider sharing any personal information with her.

"That's very kind of you, Adele. I appreciate you checking up on me." Grace pulled the dishrag from the counter and dried her hands. "And him."

"Of course! Were you able to return him to his parents? They must have been so worried."

Grace let out a sigh. Adele was known for her persistence. "He's living on the grounds of Our Lady Queen of Martyrs with his aunt. The diocese sponsored some Vietnamese refugees."

The phone crackled with silence.

"From Vietnam? Well, if that's not . . ." Adele paused. "Vietnam— that certainly is long way from here."

"Yes." Grace softened her voice. "I'm sorry . . . I know that country brings up a lot of painful memories for you and your family."

"Not just my family . . ." Adele sounded prickly. "There's a lot of families who lost someone over there." She paused again. "And what about that man Tom took under his wing? The veteran who lives above your store. You think he's not going to be upset?"

Grace's stomach flipped. She'd felt terrible that she'd forgotten to telephone Jack and cancel dinner. He always looked forward to having supper with them on the first Sunday of the month. The children told her how he'd came to the house promptly at 5:00 p.m. but left quickly when he realized something had come up. Of course, Adele still had never made the effort to remember his name.

"I have no idea . . . but they'd be wrong to be upset. This boy and the others were the people our men believed they were fighting for.

They're not the enemy. . . ." she answered quickly. She knew so little
about the politics behind the war, but truthfully, she'd been sickened
every time she picked up the paper or had watched the news. It wasn't
only the images of countless coffins being escorted off airplanes with
American flags draped over them that had upset her, but all of it. That
photograph of the child running naked in the street, her body on fire.
All the torched forests. The pain and devastation were too much.

"Bobby was just a kid. . . ."

Grace closed her eyes and tried to imagine the young man who she
had only seen snapshots of in Tom's scrapbook. He was tall and lanky
with shaggy hair just like Tom and shared a similar mischievous grin.

"I know, Adele. And this little boy is just a child. I'm going to call
over there tomorrow and see if there is anything our women's group
can do to help."

"You are always so good like that, Grace." Adele had managed to
restrain her emotions.

"I don't know how good I am, Adele . . . but I was the one who
found him. I want to make sure he's in safe hands."

Katie came into the kitchen, freshly showered and wearing a T-shirt
and pajama pants.

"Oh, good, you're off the phone. I wanted to call Annie."

"Go ahead, I'm done." Grace took a sponge to the counter.

"Who were you on the phone with?"

"Adele."

Katie made a face. "Her son, Buddy, has been hanging out with a
new boy, Clayton Mavis. . . . They're both always shooting spitballs at
Annie and me." She went to the cupboard and pulled out a cookie from
the brightly colored packaging and took a bite.

"Well, that's not right. You want me to call the teacher?"

"No, it's not that bad. Clayton's just such a bully . . . picks on Francis Wilson all the time, calling him names like 'Blubber' and 'Lard-ass' . . ."

"Katherine Rose . . ." Grace said her daughter's full name to show her disapproval. "No need for that kind of language."

"I was just stating the facts, Mom." Katie rolled her eyes and went to pick up the phone.

CHAPTER 11

THE NEXT MORNING, AFTER THE GIRLS HAD GONE OFF TO school and Tom had left for the store, Grace sat down at the kitchen table and looked up the phone number for Our Lady Queen of Martyrs.

She knew where the old brick complex was located, with its tall iron gates and the statue of the Virgin Mary in the interior courtyard. The women's group regularly dropped off their collections for clothing drives there, as the Franciscan Sisters in association with the church shipped the donations to needy Catholic communities abroad. Her own children had always found the place scary and intimidating. As much as she and Tom had encouraged their children to appreciate both their religions, it felt like they'd failed them. The girls picked the religion that suited their needs moment by moment. They suddenly became Jewish when Grace asked them if they wanted to attend Mass with her, and they became Catholic when Christmas was around the corner. But for Grace, her relationship to the Church brought up a complex bevy of emotions.

Grace didn't doubt the Sisters at Our Lady Queen of Martyrs had the best intentions with their sponsorship of the refugees, but navigating a new community in a country so different than your own would not be easy. Grace couldn't help but think her path had crossed with Bảo for a reason. She got up from the table and went to dial the main reception of the motherhouse but then hesitated. It would take far too long to explain what had transpired over the weekend. Minutes later, she was in front of her vanity, putting on her makeup and touching up her hair. Grace then put on a white knit top and light-blue skirt and got into the car.

The long driveway that led up to the large complex immediately threw her back to her days as a student at a Catholic school in Ireland. The severity of the nuns' behavior created a fear that rushed through her body every time Grace entered the classroom. For years, as a child, she was afraid her fingers would be lashed with a wooden cane for forgetting her homework or for speaking before she was called upon.

So even now, part of her tensed up as she approached the grounds. Despite the somber architecture, the surroundings were alight with color. Flower beds filled with tulips and daffodils were carefully maintained in perfect rows. The cherry trees, some so large they might have been over a hundred years old, created soft pink canopies over Grace's Pontiac wagon as it slowly inched up the driveway.

Exiting her car, Grace straightened her skirt and checked her lipstick in her silver compact mirror. She couldn't stop the immediate impulse to make sure she appeared beyond reproach as she walked up the cement steps and into the reception area.

The familiar smell of damp stone and ceremonial incense hit her immediately as her pumps struck the marble floor.

"May I help you?" A petite woman with gray hair and cat-eye glasses greeted Grace.

"Hello, I'm Grace Golden. I think we might have met before when I dropped off some clothes from the City of Hope Women's Club."

The woman smiled at Grace. "I thought you looked familiar . . . and you're one of the only locals with such a charming Irish accent."

"Thank you, that's most kind." Grace leaned in as if sharing a secret with the woman. "I'm hoping maybe you can help me. . . . You see, I'm here for a specific reason. . . ."

"I will certainly try, Mrs. Golden."

"Well, over the weekend, on my way home from Mass, actually," Grace continued, "I found a little boy alone on the street. I learned later that afternoon when we took him down to the police station that he had run away from here."

The woman's face stiffened.

"The only children we have here at the moment are those who came with their families from a Red Cross refugee camp and are sponsored by the diocese."

"Yes, that's what the social worker mentioned." Grace paused. "It's got to be about five miles from here to Maple Avenue in Bellegrove, so it concerns me the child walked so far . . . and also seemed to have spent the night sleeping outside."

"That's a long way to walk." The woman frowned. "But I can assure you all the families are getting wonderful care here."

"I was hoping I could check on him and his aunt, Anh," she explained gently. "I remember how hard it was for me to come here from Ireland not knowing a soul; I just want to show a friendly face."

"We don't typically allow unscheduled visitors, I'm afraid."

"Well, I can sit down and wait. Let me know when there might be someone in charge who can speak with me."

Grace looked over at the wooden bench outside the reception area, then glanced at her wristwatch.

It was 10:15. Katie would be getting home at 3:00 p.m., Molly at 3:30. For all practical purposes, Grace could wait there all day.

Grace sat quietly on the bench for nearly forty minutes before one of the Sisters appeared.

"Ms. Golden?" Standing in front of Grace was a middle-aged woman in a navy skirt and blazer. "I'm Sister Mary Alice," she said, extending her hand. "Apologies for keeping you waiting. We're a bit overwhelmed at the moment with our latest charges."

"Yes, I imagine you are."

"I hear you've come here to inquire about Anh and her nephew Bảo."

"Yes," she said, steadying her voice. "I was the one who found him in Bellegrove on Sunday."

"And we're very grateful that you did. We are going to keep an extra careful eye on him now."

Grace forced a smile. "It must be quite an adjustment here from his life back in Vietnam."

"Oh, yes! It really is. . . . Not just the language barrier . . . but so many things. America is foreign for them in so many ways. . . ."

"And I gather you're trying to teach them English. . . ."

"Yes, that's our priority right now. Most of them had basic English lessons in the refugee camp before they came here, but there is still so much work to be done. With the public school nearly out for the summer break, we wanted to use the next few months most effectively so the children will be able to start class there in the fall. Bảo is the oldest we have. The others are mostly toddlers."

"How old is he?"

"We believe Bảo is ten." Sister Mary Alice smiled. "It's been a bit of a whirlwind trying to get the facts straight through the refugee camp in Malaysia they were sent to before they came here."

"I can imagine," Grace agreed. "Have you any idea where his parents are?"

"Sadly, Bảo's an orphan. Anh is his guardian."

Grace's fingers touched her amulet as she remembered how she'd tried to escape the pain of Bridey's death by tucking herself against one of the old stone walls that curved along the perimeter of her village.

Bảo running away now made sense to her. "Children often try too hard to be brave," she said softly.

"Compassion like yours is a gift, Mrs. Golden."

A flicker of pain pinched inside her. Her mother curled in a tight ball in bed, her baby brother wailing, the flash of memory returned to her. Grace had often been the one to feed him, to rock him to sleep. Her mother's grief had consumed her.

"My own childhood had its fair share of sadness, but I was fortunate to know kindness, too." Delilah had died over thirty years ago, but there were times Grace could swear she felt the papery skin of the old woman's hand gripping her own.

"We are grateful that God has shown mercy and Bảo has one family member with him. He is not alone." Sister Mary unfolded her hands. "Would you like to come this way? I'll show you where they're having an English lessons right now. We have four other nuns who are helping with their instruction. Anh, actually, has become one of our best students."

"Yes, thank you," Grace said.

"It's my pleasure. And it's not entirely selfless on my part." She took a step into the room and said, "As you can see, we have quite a project here . . . with the tutoring. We could always use another hand."

The motherhouse, the Sisters' headquarters on the grounds of Our Lady Queen of Martyrs, had always appeared rather gloomy to Grace, but now it buzzed like a beehive. She followed Sister Mary Alice toward a common area where four matronly-looking women sat at different tables giving instruction to the adults while the children sat on the floor. The room smelled like apple juice, crayons, and warm bodies.

Grace spotted Bảo first. Sitting beside two small girls with pigtails, he seemed to have little interest in repeating basic words back in

English. Instead, he was pulling out tiny fibers of the rug and arranging them in a pile.

Then she saw Anh. Unlike the others, who were spread out into small groups, Anh sat alone at a desk in the corner, bent over a soft-covered workbook, her long black hair tied loosely with a scarf. The edge of two pink shower sandals peeked out from beneath the hem of her skirt.

"As I said, Anh is one of our hardest workers," Mary Alice said, noting that Grace was looking at her from afar.

"She still doesn't speak very much, but she definitely seems to understand more than the others. I suspect she made the most of the lessons back at the Red Cross camp."

Grace again looked over in Anh's direction.

"Anyway, it's been quite a challenge here," the Sister continued. "We don't understand a word of Vietnamese. And while most of them as I mentioned had a bit of lessons in the refugee camp, a few are even too shy to practice with us. We're hoping that will change soon...." She looked over at Bảo. "The boy's been a bit hard to reach. Watches a lot of television but doesn't want to practice speaking. He's still so withdrawn, but we don't want to push him too much after this weekend's incident." She took a deep breath. "Maybe you can help."

Grace watched as she went over to one of the folded bridge tables and tapped Bảo on his back, then whispered something in his ear. He looked older now that he was wearing a plaid short-sleeved shirt and khaki pants. He turned his head around after Sister Mary Alice pointed in her direction. Grace felt a warmth flow through her as Bảo's hand slowly unfurled and he offered her a tiny wave.

CHAPTER 12

Vietnam, 1976

ANH WATCHED HER SISTER PREPARE BảO'S LUNCH BOX BEFORE he set off for school, adding a small amount of fish sauce to make the modest rice gruel more flavorful and then artfully placing three sweet potato leaves on top. She'd been waiting for the right time to share her good news, but she could see how preoccupied Linh was in making sure Bảo's modest meal reflected her heart. Her sister believed that even with the barest ingredients, one could still show great care and love.

Her nephew had been struggling in school. The child always left each morning with a strained smile on his face, but Linh told Anh that he was constantly being bullied by his classmates who called him "a son of a traitor." With so few opportunities to socialize, Bảo spent most of his time with a stray dog he had named Bibo who was so starved for nourishment, he spent most of his days sleeping on the ground. But the child was devoted to him, nuzzling next to him during the hot afternoons and keeping his fur brushed and clean. Several times Linh had caught the boy taking what little food he had on his plate and slipping it into his pocket so he could later offer it to the dog.

In an effort to give his son another outlet, Chung had recently found an old bicycle with no rubber on the tires for Bảo, and the boy—despite a tremendous amount of falling and wobbling at first— miraculously learned to ride it just on the wire rims. But then one day, one of his classmates smashed the front wheel and slashed the old vinyl seat. Linh didn't need Anh to tell her that mean-spirited acts and torments were committed by the same children whose fathers harassed

Minh and Chung at the cooperative farm. How many times had Minh been blamed for a crop failure or accused of sabotaging the plantings when they didn't grow? In the poverty and widespread hunger that affected the community, everyone—adults and children alike—was looking for places to unleash their frustration.

"One more thing, bé tí," Linh said to Bảo before he departed, her voice lifting in an attempt to provide him some cheer. She reached into her apron and pulled out a small mango she'd miraculously found on the path that morning, the skin not quite golden. Despite its modest size, it was nearly perfect. She took her knife and quickly peeled off the skin and cut the flesh off the pith. "I saved this one just for you."

That afternoon, Anh confided in her sister that finally, after so many years of trying with no luck, she had missed her monthly cycle.

"Sister!" Linh rejoiced at the news. "Our ancestors have heard your prayers."

Anh beamed. It had taken a painfully long time for them to hear it, but she was now so grateful, her heart was bursting.

"No more lifting. No more pulling the cart. . . ." Linh insisted. "I will cover for you so the others don't know you're not doing as much physical labor."

"Bảo will finally have a little one to play with," she said, smiling. She had herself wished for another child, but they barely had enough food to feed Bảo.

"My sister is going to be a mother!" She threw her arms around Anh's neck and kissed her.

Over the next few months, Linh cared for Anh with renewed energy. She grated ginger root into hot water to fight any nausea. She collected betel leaves to ensure her sister had extra vitamins and massaged her feet when they became tired and swollen.

Then one morning, men in Communist uniforms arrived looking for Minh.

"There've been complaints made against your husband!" one of the men shouted at Anh. "Where is he? He needs to know that if he doesn't work harder, we'll send him up north!"

Anh froze. She knew if her husband was taken to a camp again, it would be far harsher than the one he'd been sent to the last time.

In an effort to distract the soldiers, she began evoking the protection of their ancestors very loudly, a signal to Minh to let him know there was danger and he should run.

"Tell us where your husband is!" one of the soldiers barked again. He pushed the rifle into her ribs.

"My husband isn't here," she whimpered, hoping he'd had enough time to flee from the backyard.

The men, infuriated by her answer, shook their heads and shouted at each other. They kicked over metal pails and tore down the hammocks strung outside. They found a small sack of rice and emptied it onto the dirt floor. They searched the house, throwing pots down from the kitchen shelves and laundry from the clothesline. Most painful to Anh was the destruction of the family's altar; the men shattered the small ceramic vase with its pale white flower and the plate with the mound of salt, burning incense, and piece of fruit.

As the soldiers' rampage continued, Linh—who'd heard her sister's cries—rushed to her side, grateful that Bảo had already left for school and her husband had already departed for the farm.

Suddenly, the terrible sound of a man screaming pierced through the air.

Two men in uniform emerged from the woods, dragging Minh on the ground.

The men wouldn't listen to his protests of innocence. They pulled him by his hair into the small courtyard in front of their hut.

They began kicking him in the ribs, chanting, "Capitalist traitor" until his blood soaked the parched soil. "You are lazy. You should be ashamed," another one said as he kicked Minh's head.

Linh held Anh back as they both begged the men to stop. But the beating was relentless. It took no more than five minutes of their boots striking her husband's body for the life to drain from him.

"Let's go!" the head soldier finally commanded. The men walked toward the jeep. All but one soldier, who stepped over a sobbing Anh and pushed his face close to Linh's. "Tell your husband he's next!" he hissed with narrow eyes before making sure the two sisters saw him spit inches away from Minh's body.

Anh did not remember what happened in the hours that followed. She had a vague sensation of her sister silently washing Minh's body, her hands moving deftly to remove any trace of dirt or blood from his skin. She recalled Bảo's wide eyes as his father dug a crude grave, the boy clutching the fruit his mother had given him for the spiritual offering, and finally the long incantation of prayers. But Anh had gone through the steps of the burial as though she were in a trance.

"You must eat something," Linh tried to insist after the funeral, but Anh could do nothing beyond finding a mat on the floor and curling herself into a tight ball.

"A little rice gruel—please." She held a ladle of watery liquid near Anh's lips. Each grain used to make it had been scooped up and cleaned after the attack.

Anh shook her head and refused. But when Bảo came the next morning with a small wooden bowl full of porridge, she managed to take in a few spoonfuls.

"You're a good boy," she said, her eyes full of tears. The sight of him both warmed her heart and pained her. How lucky he was to still have his father, while she would now be forced to raise her baby on her own.

* * *

Three days later, Anh awoke with terrible cramps. She pulled off the blanket and discovered her cotton pants were soaked through with blood. The child who had begun to grow inside her, the manifestation of her and Minh's love, had untethered itself from her womb while she was sleeping. As she reached between her legs, her fingers touching the crimson, clotting mass, Anh couldn't believe the gods could be so cruel. First her husband, now the baby. The two things she loved most in this world were suddenly gone.

Her despair overtook her. What had she done to deserve such a punishment?

Anh shuddered. Part of her had always been superstitious, the belief that evil spirits could inhabit a body and cause it harm. And only days earlier, just after they'd buried Minh, she'd felt a pang of resentment that her baby would not have the protection of its father, like Bảo enjoyed. Now Anh wondered if she'd caused her miscarriage by having such terrible, selfish thoughts. Had she brought about her own misfortune by jealously yearning to be more like Linh? Had she poisoned her womb with her envy?

When Linh came in carrying a cold compress for her head and some warm broth, Anh turned away from her and only groaned.

Over the next week, Linh ignored Anh's efforts to keep her at a distance. "The baby will now be with Minh," Linh said, trying again to offer some comfort to her sister.

"I wish the gods had taken me instead," Anh wept. "You are so fortunate. You still have your husband and son," she murmured to Linh. "But I've lost everything."

"Nonsense." Linh waved away such dark thoughts. "You also have Chung and me. You have Bảo." She clutched Anh's hands in hers.

"But we all must be careful now," Linh said quietly. "Your losses are terrible and unfair; but we mustn't draw any more attention to ourselves."

That night Linh held Bảo extra close, his little body curled next to hers. When her husband approached her the following morning with fear in his eyes, revealing his concern that the soldiers would come for him next, she listened intently. And when he whispered to her that he thought they should try to escape, she did not protest.

CHAPTER 13

Long Island, 1979

GRACE HANDED THE DINNER PLATES TO THE GIRLS TO SET the table.

"How was everyone's day?" Tom asked as he stepped into the busy kitchen.

"I went up to the motherhouse today. It looks like they have their hands full up there," Grace said as she arranged the chicken cutlets on a plate. "But it was good to see Bảo."

"Maybe we can we adopt him?" Molly asked. It was just like Molly to be concerned and want to strategize about ways to help a stranger. Although the youngest, she was the child who always took the lead in school with food drives, toy campaigns for needy families, or fundraisers for St. Jude. Katie scraped her dish noisily into the waste bin. "It doesn't work like that, stupid. They have agencies that care for kids like that."

"He has his aunt," Grace reminded the children. "He doesn't need to be adopted." She was still trying to sort through her thoughts from the afternoon.

"But he can't be happy at that place," Molly insisted. "Otherwise he wouldn't have run away."

"It could be that he's struggling in a new place. You can understand that, can't you, honey?" She thought about her own experience in Bellegrove and Jack who lived above the store. Fitting in when others perceived you as an outsider was never easy.

Grace felt Tom's warm hand suddenly on top of her own. "You're not eating," he said gently.

"I'm not hungry. I think I'm going to turn in early tonight. Are you heading back out to the store?"

"I was, but I can stay here if you're not feeling well."

"No, go on," she said. "Please remind Jack he has a rain check for dinner."

"I will," he said and then kissed her on her head.

When Tom arrived at the store that evening, he found Jack in the back room repairing a 1960s Breguet chronograph watch. Hunched over the long wooden table, his hair longer than typical for a grown man, he held the open timepiece in one hand and a metal tweezer in the other. Hendrix, his black Labrador, slept comfortably at Jack's feet, his slow and steady breathing adding yet another layer of calm to the room.

Jack only worked in the evenings, when the store was shuttered closed and no one could see him. He slept during the day upstairs in the apartment Tom rented out to him at a reduced rate and came down after the shop was closed and then worked into the night. The arrangement had benefited them both.

He had learned the trade quickly from Tom. First just simple work, like replacing quartz batteries, and then onto more complicated repairs like replacing worn out pinions and stripping gears. After a few years, he could do just about everything Tom could do. His presence had made life at the shop infinitely easier for Tom, who enjoyed being out in the front and chatting with customers, many of whom he had known for most of his life.

Now all Tom had to do was leave the various watches that needed repair tagged and placed in a small cardboard box on the workstation, and Jack would have them all finished by the morning. If Tom wanted to catch Jack and speak to him in person, he knew he had to stop by the store after hours.

They had met five years before, when Tom was visiting his father at the Veterans Affairs home. It was a chance meeting, the kind that can only happen on a bench in a place where the wounded outnumber the healed, in a meditative garden where the flowers were planted by retired veterans who had found peace through gardening and nurturing delicate blooms.

Tom had brought Harry to live at the VA home only a couple months before and was still struggling to deal with his father's physical and mental decline, particularly after losing his mother to cancer two years earlier. After Harry had suffered more than a dozen episodes of becoming disoriented and unable to recognize Tom, he and Grace felt they had little choice but to make sure he received supervised care. And although they struggled to believe a man in his early sixties could be suffering from dementia, the doctors at the VA attributed the premature memory issues to head trauma they found in Harry's medical records. The nursing home where they brought Harry sat behind the larger veterans hospital. A cultivated garden stretched between the two structures, its leafy green trees and shrubbery shielded from the street view.

There were no statues in the meditative garden, though from afar, certain figures seemed cut from stone. On a warm day, one could often see men in wheelchairs positioned by their nurses or loved ones in places where they could enjoy a little sun. Men with solemn faces. Some with a missing leg, others with a shirtsleeve pinned behind their back, and a few with eyes hidden by thick, dark glasses.

The first time Tom saw Jack sitting on the bench at the VA garden, he only saw his profile from the right side. Jack was a sturdy-looking man in his mid- to late twenties. He wore an olive-green army coat, jeans, and work boots. His dark curly hair was unruly and long. His head was bent over a magazine, the pages wavy and worn.

He was deep in his reading when Tom sat down next to him.

"Do you mind if I sit here?" he asked, hoping to spend a few minutes in the garden gathering his thoughts. His father had not recognized him when Tom came to visit that morning. Instead, he had called him "Jimmy" over and over again and kept asking if the fire had been put out. This imagined fire in Harry's head had been tormenting him for days. When Tom told him the fire had been extinguished, his paper-skinned hand, blue-veined and spotted, lifted up from beneath his bedsheets and cradled Tom's face. He could still feel the lingering sensation of his father's touch on his cheek.

Jack took a moment before he answered him, a beat before that flash of discovery he knew was coming. Tom would remember it always. He glanced at the worn magazine between Jack's hands, with Bruce Springsteen on the cover.

"*Born to Run* is such an incredible album."

"Yeah." Jack nodded. "Sure is."

Tom began to hum a few bars of the title song, and Jack's foot tapped on the grass as he joined in. Two strangers connected for a brief moment through a song's lyrics.

When they finished, Jack lifted his head and turned to look at Tom.

His gaze was unexpected, shocking. Jack's left eye was sealed shut. Half of his face was lost under a maze of angry red scars.

Tom fell silent.

He stared at Jack. His one sunken cheek appeared like a deflated balloon, a valley etched in trauma. The opposite side of his face was smooth, with one perfectly shaped brown iris, while the other eye was hardly visible. The lid was drooping, and a portion of his forehead was a dome of thick pink skin.

"I don't mind, brother," Jack said. "The question is, do you?"

***

Tom believed there were times in your life when you felt time moving in slow motion. These moments were rare, and Tom could count them on one hand, like the birth of his two girls or the death of his mother. Even the first time Grace had spoken to him at the mixer. His father had always said time couldn't stand still, but in all of those instances, it felt to Tom like it had.

Now he felt as though he were in a painfully slow free fall. He didn't want to look away from the man who was now facing him with so much pain sewn into his skin. But he also didn't want the man to think he was staring at him either.

"I bought that record the week it came out," he said, finally breaking the silence. "But you know what? 'Born to Run' isn't even the best song on the album. . . ."

"Yeah." Jack nodded. He looked straight ahead now. The wounded side of his face was no longer in full view. "It's 'Thunder Road,'" Jack said.

"Damn right." Tom laughed.

They both started to sing the final verse of the lyrics.

Jack still had not reopened the magazine. One palm rested on the cover, five large fingers spread open like a fan. "You can sit here if you want."

"Thanks," Tom answered. "It's been a long morning." He sat down and stretched out his bum leg and massaged it.

"You here for that leg?"

Tom's face grew warm. He always felt a wave of shame come over him whenever people thought his bad leg was from the war. "No . . . bad motorcycle accident. I shattered it in eight places."

Jack's eyes softened, and he reopened his magazine.

"Lucky you." He said it like he meant it.

**

For the next few months, whenever Tom went to see his dad and if the weather was cooperative, he'd walk into the garden and see if Jack was there. He wasn't always, but more often than not, Tom would find him there reading on the bench, just as he had seen him the first time, hunched over a magazine or a worn paperback, his army jacket covering his tall frame.

Sometimes Tom would comment on who was on the cover of the magazine; other times he found he had nothing to say except to remark a bit on the day's temperature. But regardless, soon a familiarity emerged between them.

It struck Tom how the wounds of war could be so different between men. His father's was internal. You would never know about his hauntings from what he had seen in Germany—unless you were his wife who slept next to him for forty years and heard his cries at night, or his son who now visited him and heard him lost in those memories, far more often than he wanted.

It would be five months before Tom eventually learned Jack's story, when one morning Jack folded back the paperback novel he was reading and looked Tom straight in the face. Tom no longer recoiled when he saw the damaged skin or the sealed-shut eye. He saw a man finally able to unburden himself. Perhaps even more powerfully, he saw trust.

CHAPTER 14

Allentown, Pennsylvania, 1969

On January 5, six months before his twenty-first birth-day, Jack got his papers confirming that his draft number had been called. He had hoped after he had made it past his eighteenth birthday that he'd escape being shipped off to Vietnam, but then the draft laws were changed, allowing men up to the age of twenty-one to be sent over, and now even married men were no longer exempt. Jack had never considered himself particularly lucky, so part of him almost expected that the army would call him up only a few months before he turned twenty-one. It wasn't Murphy's law, he liked to jest. It was "Jack's law." If something unlucky were to happen, it happened to Jack so often that it had become an inside joke with his buddies.

The envelope was waiting for him on the kitchen table. His mother sat across from it with a cup of black coffee in her hand. It looked like she had been having a conversation with it for hours.

He had been working at Auggie's Auto since he graduated high school, and the extra income helped with the house payments. At the end of the month, he'd take the remaining cash and store it away. He was hoping to someday have enough money to buy a new Stratocaster guitar and get a place of his own.

When he entered the kitchen, he knew without either of them exchanging a single word what was in that letter.

"Aw, Ma . . ."

She lifted the paper. Her eyes were glassy. Her face was white.

She started to say something, but the words caught in her throat.

He stepped toward her. Trying to act like a man, he pushed his shoulders back and reached for the letter, pulling it out of the envelope and reading it over quickly.

"Looks like my number got called." He let out a nervous laugh because he didn't know how else to fill the air.

Days later, he packed his duffel bag with only what he thought he needed. The underwear and shirts. The white socks. The dark brown shoes. The money he had earned from Auggie's remained stored in a peanut butter jar.

He brought the jar over when he came in to say goodbye to his mother. "This is for you," he told her. "Looks like I won't be getting that new Strat anytime soon, Ma."

"You're going to come back." Her voice broke. "You're going to get yourself that damn guitar."

He thought about his dad, who didn't come back from work one evening sixteen years before. Never even came back to pack a suitcase. He only had a vague memory of his father. The work boots that sounded heavy on the floorboards when he came in late at night. The face that was never clean-shaven. His cologne, the smell of Budweiser.

He had left him and his mother when Jack was only five. Now Jack was the one leaving his mother, and it gutted him.

"I love you, Jack," she told him. He knew she meant it. She was the kind of woman who saved her words, believing it easier to speak plainly.

Jack leaned over her armchair to kiss her goodbye. Her breath smelled like coffee and cigarettes. "Promise me you'll come home." She reached for his hand and grabbed it tightly in her fist.

"I promise," he answered. He had promised the same thing to Becky the night before when they lay huddled in her bedroom, his body pressed against hers.

He had not wanted to get up from her bed and leave her. The curve of her body was so beautiful. He lifted his hand and traced her silhouette from the top of her shoulder, through the dip in her waist, to the cliff of her hips.

"Becky . . ."

Her face was half-veiled by the curtain of long chestnut-colored hair. She leaned in closer and adjusted her bangs so he could see her face more clearly. Her green eyes were smooth as stones from a river. Her expression just as calm.

"What if I don't come back?"

His heart hurt inside his chest. He didn't want to believe this might be the last time he held Becky in his arms.

"Don't say such a thing," she said firmly. She pulled him close and kissed him on the mouth. Her lips were so soft and gentle, he had to force himself not to cry.

In this naked moment of intimacy before he left, he wanted to shed everything that weighed on him. He wanted to tell her he was afraid. He didn't want to come home in a body bag. He didn't want to lose a limb and spend the rest of life in a wheelchair. But he couldn't come undone in front of Becky. He wanted her to think him strong and invincible. He wanted to be seen as brave.

He shifted the conversation to the practicalities and tried to gather himself. "You'll check in with Ma while I'm gone?"

"Of course," she said, as though it was a given.

He was happy she was continuing her education. He would be away for nearly two years, and she would focus on her studies. No one would be a better teacher than his beautiful Becky. Jack could already imagine her in front of a classroom with all the children looking up at her with adoration.

What he didn't say to her was that when he returned, *if he even did return*, he was going to ask her to marry him. They had been dating since the beginning of senior year, when he finally worked up the nerve to ask her to homecoming. That afternoon he felt like he had won the prize. Becky Dougherty. The girl that lit up the homecoming parade with her perfect white smile and gentle wave. He would soon learn she liked all the things he liked. Rock and roll. Jelly donuts. Buttermilk pancakes and movies at the old drive-in on dollar night.

Now that Jack's last hours in Allentown were slipping away, everything seemed suddenly crystal clear. Becky was the woman he wanted to have children with. He had never been good in school like her, but their children would take after her. They'd be smart and beautiful.

If he got home, their life would be good. They'd be perfect together, like a slice of pizza and an ice-cold Coke. He pulled her close again and felt her heart beat next to his chest.

"I love you, Becky."

He would remember always how she told him she loved him. She put his face between her palms. Kissed him again, this time so deeply, he felt her warmth spreading through his entire body. He made love to her one last time before getting dressed.

As he zipped up his jeans, she stared at him from the bed. "I'm going to write to you every day, I promise."

"Who even knows what the mail will be like. . . ."

"Of course there will be mail, Jack. I'll send care packages, too."

"Don't worry about me. I'm worried about my mother. I'm worried about *you*."

"I'll be fine. She'll be fine. . . ." She rolled onto her back and stared at the ceiling. "You're the one that we'll both be worrying about."

She placed a flat palm on her belly, where minutes before he had kissed her.

"My mom saved all the letters my dad wrote to her when he was in Germany. I'm going to save every one you write, too."

He had forgotten until Becky mentioned it that her father had been in World War II. He had died when she was five from stomach cancer. Her mother had remarried a few years later, but Becky had showed him a photograph of her father dressed in his Army Air Corps uniform when they began dating. "I have only a handful of memories of him," she confessed as she held the portrait. "But in some ways, he's still my hero. I only wish I had the chance to get to know him better."

Jack was grateful she hadn't brought up any anti-war sentiment when he learned he was being shipped off. So many of the kids going off to college were already engaged in protests. He would have hated spending his last days with Becky fighting about whether America should be in the war. He loved her more for not making his departure feel worse than it already did.

He was now fully dressed. He tucked in his shirt and sucked in his breath. He gazed upon her nakedness one last time, trying to commit it to memory.

"Promise me, Jack—you'll come back in one piece." She pulled herself to her knees and extended her arms, beckoning him over, lassoing him around his neck. Planting one last kiss.

He knew she wouldn't let him go until made the vow. But in his mind, he couldn't help but imagine the photographs printed in the newspapers and the footage that was broadcast on every major news channel. Body bags hoisted onto helicopters, tarmacs lined with coffins draped with American flags. He bet each and every one of those men had made promises to their mothers or girlfriends that they'd come home in one piece.

"I promise," he said. He loved her so much. The words were uttered like a gift.

He spent eight weeks in basic training at Parris Island, then eight more in infantry training in Camp Lejeune before being given his first leave home. Needing more live bodies in the Marine Corps, someone at a desk somewhere had made the executive decision to make him part of that prestigious group rather than including him with the rest of the men drafted into the army.

In training, they beat the boy out of him. He learned to take orders. To take punishment. To eat food that had no taste. He had grown up in a household without a father or brother, and now he learned to live and sleep in the constant company of men.

He was grateful his lean build had saved him from the barbs of the drill sergeant, who tormented those carrying any excess pounds. And while he was not exempt from being called a "shitbird," one of the drill instructors' favorite slurs for anyone who failed at an order, Jack was among the few recruits who could finish a twelve-hour run holding a rifle, four canteens of water, a helmet, and a heavy pack.

When he wasn't doing close order drills, physical training, or weapons classes, Becky floated in the back of his mind. She had kept her promise and written to him almost daily. Her letters were always written on pretty stationery, sometimes on daffodil-colored paper, other times on cheery pink. When he read them, he tried to imagine her saying the words. *My dearest Jack . . .* She always began in her big loopy handwriting. She signed off with love and kisses, decorating the remaining space on the page with *x*'s and *o*'s.

During his two-week home leave following his infantry training at Camp Lejeune, they had spent as much time together as possible. They drove to Atlantic City, and he blasted the radio, and Becky pulled her hair out of her ponytail to let it whip free in the wind. Jack splurged on lobster dinners for each of them. He loaded his baked potato with sour cream and butter and ate every single kernel of his corn on the cob. Every sensation seemed heightened to him. The smell of Becky's perfume. The flash of light in her eyes when she threw her head back and laughed.

After dinner, in the soft, hazy twilight, they walked down the boardwalk hand in hand. The smell of the Atlantic filled Jack's nostrils, and the briny salt air made him feel alive. He was happy the Corps no longer made it a requirement for marines to be in uniform when they were on leave. Too many incidents had occurred with peace activists attacking men in uniform. So Jack wore a soft flannel shirt and his favorite pair of jeans, happy to return to his old, familiar skin. They found one of those instant photo booths. She made funny faces and planted kisses on his face. His favorite one was of her in profile with her eyes closed, her lips pressed firmly on his cheek.

The following morning, they drove back to Allentown so he could spend time with his mother. In the months he was away, his mother appeared to have aged terribly.

She walked toward Jack and wrapped her arms around him.

"My sweet boy..." She sighed as she looked up to him. Her short corn silk hair was parted on the side, her blue eyes rippled with emotion. "You look like a man now." She touched his cheek with her hand.

"Aw, Ma..." he answered and kissed her on top of her head.

"You're going to stay here the rest of your leave, right? I told Walter that I wasn't going back to work until you left for Camp Pendleton."

"You didn't need to do that, Ma," he said and hugged her tight.

"Why? I haven't taken a vacation in years," she joked. "I think I deserve a little more time with my son."

He would stay with her, and they'd watch TV together, all the shows she enjoyed, like *Carol Burnett* and *The Ed Sullivan Show*. She loved Kentucky Fried Chicken and mashed potatoes, so they'd get an entire bucket and eat the leftovers cold the next day.

At night, when his mother had fallen asleep in her big comfy chair, the television's white noise still churning in the background,

Jack would empty her ashtray of extinguished cigarettes and drape an old afghan blanket over her legs before quietly leaving the house. The moon would be bright against the night sky as he drove over to Becky's small apartment, where he'd find her asleep with a book open beside her pillow. He unbuckled his belt, shed his jeans, and slipped next to her. His body folding into hers.

The sweet memory of being in Becky's arms would be the last time he saw her. After his leave from Camp Lejeune, he would spend eight weeks in Camp Pendleton, where he was literally run into the ground and toughened up both physically and emotionally for what was to come. After his second month there, he received his orders to join a rifle company in Vietnam, and a week later he shipped out with several hundred men to Da Nang.

During one of his first days in Vietnam, Jack headed north, packed into an olive-drab transport truck with the members of his new platoon. Beside him sat a shy-looking private by the name of Stanley Coates. His head bowed toward his lap, his rifle tucked between his knees. Jack had hardly noticed him back in training camp, but earlier that morning after the young man pulled out a small, leather-bound Bible, his innocence stood out in high relief to Jack. He watched Stanley quietly, almost in awe, as the boy whispered a psalm, his lips moving as his index finger traced the words.

Amid the crude talk and the harsh jungle conditions, Stanley stood out. He had large blue eyes that bulged slightly, making him appear as though he was locked in a perpetual state of wonder.

"Where you from?" Jack asked as the vehicle bumped along Highway 1.

"Bet you never heard of it. . . ." Stanley smiled. "Bell Buckle, Tennessee."

Jack clasped his rifle between both hands and grinned. "You're right, man. I never have." Jack looked at Stanley from the corner of his eye. He was tall and lanky, with hardly any muscle on his bones. So fair, his skin looked as white as milk. "You don't look like you're even old enough to go to high school."

Stanley's laugh was soft and low. "That's what the everybody said back at Pendleton. It's not true, though. I enlisted three days after I turned seventeen."

The men in the truck were packed shoulder to shoulder, the heat so oppressive that as the sweat rolled down their cheeks, it made them look like they were crying. Stanley pulled his shoulders inward, creating a slight space between him and the others.

"Can I ask you something?" Stanley probed.

Jack shrugged. "Sure."

"Do you ever pray?" His gaze looked hopeful and painfully childlike—as though he was searching for a friend to anchor himself to in his strange new surroundings. "I noticed back at Pendleton, you were one of the only guys not talking trash about women."

"Nah," Jack muttered. "That's not something I do."

Stanley grew quiet. As he turned toward Jack, a ray of sharp sunlight hit the truck for a moment, and he appeared eerily illuminated. "My daddy's a Baptist preacher. He didn't want me to come fight out here, but I wanted to show him I'm no baby." He nibbled a little on his bottom lip. "I thought signing up was the best way to prove to him I was a man."

Jack raised an eyebrow. "You needed to come all the way to Vietnam for that? Couldn't you have just shot a deer and brought it home for dinner or something?"

Stanley shrugged. "I dunno, maybe . . . but I'm here now anyway. Right?" His pale hand lifted up to adjust his helmet. "No looking back, that's what they say. . . ."

Jack was only half listening to Stanley now; instead, he was distracted by the unfurling new landscape: the thatched villages, thick tropical trees, and water buffalo hitched to carts.

"You know, I've never even had a beer," Stanley added, though at this point, it seemed to Jack that the boy was actually talking to himself.

"Did you hear that?" one of the other men interrupted, slapping his hand down on the seat. "Fucking Stanley never even had a beer!"

Everyone on the truck began to laugh. Everyone except Jack, who didn't find it funny at all.

The steel helmet. The flak jacket. The heavy boots. The four canteens of water, the five grenades. The bandolier that held his ammunition and essential M16 rifle. All of it is heavy. But none of it is as burdensome as the twenty-five-pound PRC-25 radio he carries on his back. Every platoon has a single radio transmitting operator, and that responsibility is given to Jack. Lance Corporal Jack Grady from Allentown, Pennsylvania.

Six foot two. Tawny-brown hair and a face like a movie star. Crystal-blue eyes that twinkle when he laughs. *Hollywood*—that's the nickname his buddies call him at first, and then it sticks.

He doesn't ask for help when lugging the radio, even though his pack is heavy and the heat diabolical. Nor does he tell his buddies that he carries his sweetheart's most recent letter tucked into the mesh of his helmet. The photograph from Atlantic City is also slipped inside, now creased and faded from his perspiration.

Some days it reaches over a hundred degrees, and the platoon collapses on the ground, peeling off their sweat-soaked gear. Their feet swelter in their boots, drenched from walking in rice paddies. Jungle rot eats away at their skin and the lieutenant orders them when they take a rest to pull their boots off, wring out their socks, and air out their feet.

There are fourteen men in his squad, three fire teams, and as they set out in patrol, they walk in single file. He is protected by a few men walking in front of him. Those men are the ones who must cut the jungle down as they walk. Sometimes with a machete. Other times with just their standard-issue knife. It is not a coveted position to be the first two men in line. The first man has the highest risk stepping on a booby trap or land mine. The second will most likely be killed in the blast as well. But Jack is somewhere in the middle, protected by the five or six men in front of him. He walks behind the second lieutenant, his platoon commander, Franklin L. Bates. Jack must be within arm's length from Bates at all times in case he needs to reach the company headquarters and call in for an artillery strike or medical evacuation.

When the radio is needed, Jack will slip it off his back and give Lieutenant Bates the hand receiver. He carries the radio just for him.

Sometimes he hears music in his head when the platoon is route marching. Sometimes he pretends that the radio on his back is going to play Jimi Hendrix or the Doors. The Rolling Stones. The Kinks. The Who. It's going to be a jukebox, calling the men to song, not to war.

He finally pulls it off his back. Picks up the receiver, calls in, and Bates reports their coordinates. They pause for instructions, praying they're not blown to pieces while they wait.

Around them, the jungle teems with creatures that are all against them. The mosquitoes, the leeches. The enemy hidden under the brush.

He sleeps fitfully, never deeply. He hears the enemy everywhere.

He carries the radio like a lifeline. He learns to shimmy across the dirt, extending the telephone-like receiver to his commanding officer. He keeps the radio on even in a foxhole, for it's his responsibility. The

radio is the only thing they have to summon help. To ask for backup
or covering gunfire, to ask to help retrieve the wounded and the dead.

He realizes early on his life is not what is the most valuable. It is the
thing strapped to his back. Without it, they are all lost.

CHAPTER 15

Vietnam, 1978

IN THE DAYS LEADING UP TO THEIR ESCAPE, LINH TRIES TO MAKE nothing seem out of the ordinary for Bảo. The firewood is stacked outside the house, the laundry is washed and placed on a clothesline, and the water jugs are full. She sends him off to school each morning.

This type of planning has been her and Chung's mindset for nearly a year and half. It was well known that the Communists watched everything from afar. If people suddenly placed too much money in the bank, or if a neighbor reported that they heard a family was quickly selling off all their belongings, an arrest could be ordered solely on the suspicion they were preparing to flee.

So for just over a year, they have worked slowly and carefully. Chung took on more responsibilities at the collective farm to prove his loyalty. Linh found a job picking fruit at the orchard that had been her family's until the takeover. At night, she and Anh wove baskets, using strips of bamboo from the garden, then sold them at a weekend market several miles away. Every bit of money they saved was buried underneath the earthen jars behind their house.

They have already paid all they have to the latest smuggler who has agreed to get them out of Vietnam. Two other fishermen had previously promised Linh they would get the four of them out. Each of them took the first payment from her but never reappeared for the second. But now things are different, for it is the first time Linh has paid the second of the three payments. The last one is to be made on the day of their journey.

Five days before they are set to leave, Linh and Chung realize they don't have enough money to make the final payment. They continue to calculate the missing sum in their mind, struggling to figure out a way to get the needed funds. It is late at night when the couple find themselves staring at their hands.

Their gold wedding bands glimmer on their fingers. Sacred to them in the most holy way, for they believe the rings are a symbol of their marriage and love. The thought of selling them causes them both tremendous anguish.

"We'll replace them as soon as we can," Chung promises. He slides his off and hands it to his wife.

Linh holds the ring in her palm then closes her fingers around the gold circle. The last time she held the ring in her grip was on her wedding day, when she and Chung took vows that bound themselves to each other for eternity.

"It will bring us bad luck if we sell them," she whispers.

"We cannot stay," Chung reminds her.

"But will it even be enough?"

Chung does a rough calculation in his head. "I think we might need to ask Anh to sell hers, too."

Linh shakes her head. "No, we can't. She's already lost so much."

He doesn't answer at first. Then Chung's face becomes resolved. "I will ask her, then."

The next morning Linh rises early. She dresses in her traditional *áo bà ba*, the long white tunic and flowing pants. She brushes her long black hair and adjusts her conical hat to cover her eyes. On her left hand, she still wears her gold wedding band. In a small silk coin purse, she carries her husband's as well as the ring Anh has stoically given her.

Three hours later, she walks home with the amount of money they need for the journey, but the sight of her bare finger, and the realization that Chung's and Anh's are now bare too, breaks her heart.

On the morning of their escape, Chung, nervous to draw any attention to him and his family, goes to work as usual and harnesses the village's half-starved water buffalo to a plow while the women plan their separate departure.

The sisters move quickly after Chung departs. Bảo does as his mother instructs, wearing a second pair of clothing underneath his normal cotton shirt and pants. His mother doesn't protest this time when he takes some food she's left in the kitchen and puts it on a plate for Bibo.

"See you soon," he tells the dog as he kisses him by his matted ear and tenderly rubs his spotty brown coat. He thinks they are only going on a trip and will be back in a few short days.

Anh has packed a pot, three lemons, a box of sugar, and some triangles of pressed rice wrapped in leaves into a tightly folded kerchief. Linh carries a thermos of water, some kerosene, and more food as well. They walk slowly down dirt paths and through patches of forest.

"Mama, are we almost there?" he asks after two hours of trekking.

"Yes," Linh replies. "We are almost there." But she stretches the truth. They continue to walk for another hour. Just when Bảo doesn't think he can go one step farther, his mother points to a small wooden house.

"It's just over there," she indicates.

The house is long and narrow. Mud floor. Corrugated metal walls. A little girl in a torn yellow dress is in the back, drying banana leaves.

Linh tells Bảo to go in the back and help the girl. "Make a new friend," she says.

A man emerges from the house and waves Linh and Anh inside.

Within the dark, dank interior, Linh takes out a can from the things she has packed. She opens it and spills out some coffee. Within the dark grains, two small gold bars are revealed. She takes another can out, and two more sparkling bars emerge.

The man takes them and dusts off the coffee by polishing the bars on his pant leg.

Anh excuses herself and goes outside. She hears the little girl pepper Bảo with questions. She looks younger than him. Her hair is long and tangled; her face is smudged a little with dirt.

"My name is Mai," she says. "Are you here for my father?" she asks. "People come here and bring him gold."

Anh is silent as Linh tells Bảo they are both leaving him and will meet him later after it is dark. "Your father will meet us there too. It is too dangerous for us all to travel together, so we need to arrive there separately."

She watches as Linh crouches down to kiss him on the head. "That little girl in the back is the daughter of the man who is arranging our special voyage," she whispers. "Her father is a friend of the captain. She knows the meeting spot where the boat will come."

He reaches to touch his mother, and the sight of his fingers reaching for Linh's cheek guts Anh to her core. Her sister is kneeling, her arms stretched out to him. Her black hair is tied back, and the light catches his reflection in her eyes.

"I want to go with you," he begs. "I don't want to stay here alone."

Linh fights back tears. "I know, bé tí, I know." She struggles to soothe him, to make him feel safe, like she has always done in the past.

She reaches into one of the baskets that she is carrying on her pole, and she hands him a mango.

"Everything will be fine," she offers, trying to smile through her tears.

Anh turns away. For years, she has believed her sister's promises, but now she cannot help but feel uncertain. Still, as she listens to Linh's parting words to her son, she knows they are true.

"Bảo, you know your ma always saves the sweetest fruit for you."

Anh and Linh quietly trudge through the woods, not a word exchanged between them. They know the plan. They have imagined it for weeks. Now each step must fall into place, and they pray for no unforeseen problems that might derail their escape.

The biggest risk is leaving Bảo alone with the fisherman and his daughter. Anh knows Linh must surrender to this part of their escape—that her brother-in-law has stressed that they must separate as a family to avoid suspicion.

But it is an oppressive request. Her sister must put her trust a complete stranger and hope he does what they've bribed him to do—to bring Bảo to the place where their boat will depart.

Anh takes a step closer to her sister, lets the cloth with her few belongings slide from her shoulders. "He will be there waiting for us," she promises. Her hand reaches to squeeze Linh's fingers.

For her whole life, it's been her sister who has reassured her. But now their roles are reversed.

Linh turns to her, the whites of her eyes shining against the dark sky. She grips Anh's hand in her own. But she says nothing. For the first time since Anh can remember, her sister has no words.

CHAPTER 16

AT NIGHTFALL THE FISHERMAN TELLS HIS DAUGHTER, MAI, to take the little boy to where they fish after sunset.

Bảo follows the girl. Her yellow dress is like a lantern in the evening sky.

As they approach the shore, he notices a few small fishing boats already there, but Bảo does not see his mother or father.

"Is that our boat?" he asks Mai as he points to the tiny wooden crafts bobbing in the dark water.

"No," she answers. She giggles as if she is still playing a game.

"Is that our boat?" he asks again, indicating to another one that looks empty anchored closer to the shore.

"No," she answers again.

Fear washes over him. Neither his mother nor his father nor Anh has come over to meet him, and he wonders if Mai's father has somehow tricked his parents, taken their gold and separated them from him in the process of this hoax.

"Where is your father?" Bảo now begs the little girl. "He promised to help my parents."

Her face glows in the moonlight. Her eyes are wide and empty. "I don't know," she says. "Where is yours?"

Bảo has no answer. He last saw his father at sunrise as he headed out, a pole with two baskets balanced on his back. "We are going on a journey," Chung told him. But he still doesn't understand why they've left him here all alone.

***

Night falls and the air cools. Two layers on his body, but no blanket for warmth, Bảo curls himself tightly into a ball and closes his eyes. Mai has left. He is hungry and imagines a bowl of rice in his hands, counting each grain to make the hours go by more quickly. He tells himself when morning comes, he will convince the captain's daughter to take him back to their hut. If his mother doesn't arrive as she promised, he must think of another plan to ensure they are somehow reunited.

An hour later, he hears a rustle in the grass, and Bảo sees his mother walking toward him. Bảo rushes over and embraces her. She wraps her arms around him and pulls him close. Her warmth flows over him like a blanket. He begins to cry, unable to stifle the emotion that he had fought to control.

"I didn't think you'd ever come," he utters through his tears.

She pulls him again closer to her. "Nothing would keep me from you, bé tí." Minutes later, his aunt emerges from the forest, having followed Linh's path. She walks toward them.

In the grass, mosquitoes buzz and bite. Now, the three of them united, they wait, frozen as statues.

Soon two more adults appear. Like Linh, they are carrying provisions wrapped in cloth. One person is clasping a carved statue of the Virgin Mary to their breast. Another is carrying kerosene.

They all crouch low, looking out to the water, waiting for a sign that their boat is near.

Lastly, Chung arrives. Bảo sees his father approaching through the tall grass, his bamboo pole with its loaded baskets sags across his back. His eyes are lit and flickering in the darkness.

His mother does not move, but Bảo can sense her relief. She turns to him and places a finger over her mouth. But her lips are now curled in a smile. She reaches into her blouse and takes out a yellow handkerchief, which she lifts in the air like a small flag. His father lays his pole down in the tall grass and moves toward them. Anh is a few steps behind.

The light flashes like a beacon from the boat before melting into the shadow of the night.

It was the sign they have been waiting for. Slowly they wade into the river toward a small fishing boat. They walk until the water is waist deep. Linh and Chung lift the cloth-tied bundles of food above their heads. Bảo stays at his mother's side, holding on to her pant leg. None of them can swim, and he's never been so deeply submerged in water before.

Everyone scrambles to try to get on board the boat. The person carrying the statue of the Virgin Mary pushes ahead. The single fisherman, with the light strapped to his head, pulls them each onto the boat, telling them they have all brought too much.

The boat bobs up and down; water laps at its wooden edge.

Bảo is lifted on board, then Linh, then Anh. The men are last. They crouch next to the others, shoulder to shoulder, fitted together to occupy nearly every inch of space.

Chung wraps an arm around his son. Between his knees, he safeguards what they have brought for the journey. Linh's face tips to the moonlight, and Anh watches her sister's family with longing. The ache inside her is overwhelming. She looks back at the strip of land, the country she has known her whole life and the soil in which her husband is buried beneath, the ancestral shrine she has devoted to her prayers for those she has lost, her husband and their baby. She glances at her own naked ring finger, then her sister's and Chung's. She prays that the act of selling their rings won't bring them bad luck.

Her brother-in-law draws Bảo close.

"Is America far?" her nephew asks sweetly. Chung shakes his head. Like the rest of them, he believes America is only a few days' distance by boat. The other side of the world is just next door.

The captain takes a large tarp and throws it over them so that no one can see he is carrying human cargo.

"It's only until we get farther from shore and away from the patrols," Chung whispers to Bảo.

Beneath the tarp, huddled together, they struggle to breathe. Their heads are bowed to their knees, the smells of packed bodies and food is stifling. The small motor in the back of the boat putters softly as the captain begins to head into deeper waters, the shoreline fading into the distance.

Hours later, after the tarp has been removed and most of the passengers drift into sleep, the waves get bigger as they approach the mouth of the South China Sea. They will be awakened by the sensation of the boat rocking back and forth. Water slaps against the vessel's wooden sides, some of it spilling over into the hull.

One of the women has positioned the wooden Virgin Mary at the front of the boat in an effort to create a powerful maidenhead she believes will bring them luck and steer them to safety. But the waves continue to intensify, and the others are panicking as they try to scoop the water out of the boat. The captain calls on her to return to the back.

"I'm going to throw it overboard," the captain hollers to her, but she remains at the front, holding the statue as the wind whips through her hair and the water crashes at the bow.

"Sit down!" another man cries from the back.

Finally, one of the men stands up and hurtles toward her, rushing to remove the statue that he thinks is causing the boat to become unstable. But his own movements only increase the boat's instability. As he reaches for the statue, the boat keels to the side.

Anh is cast starboard, pinned to the side between two men, while Bảo, Linh, and Chung are thrown into the cold water. Chung, hearing his son's screams for help, finds his own arms and legs instinctively thrashing and kicking as he searches the dark water to find him. He seizes Bảo and drags him to the boat's edge, focused solely on getting him to safety. The cold water is up to his chin.

But Bảo continues to grip his arm.

"Let me go, I need to get your mother," his father yells now at Bảo.

But Bảo refuses. The boy's fingers dig into Chung's slippery flesh.

"You have to let me go," he pleads one more time to his son. He then bites Bảo's arm, like an animal determined to be freed.

Chung falls back into the water in search of Linh. The water swallowing both of them into the night.

PART II

CHAPTER 17

Long Island, 1979

Grace left the motherhouse promising Sister Mary Alice she would come at least twice a week to help tutor Bảo and the other children with their reading. She could do that easily and also maintain her own household obligations. It was a chance for her to give back in a meaningful way. But she also knew that seeing the Sisters at work had awakened her own yearning to do more than the daily drudgery of cooking, cleaning, and driving.

She had stored many of Katie and Molly's old picture books in the attic, and Grace knew if she made a few calls around the neighborhood, she'd be able to fill the whole Pontiac wagon with boxes of old books and toys.

That afternoon, she was eager to share the good news with the girls when they came home from school. But to her distress, Katie didn't seem to have any interest at all in her mother's new volunteer endeavors, and Molly seemed more concerned about how nuns could actually shelter men inside the motherhouse.

"They're not sharing rooms with the nuns, sweetheart. All the families are living in a separate building."

"Oh." Molly seemed mildly disappointed.

"Can you do me a favor and go to the attic and bring down some of those boxes of your old picture books? You too, Katie."

Katie was buried in the open refrigerator, pulling out snacks of Jell-O pudding. She didn't bother responding to Grace.

Grace felt her chest tighten. No one had told her it would be this difficult to raise a teenage girl. Every day she wondered how Katie would act once she got home from school. Her moodiness was often unleashed on Grace. The little girl who used to rush off the elementary school bus into her mother's arms had long since vanished, transformed into a sullen, sarcastic young woman. Grace missed the old Katie.

"I need you to help your sister with the books, Katherine. Those boxes will be heavy."

Katie licked the chocolate off her spoon. "In a second, Mom. I need to relax. I just got home."

"Fine, but once you're done eating . . ."

Katie rolled her eyes. "Okay, but first I need to call Amy about history homework and Maggie about . . ."

Grace bit her lip. Her daughter had a thousand excuses ready just to avoid helping out. And Grace thought even one was too much.

Grace had not been prepared for a snarky teenager at home, a body that had grown soft in various places, and her own racing mind that often made it difficult for her to sleep.

It felt like some sort of cruel joke that she would feel her own attractiveness slipping away just as her two daughters were coming into their own. Although Katie had yet to recognize her nascent beauty, Grace could see it pushing forth like a spring bulb, each day closer to its full bloom. Katie was tall and slender, and her years of swimming at the local beach club had made her shoulders broad and her legs lean. With her blond hair pulled back into a high ponytail, it was easy to see the strong chiseled features of Tom's mother, Rosie. Her high forehead and small, straight nose.

Grace desperately wanted to take a washcloth and scrub off all the Maybelline mascara and raspberry-pink lip gloss that Katie put on whenever she went out with her friends on the weekend. Didn't Katie realize how beautiful she looked without it? She wished her daughter would appreciate how lucky she was to just be able to roll out of bed and run a comb through her hair.

Grace now viewed her own face like a daily science experiment. She never had bags under her eyes before, not even when the girls were in diapers and she would spend all night trying to soothe them back to sleep. Yet here she was with little pillows underneath her eyes, and though she tried to encourage her teenage daughter to embrace the face God had given her, she spent increasingly more time each morning armed with her concealer stick in hand.

She heard a voice in her head telling her how shallow she was to be so preoccupied by maintaining her appearance. The women of her childhood village never spent time in front of mirrors appraising every inch of their faces or their figures. She had no idea if her mother had even owned a tube of lipstick.

She told herself perhaps she wasn't busy enough. Everyone seemed to need her less and less these days. Molly was no longer a baby, and middle school had catapulted her closer to being a teenager like her older sister. The math was easy enough to do on her fingers. In six years, she and Tom would have an empty house, and she'd be that much older, approaching her midforties. Her mother had died when she was barely fifty-five. That age had seemed neither old nor young to Grace when she returned to her village, pregnant with Molly for her mother's funeral. On that trip, it seemed to Grace that nearly every young woman in the town was pregnant. Even her shy baby brother, Joe, had managed to find himself a wife, and her sister-in-law greeted her with a big round belly and a cup of tea.

It was a strange and painful trip to be home, despite the excitement of her second pregnancy, the wounds of never having made peace with her mother still ran deep.

"How can you do this to us, Gracie?" her mother had sobbed on the telephone when she first shared the news of her engagement to Tom. A terrible pause followed, filled with the static of the long-distance connection.

"I already lost one daughter." Her mother's voice heaved with pain. "Now I'm losing two."

Grace knew it would upset her parents when they heard she was marrying outside the Church. But she still retained her optimism, hoping that when they met Tom, they'd both recognize what a good man he was.

"You're not losing me," she insisted. "I am still your daughter. I will still go to Mass. Still go to confession."

"And your children?" Her mother's voice was now all but inconsolable. "Without a baptism, do you know where they'll end up?"

Grace's throat tightened.

She wondered if her mother had forgotten how not a single person in the village—except for Delilah—would help bury Bridey, despite her having two devout parents.

How Christian had every one of the other men and women of Glennagalt been when they cast out an innocent child? Not very Christian at all.

In their shared family house, her brother Joe's fishing jacket hung on a peg next to her father's. Two pairs of tall rubber boots stood beside her nephew's smaller pair. When they buried her mother, it was next to Bridey's small grave, now weathered from so many years of wind and beating rain.

Her father's stoic veneer vanished during her mother's funeral. Standing in front of the two tombstones, he seemed to finally realize that life, no matter how many years you lived, always seemed far too short in the end.

Tom had quietly shadowed Grace during the trip, making sure she took rests so her feet didn't swell and reminding her to eat despite her lack of appetite. Their baby had just started to kick, and when they lay next to each other at night, tucked together in the room of the small bed-and-breakfast, Tom told her how meaningful it was for him to finally see where Grace came from.

"I can almost taste the salt in the air," he said, turning to her and placing a palm on her belly. "And it's so easy to imagine you as a little girl picking flowers in the glen."

She smiled, warming at his touch. "I'm glad you're here with me now. It's so hard to be pregnant and burying my mother at the same time. And my dad . . . he looks at me with such sadness. . . ."

Tom lifted his hand and caressed the side of her cheek. The sound of his wristwatch ticked in her ear.

"This has to be tough on him, Gracie. I saw your mother's wedding portrait today, and I had to do a double take—for a second there, I thought I was looking at your twin."

Grace closed her eyes. "People used to tell me that a lot when I was a teenager."

"I bet there's a part of him that sees your mother. . . ."

He found her hand and squeezed her fingers. "You're pregnant and you're at this exciting new crossroads, and he's not looking forward at all, Grace. He's looking backward, and, God, it must be gutting."

She knew Tom was right, so in the few days they had left in the village, she let her heart soften and put aside the pain of how her parents, particularly her mother, had reacted when she and Tom announced their engagement.

On their trip, she felt she witnessed her father's heart cracking open just far enough to realize that she had married a good man.

"Take good care of my Gracie," he told Tom the night before they departed. "She's the only girl I have left."

Four years after her mother's funeral, she returned to Ireland to bury her father. His death felt harder somehow than when they had buried her mother. As she stood in the rain—clasping the hands of both of her girls, Tom's umbrella held over them—it struck Grace, as her father's coffin was lowered into the ground, that she would never be someone's little girl again. Her daughters' warm fingers wiggled inside her own, and she gripped them even more tightly. The girls' restlessness, their vitality that rose from their every pore, seemed so precious to Grace at that moment. The weight of death and the cycle of life flowed through her as the priest read the burial rites. The torch had been passed on, and she knew one day her daughters would be mothers themselves, and if she lived long enough, she would find herself with aching bones and liver-spotted skin just like everyone else.

Grace took comfort in that last trip to Ireland before her father passed away. She was grateful that Tom had encouraged her to have empathy for her dad, to try to heal the wounds between them. During her final days in Glennagalt, she had gone down to the docks with Joe and her father and helped them paint the family's old fishing boat. It was positioned on cement blocks, its wooden belly no longer submerged in the icy Atlantic waters, and had already been stripped and sanded.

They bought two cans of bright blue paint and a smaller yellow one for the trim. They each clasped the handle of a single fat brush to coat the wood with the exact shade Grace had picked to match the bluest sky.

"Dad wants to finally put a name on the boat when we're done painting," her brother whispered in her ear that afternoon. It was something her father had always mocked when they were younger: "A boat is just a boat," he'd answer whenever asked if his skiff had a name. Now, after all this time, she assumed sentimentality had gotten the best of him. Grace imagined that perhaps her father would now choose to call it *Bridey*, to show her sister's name had finally managed to rise above the sea after all these years. Or perhaps name it after her late mother, in honor of her quiet endurance. But when Joe finally offered him a jar and a thin brush for the dedication, her father's weathered hand wrote the five letters out carefully. He named the boat *Grace*.

CHAPTER 18

KATIE GOLDEN HAD GROWN WEARY OF HER BEDROOM. THE COT-
ton candy–pink walls, the canopied bed with its calico-flowered bed-
spread and matching rosebud curtains, all of it felt oppressively cloying
to her in recent weeks. Now, with her second year of high school behind
her, Katie found herself impatient for something more sophisticated.
Her friend Abigail had recently convinced her mother to repaint her
room a wisteria purple, and Katie kept dreaming of how much better
her bedroom would be if hers was also updated. It just seemed so painfully childish now.

It wasn't just her bedroom that she imagined reinvented, it was
herself as well. She had promised herself that big changes were coming this summer. She already had enough foresight to go down to the
beach club and apply for a lifeguard position. For as long as she could
remember, she'd been obsessed with the older girls at the club who were
lifeguards. Dressed in their fire engine–red swimsuits, they sat high on
the wooden watchtower of the main pool with a whistle around their
necks and an enviable pair of Ray-Ban sunglasses. How many times
had she jealously watched those girls descend from their towers during
their lunch break into the waiting arms of one of their male counter-
parts, the tan, shirtless boys who always seemed eager to offer an extra
application of Bain de Soleil on their backs or bring them an icy Coke
from the canteen. Popularity seemed suddenly within reach, and Katie
couldn't help but feel giddy with anticipation.

She just had to make sure her mother's latest pity project didn't
cramp her carefully planned social ascent this summer.

For certain, Katie had grown tired of her parents' incessant need to prove how good and selfless they were. Her mother had just found a Vietnamese orphan on the street, and within seconds of seeing the lost boy in the kitchen, Katie could sense her mother's inclination to take the poor, wounded bird under her wing. It was all part of an annoying pattern. How many times had she heard her mother tell the story of seeing her dad with his bad leg at the Irish dance and falling in love with him despite their different backgrounds? What miracle would her mother try for next? Was she going to ask the nuns if she could bring Bảo home and live with them? Didn't her mother realize her father had already taken the prize when he found a wounded Vietnam vet missing nearly half his face at the veterans home where Grandpa Harry spent his last days?

It had taken Katie five years, two of which were in the hardest years of middle school, to get over being ridiculed at school for her father's association with "the one-eyed monster," as so many of her classmates liked to call Jack.

Jack hardly ever left the seclusion of his apartment or the safety of the store, and when he did venture outside, he always wore a large, hooded sweatshirt to shield his disfigured face from view. Shoulders slumped, the tips of his work boots protruding from frayed jeans, he shuffled along the pavement with his dog always by his side. He had been known to pick up a slice of pizza at Nino's (Scottie Demarco reported to the cafeteria lunch table that the one-eyed monster liked root beer with his pizza) or at Kepler's for his groceries (according to Daisy Ludlum, the one-eyed monster liked Ritz crackers, Welch's grape jelly, and Kraft macaroni and cheese). The Gallo twins, whose parents owned the local laundromat, shared with great relish, as if they had the juiciest tidbits of information, that Jack came with his sack of laundry every other Sunday, and always two hours before it closed. It was also noted, by Lucy Crowley, the school's token know-it-all, that Jack never lingered while his wash was in the machine or when it was in the dryer. Like clockwork, he arrived just as the buzzer went off.

And so it was established from the very beginning, when Jack first came to live above Katie's father's shop, that his movements around town were contained yet predictable. Still, he would come to have an almost-mythical aura with the children of Bellegrove. His dog, too, would come to be part of the myth. For the part Katie did not share with anyone at the cafeteria table was that she knew Jack walked Hendrix late each night, sometimes so late, it was almost morning. After he was done with all the repairs, he'd clip Hendrix's leash onto his red leather collar and take the dog for a long walk, not through the empty streets of the town, but rather through the serpentine paths that bordered it. She had learned that small fact over dinner one night, and it was the image she held on to about Jack. Her private piece of the puzzle that she would never share with anyone, even if it would make her seem cool.

Once a month, since her father first brought him to Bellegrove, her mom invited Jack to Sunday dinner. Jack always brought Hendrix with him. The dog, at least, was a welcome distraction, as it had been hard at first not to stare at Jack's scars during the meal. She had been envious of how her little sister did not seem at all disturbed by the man's wounds. Molly continued to chatter as if there were nothing unusual about Jack's face. They had learned from her father that Jack had worked as a night janitor at an elementary school in Foxton, two towns over, after he had recovered from several painful surgeries and skin grafts to repair his face, and Molly couldn't stop asking him questions about what was the grossest thing he ever cleaned up at school.

Molly had peppered the conversation with such verbal gems like: "You didn't get grossed out mopping up kids' messes, like puke and stuff?"

Jack, who had hardly said a word when he sat down for dinner, clearly uneasy about being in such an intimate family setting, found Molly's questions amusing, much to everyone's relief at the table.

As he laughed, Katie had noticed how half his face softened in its expression, while the other half always remained taut and incapable of movement. She knew she wasn't supposed to stare, but she found herself stealing the chance to look at his face whenever she saw he was busy eating.

It wasn't until nearly a year later, after Jack was settled into his routine in Bellegrove, that the subject of his nightly walks come up.

"Do you like Bellegrove?" Molly had asked as she forked a spoonful of peas into her mouth. "I mean . . . do you like it more than where you grew up?"

Jack grew pensive. "Well, it's different. . . . Of course, I wasn't the same person back home."

Grace glanced over at Molly and gave her a firm eye, as if willing her not to ask any more questions. But Jack seemed to take the little girl's curiosity to heart.

"The best thing about Bellegrove is something I bet you don't even know, Molly."

"What's that?" Molly asked.

"Well, first of all, it's most beautiful past midnight, when the moon lights up the whole sky. I like the sounds of night, and so does Hendrix." He reached down and gave the dog a little pat.

"It's so quiet, you can hear the wind rustle through the trees, and there's this little path behind the shopping center's parking lot that takes you all the way up to the town's reservoir. I go there with Hendrix, and we watch the reflection on the water, and sometimes the moon looks like it's sitting right there on top of its surface. The ripples and stuff . . . it's so pretty and peaceful."

It was a strange thing to hear him speak like that. Even though Katie was barely eleven years old at the time, it had left an impression on her. It was the first time she realized that sometimes when people spoke, they had the power to make everything else disappear.

At that moment, she no longer saw the wounds on Jack's face. She only heard his words.

When he went to say goodbye to them that night, Katie felt that he had gifted them all a secret. It was something she sensed was sacred. She would never share it with anyone, not even in order to sit closer to the popular girls at lunch.

Jack was now an established extension of her family. The other kids talked less about Jack once they reached high school, but his shadowy figure remained in their imagination.

But with the latest development of her mother meeting Bảo on the street, Katie began to fear that both her parents were heading to become the adopt-the-freaks couple of the neighborhood.

She had no idea why they couldn't be like everyone else's parents in Bellegrove. Everyone went to church. Everyone gave generously to the poor box and the needy. But why did only her parents feel the need to bring every stray home? With Molly and all her stuffed animals and Barbie dolls, and her father with all the clocks he brought back from the store, wasn't the house already crowded enough?

CHAPTER 19

Vietnam, 1969

AT NIGHT, WHEN HE WAS BACK AT BASE CAMP WITH A TORCH lamp beside him, while the others smoked cigarettes and Stanley prayed, he would reread Becky's latest letter.

Dear Jack,

We had our first snowfall yesterday, and the streets look like they're covered in powdered sugar. How are you? I hope you're not in too much danger. I worry a lot about you and it's hard for me to imagine what it's like over there. Is it still as hot as you said in your last letter? When I look at the snow outside my window, I think of you and wish I could scoop up a snowball and send it to you! I bet a cold snowball in the jungle would feel so good right now.

Did you get the candy I sent you? I chose hard candies so they wouldn't melt. There isn't that much new here. I checked on your mom, and she was a bit down knowing you'd be away for Easter this year. She has a little cough, but don't worry! I was sick after finals, too. Classes here are so much harder than high school, and I don't have much time to do anything else except study. There's been a lot of protests on campus about the war. The other day police were called because people started throwing rocks at some men from the ROTC who were walking through campus. I wonder what you're doing every day and try

*to imagine you here beside me, listening to records and playing
with my hair.*

*Love,
Becky*

Jack was not that good at writing letters back. As much as he
missed her, loved her, even, he couldn't just pull out a sheet of paper
and tell her casually what he had to endure. 'Nam was like being in
hell, and he knew if he opened up all the emotions he pushed down
each day, he'd go out of his mind.

Jack found himself starting to numb. He knew almost nothing
except hunger, exhaustion, and fear. He'd become almost robotic
in his movements. He dug trenches and filled sandbags. He did all
the grunt work he was ordered to do. But that was the easy part. It
was when his platoon was ordered to go to the bush, that was when
the misery began, the adrenaline pumping through his body telling
him that any second, a hidden Vietcong could open fire and ambush
them all.

He didn't want Becky to know that his job as a radio man made
him a walking human target or that his body was in a state of constant
exhaustion and pain. So he only wrote to her about the banal. He asked
Becky to check up on his mother, who he knew wasn't good at taking
care of herself. Too many cigarettes. Never much of a cook. He knew
she was probably spending too much time in front of the television
instead of getting outside. She had mentioned she had a bit of a nag-
ging cough.

Tell her I love her, he wrote to Becky. It felt harder to write those
words than when he wrote the same sentiment to Becky. That always
just came floating off his pen. He would write to his mother separately,
but somehow he felt Becky was an easier conduit for his feelings. She

was so soft and lovely. He could close his eyes and almost feel the sensation of her skin beneath his hands.

In the Vietnamese jungle, twenty-five miles north of Da Nang, they walk through a maze of bamboo and thick vines, thwacking away the leafy coverage with their knives and rifles. It has been several days that Jack has been out on patrol, and as he pushes up the ridge, he can hear his own heavy breathing rising and falling in his chest.

He takes a cigarette from his flak jacket and lights it.

He is bone-tired. Every step brings with it the threat of a land mine or a punji trap underfoot. He hasn't yet seen a man getting blown up in front of him, but back at the camp, he's seen men pulled off the medivac copters looking like they're missing more pieces than they have left.

After two hours of walking uphill in the jungle's oppressive heat with his twenty-five-pound radio, his body is soaked with perspiration. He keeps the latest letter from Becky folded in the mesh liner of his helmet.

How is my love? she has written. *Do you think of me as much as I think of you?*

She does not know, because he cannot convey it in words, how often he actually does think of her. When he's not thinking about keeping out of enemy crossfire or stepping into a leg trap, when he's not thinking of how damn hungry he is, Becky Dougherty is the first thing that comes into his head and soothes him. He keeps a vivid image of her in his mind at all times, like a snapshot. She is sitting on his bed wearing his old T-shirt. A few wisps of auburn hair fall over her face. He imagines his finger moving that curtain of hair. A smile on her face that lights up a room. He wants to tell her, but he is unsure how to write it in a letter, that she is his beacon. His sunshine at midnight.

When he takes his helmet off, the ink from her envelope has bled from his sweat.

He hates that he has ruined something she sent. He tells himself he will wrap her next letter in some foraged plastic.

He wonders what she does with his letters, whether she saves them and then reads them over and over as he does hers.

He imagines her in class. He sees her laughing with her head tilted upward, a knapsack on her back as she walks through campus. In it, she carries her books and maybe a pencil case filled with a gum eraser and a highlighter. Maybe even a small transistor radio for when she and her friends have a break and are able to sit outside.

He, too, carries a backpack. But he will not reveal to Becky that the radio on his back, with its four-foot antenna, makes him a bull's-eye target for the Vietcong. In his harness he has a pistol, a knife. An M16 strung across his chest. A belt of ammunition.

How could he write and tell her that?

They had now been up on Hill 35 for two days. A squad of twelve men had been taken out, led by Wes Sandoval, their point man. Sandoval was a six-foot-four Native American man from Sioux City who they affectionately called "Chief." Since they left base, they hadn't seen a single Vietcong. But after several hours scouting, there was a slight rustle in the trees. Stanley was the first to fire a burst, and immediately, down fell a VC.

When they felt secure enough that there were no other VC in the vicinity, the men went over to examine the dead man. Larini took his rifle and poked the body.

Lying on the earthen floor, the young man looked to be about Stanley's age, no older than seventeen. He'd been shot through the chest, the blood soaking the front of his shirt. His eyes were staring straight ahead, vacant and without judgment. There was simply no longer any life behind them.

"Damn, Coates, you're a good shot," Flannery said as he poked his rifle at the man's heart. "Where did you learn to do that?"

Stanley stood away from the dead man. His pale skin had now turned a sickly shade of green.

"You're a fucking Kong Killer, Coates," said Flannery, beating his chest to mimic King Kong.

Stanley didn't answer to the name, even as some of the men began to chant, "Kong Killer! Kong Killer!"

That evening, when Stanley was sitting outside his tent, his head bowed toward his Bible and holding a flashlight over the open pages, one of the men leaned in to the others.

"I've got an idea," Flannery announced proudly. "Anybody got a marker on them?"

Some of the men searched their pockets while others reached into their packs. Larini was the first to find one and give it to him.

"Jesus, Flannery, what are you planning?" Mike Djiokonski, the platoon's medic, who they all called "Doc," couldn't hide his skepticism.

"Just leave him alone, for God's sake," Jack muttered.

"Yeah," Doc agreed. "It's not easy seeing your first corpse. Especially if you're the one who iced him."

No one but Jack or maybe Chief thought about the fact that Stanley had broken one of the Ten Commandments that afternoon and how hard that must be for him.

Still, some of his squad couldn't resist what they thought would be at least a good diversion from the drudgery and their exhaustion. Flannery took the marker and snuck off to find Stanley's helmet. Once he had it in hand, he boldly wrote the words *Kong Killer* on the fabric cover.

Hours later, when Stanley went to retrieve his helmet for night patrol, he discovered it defiled with the words of his new nickname.

The others watched as he placed it solemnly on his head and buckled the strap beneath his chin.

He remained silent, not condemning those who wrote the words he despised on his own equipment. Rather, without incident, without anger, he adjusted the helmet and walked over to his post. But Jack could see how Stanley had lowered his eyes toward his boots and shuffled quietly over the muddy terrain, that he wore it with a deep sense of shame.

CHAPTER 20

Long Island, 1979

ANOTHER CASE OF BOYS BEHAVING BADLY—THAT'S WHAT CAME to Grace's mind again when she saw Katie's face after school and could read her annoyances.

"Buddy bothering you again?"

Katie nodded.

"He's always been difficult." Grace shook her head. Just remembering all the little incidents with him over the years made her irritated. It was made worse by Adele's inability to set boundaries with him and her husband, Pat, always traveling for work.

Still, despite their differences, Grace tried to have empathy for the pain in Adele's family. She could never forget that morning when she saw the military car drive down the street toward the O'Rourke family home. Grace had just put Katie in her crib for her nap when she saw the car pass in front of her window, and Tom had not yet left for work.

"Oh, Jesus . . . no . . ." she remembered hearing him say out loud, followed by a terrible moan. She stepped closer to her husband and knew instantly the men in uniform had to be bringing bad news about his friend Bobby O'Rourke.

Grace's stomach sank. Just like her husband, she knew that the sight of that car was like watching a hearse pull into the town.

Even before the news of his uncle's death hit Bellegrove, "Buddy," as he became nicknamed, had not been an easy child for Adele. With their delivery dates so close to each other, Grace had been hopeful she and Adele could go on walks together with their babies bundled up in their prams, but even that was a challenge. Buddy wailed constantly, his expression defiant, and nothing, neither bottle nor cuddling, could soothe him.

"He's no piece of cake," Adele confessed in a rare moment of vulnerability. "He wails like a demon in the morning when he's hungry and punches his tiny fists into the air like a boxer."

It had been Adele's parents' idea that she name the baby after her brother, Bobby, who'd enlisted eight weeks before the birth; the entire clan was so fraught with worry that he might be killed in combat. When the boy was born with flaming red hair, so unlike Bobby's dark curls, the family seemed perplexed, as if this little howling baby had somehow betrayed their expectations that he be born the spitting image of their brother and son.

"My mother's painted the nursery the same the same shade of blue that Bobby had in his childhood room," Adele confided to Grace one afternoon as they walked with their prams into town. "She's even taken his old books and filled them on the shelves." Adele had reached over to try to console Buddy, who was fussing with a little wet fist in the air. "She just doesn't know what to do to calm her nerves with Bobby being shipped off and the headlines getting worse every day."

But when he was only six months old, the news of his uncle's death would devastate the entire O'Rourke family. After the terrible news, their grief became refocused on the newest boy baby added to the family tree. The following Christmas, Buddy was given his late uncle's American Flyer set, all the tracks, switches, and train cars repackaged in their original boxes and wrapped for the occasion with festive paper and red satin ribbon. Adele did not have the heart to tell her mother that after her husband had taken hours to reconstruct the whole train-scape on the floor, Buddy had taken one of his Lincoln Logs and smashed the steam engine right off its dark black rails, permanently breaking one of its wheels.

Although the mothers of Bellegrove would never say it out loud, they all knew that Buddy was not the kid you wanted your child to invite home. When a rock mysteriously broke through the Finnegans' window one afternoon, most people believed it had to have been the work of eight-year-old Buddy, who lived next door. No evidence against him could ever be found, and the Finnegans ended up having to file a costly insurance claim to get it replaced.

Grace loathed to exclude any child when she gave birthday parties for each of her daughters. But when Buddy tore the pin-the-tail-on-the-donkey sheet off the wall when he thought no one was looking, she caught him red-handed.

She confronted Buddy directly, not going to Adele first, who sipped punch from a plastic tumbler, her legs crossed beneath her cherry-red dress and white sweater.

"Now, why did you do such a naughty thing, young man?" Grace cornered young Buddy in the living room as other children zoomed by, holding the plastic pinwheels she had handed out as favors.

"Dunno what you're talking about, Mrs. Golden," he answered, making his green eyes wider in an effort to appear more innocent. It was a well-practiced look.

"I saw you with my own two eyes, Buddy." She held out the ripped paper sheet with the donkey printed on it. "You went right up to it and tore a piece from it."

"Wasn't me . . ." he insisted with such conviction that his ability to lie sent a nervous chill right through her.

Adele must have seen the two of them exchanging words because seconds later, she was standing in front of Grace with her hands on her hips. A few droplets of punch had spattered on her white sweater.

"What's the matter, Gracie? You look like you're upset about something."

"We've had a little incident with the donkey poster." She tried to force a smile while raising the torn sheet for Adele to see.

"Well, that's just awful. But you don't think Buddy did that, *do you?*" Her voice grew louder in disbelief. "I mean . . . there are just so many children here. How could you *really know* who did it?"

"I actually saw him do it, Adele."

Buddy slithered to his mother's side.

"He's always being wrongly accused. . . ." Adele pulled him close to her side, and Grace was sure Buddy had looked up at her and narrowed his eyes and smiled.

"Let's go home now, Buddy. . . ." Adele said, taking her son protectively to her side.

"I really didn't want to make a big deal out of this, Adele," Grace tried to explain. "That's why I chose to speak to him directly."

But Adele was no longer listening. She had suddenly become distracted by the punch stain on her sweater. Visibly distraught by the string of red droplets, which no doubt would be difficult to remove, she fled the party with her son. Grace was hopeful that Adele wouldn't remember their uncomfortable exchange the next morning, for the sweater seemed a far more pressing matter.

CHAPTER 21

GRACE WAS ANNOYED BUT NOT SURPRISED TO LEARN BUDDY was causing trouble yet again for Katie and her friend. His shenanigans had been going on for as long as she could remember. Since her eldest had started school, Grace always held her breath on the first day, hoping Katie wouldn't be in a class with him. In the years she did, it only meant a series of phone calls to the school to complain to the principal. Adele had lost more friends than she would have liked because of Buddy's attraction to mischief. Recently, the boy had grown taller than his father and Katie told her he was telling people he was going to get a motorcycle when he turned sixteen. Grace could only imagine how that conversation might go down at the family's dinner table.

Now that it was late May, Grace was looking forward to putting the school year behind them and having the next few months to recharge. Summer was always the best time in Bellegrove. The proximity of the town's bay club made life easy for her. She'd pile the girls into the old Pontiac, never earlier than 10:00 a.m. so they could sleep late and she could get another round of laundry washed and folded, and they'd spend the rest of the day by one of the two pools. They ordered inexpensive tuna sandwiches from the canteen and tall glasses of iced tea. Grace would rub Coppertone onto the girls' backs and comb out the youngest's hair. Although Katie now refused to wear matching bathing suits with her little sister, the image of them spending hours together without the stress of papers or exams was a welcome relief.

She could hardly believe Katie was now old enough to be one of the lifeguards. How could it be that if she got the job this year, she'd be seated high up on one of those metal towers rather than on one of the plastic lounge chairs with her and Molly? When Grace imagined that, the distance she had been sensing between her and Katie seemed to grow more pronounced.

But if Katie was getting a job and growing more independent, then it was yet one more sign that Grace needed to find more for herself outside the home. Hadn't the priest in last week's sermon told them that having purpose in their life would bring a greater sense of peace and well-being to their hearts and homes? Grace considered her crossing paths with Bảo might be some kind of sign from above.

Having collected the children's old picture books from the attic, she put into motion her promise to Sister Mary Alice to help tutor at the motherhouse. She promised to go twice a week, but she wasn't sure how many hours she should put aside. She'd have to talk to Tom about it, as he had a good sense about these things.

One of the qualities she loved most about Tom was his big heart that he had demonstrated so often over the years. Like when he offered Jack the apartment over the store and then spent hours teaching him the trade. Now this damaged man, who had endured so much suffering, had skills of his own.

This line of thought led her to wonder if the Sisters of Our Lady Queen of Martyrs would even let her bring Bảo and Anh back to the house, where they could practice English in a more comfortable setting. She knew she was already getting ahead of herself, but she savored her new sense of purpose. It made her feel alive.

That Monday, Grace woke up energized. Over the weekend, she had organized the boxes of books she had collected from the attic. Next, she found her daughters' black-and-white composition books from the year before that still had several blank sheets in them and pulled out the used pages so what remained between the cardboard covers was crisp and pristine. But most importantly, she mulled over how she was going to put her free time to better use.

After Katie and Molly were picked up by their school buses, Grace dressed herself in a pretty celery-colored dress, tied her hair back in a white silk scarf, and applied her makeup, choosing a particularly bright shade of pink lipstick to perk up her face.

Before grabbing the carton of books and heading over to the car, she pulled a package of Oreos from the cupboard, thinking how her own children's homework was always easier with a snack. When she sat down behind the steering wheel of her Pontiac wagon, she turned on the radio and checked her face in the mirror. She didn't see in her reflection the fatigue of motherhood or the expression of melancholy she often saw when it rained; instead, she saw herself reinvigorated and happy. Grace turned up the volume and set out to the motherhouse with the windows of the station wagon rolled down and the edges of her silk scarf rippling in the air.

Grace's memory of the Sisters teaching English to those in their care was wholly different from what she discovered this time around.

Bảo was now nestled in one of the larger upholstered chairs, quietly watching the television. The image of Shazam brightly lit up the screen.

The room bristled with restlessness. When Sister Mary Alice now approached Grace, she did not look like the same woman Grace had seen only a few days earlier. She looked frazzled and exhausted.

"Ms. Golden . . ." Sister Mary Alice hurried over to her. "I'm so happy you've come this morning. . . . We could really use an extra pair of hands."

"I brought some books that might help. . . ." Grace lifted the box.

"We're only using picture books now.... Is that what you brought?" She peered into the box. "I fear we're going to have to leave the phonetics to the professionals."

Sister Mary Alice pointed to the children of varying ages spread out on the couches and gave a little nervous laugh. "As you can see, some days are better than others."

Grace scanned the room. It seemed suddenly more claustrophobic and certainly less structured than she remembered. She felt naive in her cheery sundress and with her carton of books with the cookies casually thrown on top. What did she think would actually happen? That she could drive over here and make the lives of these children, who had journeyed thousands of miles from their home, suddenly easier with bright lipstick and some snacks? How foolish was she?

"I came to help," she muttered quietly, though all of the confidence she had on the ride over had now vanished. "But I don't know if I'm qualified to do any of this, either."

Sister Mary Alice looked at her serenely. "I'm not sure any of us are actually qualified, but we must go with what our hearts tell us."

She looked over her shoulder to where Bảo was in his chair, looking listlessly at the TV.

"Where's Anh?" Grace asked.

Sister Mary Alice pointed toward the door on the left. "She's preparing lunch. That young lady's just amazing. She can make the most delicious meals out of even the sparsest ingredients. We've been having wonderful meals with her cooking... a welcome change from frozen string beans and casseroles."

Grace inhaled deeply. She'd noticed a refreshing aromatic scent of herbs when she came into the room. "Just the smell makes me hungry," she said. Her nose detected the fragrance of fresh ginger and coriander. Grace's stomach grumbled.

"She is devoted to him," Sister Mary added. "She walked from the motherhouse into town this morning just to see if she could find some fruit for his breakfast. But he's so withdrawn. All he wants to do is watch television."

"It's a problem even with my Molly," Grace said, thinking of her youngest, who could spend hours in front of the TV.

Sister Mary shook her head. "We have other children here, but somehow his preoccupation with it seems different than the others." She looked over toward Bảo again. "Can you believe the other day one of the sisters caught him trying to unscrew the back? He was determined to try to get a look inside." She let out a little laugh. "Luckily, he was caught before he did any real damage."

"Sounds like Bảo's a bit of a tinkerer. I know the type well." Grace couldn't help but think of Harry and Tom, even Jack. They were all endlessly curious how one piece fit into the next, how a hundred little pieces went into making something functional and whole.

"It's a fascination, that's for certain," Sister Mary Alice agreed as she again glanced at Bảo glued to the television. "Look how he's completely transfixed."

CHAPTER 22

IN THE COMMON ROOM OF THE MOTHERHOUSE, Bảo ADJUSTS himself into the contours of a roomy chair, his eyes glued to the television screen. His fingernails are still raw from hours earlier, when he tried to pry off the rear plate without the tools his father used on his radio back home.

He misses his father. He remembers his nimble hands, how he would unscrew the metal backing of his radio and adjust the miniature tubes like a surgeon who knew the intricate workings of anatomy. Bảo marveled as the sounds ultimately emerged. First the uncomfortable whirl of static, and then voices that were so crystal clear, he thought that small people must be trapped inside. Now the television offers a similar reprieve; Bảo slips into the magical world of superheroes and battles. His mind welcomes the distraction. He does not want to remember his mother counting the gold in the fisherman's hut. He does not want to think about the girl in the yellow cotton dress skipping through the reeds. And most of all, he does not want to recollect the boat keeling over and him and his parents slipping into the cold, dark sea. He still imagines there is a way to bring his parents back to life. To resurrect them out from the water. He believes if he studies these sorcerer-like warriors on the television, he will learn their secrets and can then retrieve his mother and father from the other world.

The characters in the television echo the mythical champions from the stories his mother loved to tell him back home. His favorite was the one about the old woman who was pregnant for three years and finally gave birth to a little boy she named Giong, who, instead of waking and playing like all the other children in the village, slept for fifteen years. It was only when danger fell upon the country that Giong suddenly awakened and rose up to accept the challenges that faced him. He requested an iron sword and an iron horse that breathed fire, both of which he used with great skill to defeat the enemy.

Bảo believes the story of Giong to be true. After all, his mother told him that the village of Sóc Sơn still had a bamboo grove where the stalks were not green like the rest of the country but rather orange from where Giong's horse had breathed fire onto them.

"There are certain boys who are born with magical gifts," she had told him before kissing him good night. Bảo now hears her voice whispering those words in his head. He has managed to use them to replace their cries from the boat that night.

It was Anh who had pulled Bảo up from the water after Chung struggled to bring him over to the boat. Her fingers were the ones that fiercely grasped his and hauled him back on board after Chung had bitten him to release the boy's grip.

She went back over to the edge, hoping to pull Chung and Linh out too. She screamed their names while urging the others still on board to do the same. But Anh's desperate pleas fell upon deaf ears. The captain was focusing all his attention on trying to save his boat from sinking, demanding all the passengers to use whatever they could find to bail the water that had flooded the deck.

Bảo lay in her arms, soaking wet. Long red ribbons of blood snaked down his arm from where he was bitten, and the wound was starting to swell. Someone had brought some betel leaves with them, which had antibacterial properties, so Anh placed one of the leaves on the wound before wrapping his arm in some cloth she tore from her shirt. Dressed in layers, she peeled off her dark cotton top and replaced Bảo's wet clothes with her dryer ones. Those who remained on the boat were crying while others were yelling at the captain, who hissed that they would all be captured and killed if they didn't stop their wailing.

For the rest of the evening, the boat motor chugged deeper into the South China Sea. Two people lighter than when they began, those on board whispered of a curse. Anh held Bảo tightly in her arms as he drifted in and out of consciousness. Not knowing what to do, she prayed to her ancestors for help and made promises to Chung and Linh of her devotion.

When Bảo finally awoke, he asked repeatedly where his parents were.

"They are in heaven with our ancestors," she said, using the same words Linh had once used to comfort her.

He began to sob, large, violent cries that caused his whole body to shake.

"My arm . . ." He looked down at his forearm that was now bandaged with a piece of Anh's undershirt. He was still unsure if the flashes of his father's last moments were real or not.

Anh remained silent. She had neither the heart nor the words to tell him.

CHAPTER 23

JACK PLACED HIS BOOK ON HIS NIGHTSTAND AND GLANCED UP at the wall clock. It was nearly 6:30 p.m. In a few minutes, Tom would be finishing up at the store, packing up his things, and returning home to his family for supper. He would put his tools away and neatly place all the paperwork on his desk, but he would leave the brass desk lamp on for Jack. The first time Tom gave him the keys to the store and told him he could let himself in whenever he wanted after hours, Jack thought Tom had simply forgotten to shut that light off. But the soft illumination that greeted him that first evening soon became a consistent, silent invitation to enter a space that had since become sacred to him.

Jack did not consider himself a spiritual man, but it was undeniable that Tom had come into his life when he needed it the most. He had given Jack a place to stay and the means to support himself. Working at the shop had restored a crucial part of him, the part that was most vulnerable yet the least visible.

His dignity.

Before Tom offered him the apprenticeship, Jack had been employed at Foxton Elementary School as a night janitor. He had taken the job for a few reasons, one being that he could do it after regular operating hours when the school was nearly deserted. He had struggled in school his whole life. He was a late reader. The words on the page were a code that took him months longer than other children to unlock. He preferred to sit in the back of the class, far from the blackboard and the teacher's desk, where he thought no one would notice him. In high school, Becky had been the one who thrived in that environment, not he.

Working as a janitor, though, proved to be far more enjoyable than he imagined. Each night when the school was empty and he freely wheeled his trolley from classroom to classroom, he couldn't help but smile when he saw all the beautiful signs of life from the children or the brightly colored bulletin boards that revealed the care the teachers had all so clearly taken to make learning fun.

He worked there for two years, wiping down desks, polishing the sticky doorknobs, emptying trash cans, and cleaning the toilets. It had been just the kind of job he needed, offering steady pay and late hours that enabled him to be close enough to life without having to actually engage with it. He breathed in the innocence of those children through the pencil drawings on their desks and the apple cores they tossed in the trash cans. All of it spoke to him of a lightheartedness that had escaped him in his own childhood and the years thereafter.

He especially loved classroom 8, at the end of the hall. On the front door hung a greeting that proclaimed *Magic begins behind this door!* Long yellow wands with sparkly glue, top hats cut out of black and gold construction paper, and stars crafted from aluminum foil adorned the entranceway. Jack knew that had he been a student in classroom 8, he would have loved learning a lot more than he had back in Allentown.

Of all the things he would miss at Foxton, it would be the proximity to that classroom. He always went to greater lengths to clean it more carefully than he did all the others. It was easy to love this particular teacher from afar because it was so clear how much she loved her students and her job.

So when Billy Flodstrom, the head of the school's grounds crew, sat him down at the end of that June and informed him that they had to let him go, Jack was devastated. He felt as though he had lost the only remaining good thing in his life, particularly the chance to enter classroom 8 each night. He truly believed that, as the sign said, there was magic behind that door.

"With all the budget cuts in the district this year, there's money for only one night janitor next fall," Billy said quietly. "I'm sorry, I really am." He stared down at his hands folded on the metal desk, avoiding eye contact with Jack, his discomfort rising off his skin like perspiration.

Jack sat calmly across from him, his back straight and his eyes focused straight ahead, a position he fell into during times of stress. This had proven to be one of the more positive remnants of the war for him.

"I'd appreciate it if, when you're firing me, you looked me straight in the face. It's the decent thing to do."

Billy reluctantly lifted his eyes. "I feel very badly about this, Jack. You've always done a great job here."

Jack watched as Billy fidgeted and his gaze shifted away. He had always proved unable to focus on Jack's face for more than a second, and now his eyes traveled in the direction of the window. It was easier to fire a man who was invisible.

Jack wondered if anyone at Foxton had ever really seen him at all.

For Jack, life since coming home had been a series of challenges that offered unexpected gifts of healing. Five years after Tom had first sat down next to him at the VA hospital, Jack was now well aware the extent to which that meeting had shaped his life for the better. He often questioned whether he'd still be alive if had Tom not started a conversation with him that day.

For on that afternoon, Jack was not actually reading his copy of *Rolling Stone*. Instead, he had buried his face in the pages of the magazine as a shield, contemplating whether he still had the strength to go on living. He had endured several painful skin grafts after his injury, and he still struggled to come to terms with the fact that the doctors had repaired as much of his facial trauma as they could. The only thing that had gotten him out of bed once he had moved back East was his job at Foxton Elementary. But now, that had been taken from him as well.

So what Tom probably believed was merely a simple exchange between two strangers regarding the lyrics of a powerful new song had a far greater meaning for Jack. Tom's eyes had never floated away from Jack's face that day, even after he saw the full devastation of his injuries. They remained there as he excitedly spoke about Bruce Springsteen, rattling off several other songs he liked by the E Street Band. It was both mundane and extraordinary at the same time. Tom had treated Jack as if he were just any other guy.

CHAPTER 24

It was in the garden outside the veterans home that Tom opened up to Jack how the Golden Hours came to be. "Its first seeds probably began just before my dad shipped off to go fight in Europe," he said. He shared how, on that afternoon, his mother gave his father a box with a first-rate military Bulova inside. Tucked within the case, in her perfect, scrolling script, she'd written, *I'm keeping time until you return home to me.*

But when his dad returned from the Second World War, Harry wasn't the same man he'd been when he'd left. He'd seen the devastation of the killings and the bombings, not to mention the gut-wrenching photographs taken by fellow soldiers of the camps with the countless corpses of Jewish souls piled high and his own best friend senselessly killed before his very eyes. He was plagued by night terrors.

Tom explained it was his maternal grandfather, Sam, who first noticed Harry gravitating toward broken timepieces after he came home from the war. Sam saw Harry take the old Ingraham clock on the family's mantel that had sat inactive for years and become fixated in getting the clock to start working again. Harry took it apart and spent hours learning how each piece fit into the next, spreading them all out on their dining room table and filling the surface with a myriad of small, intricate parts: the various wheels and pinions, the elegant numbered dial, and the two brass plates.

Eventually, after checking out several repair manuals from the library and countless hours of trial and error, he succeeded. "I think you've got a talent there, Harry," Tom's granddad told him.

Having himself served in France during the First World War, Sam knew how important it was to discover a vocation where Harry could drown out the ghosts of war. Those who had never served thought the hardest thing for a soldier was surviving battle. But no one ever spoke about how difficult it was to come home.

Harry's watch collecting began as a hobby at first. He drove all over Connecticut and as far as Northampton, Massachusetts, harvesting from antique stores old clocks that no longer worked. He studied how to diagnose mechanical issues and read guides on cleaning gears and replacing pins. He bought old books on the history of clocks and educated himself on the different styles and their various details. He took courses in Manhattan on watch and clock repair, learning the trade through hard work and practice.

But it was his night classes in horology that ultimately opened up a whole new world for him. His teacher there spoke about the history of "time collection." What began with mankind using the sky to mark the periods within a day eventually morphed into sundials, where the stretch of shadows could help calculate the hours. Harry was fascinated by the balance of daylight against darkness, how each minute ran into the next, how hours accumulated to form days. Behind a watch's face, there was an entire universe composed of metal pins and wheels, all its components engaged in a unique dance to achieve perfect balance and movement. Harry gravitated toward this, for he yearned to put his mind at ease again, to placate what had been altered by the war.

For several months, as he tried to get his footing, Harry tinkered with all the clocks he had acquired until he got them moving again. He found the work restorative, the ability to bring life back to something that had fallen dormant. He was happy to work long into the night rather than lying in bed, unable to sleep. Or worse, to wake up from one of his nightmares.

"The hands of time must always move forward," he had told Tom from the moment he was old enough to understand. It was the metaphor he used whenever he was faced with a challenge. It always comforted him. And in some ways, he believed it had saved him.

Tom knew it was a natural extension of the Golden Hours to offer Jack a job there. Perhaps learning the craft that had saved his father could help save another veteran, too.

CHAPTER 25

JACK AND TOM HAVE WORKED THIS WAY FOR SEVERAL YEARS now, incorporating a natural rhythm into what works best for them. Theirs is a synchronized band of movements, as one of them enters the space just as the other is leaving it.

Jack softens when he walks through the threshold, and Hendrix trots in beside him. Jack isn't quite sure what it is, but there is something to the space that enables him to shed his protective armor and the weight of his memories. He immediately feels at ease as he walks deeper into the workshop. Perhaps it's the special light coming from the evening sky outside the shop's windows or the soft ticking of the clocks beating in unison. Maybe it's the sense of purpose Tom has given him by introducing him to the craft. But what is certain is that, unlike his apartment, where his memories plague him when he sleeps, in this workshop, he feels unburdened. He feels free.

Hendrix follows him into the back room and flops to the ground while Jack flips the radio on, the FM dial already tuned to his and Tom's favorite station. Music fills the air as he sits down to work, breathing in the solitude like it's oxygen.

The lush sounds of "Lucy in the Sky with Diamonds" rolls into the background.

When he hears the lyrics about the kaleidoscope-eyed girl, a knot tightens in his throat.

And right then and there, just as he thought he was going to lose himself in his work—with the screwdrivers all lined up and the dust cloths, tweezers, and calipers primed for his use—she returns to him.

Becky.

She is now in the air. The memory of her invades him, penetrating his heart like a sharp blade. He looks down at Hendrix, with his long snout resting on his black, velvety paws. His large eyes look up at Jack as though he, too, senses a shift in the room. Perhaps he notices the change of his master's heartbeat, as though it is a clock of its own. Perhaps it's in his change in breathing. The song brings him back to a time when he held Becky's face next to his own. Her eyes—they did dazzle like kaleidoscopes. Prisms of green-and-gold light.

Even though it has been years since he has seen her face up close, he can still shut his eyes and remember every detail.

Taped on the wall of the old workbench is a piece of a faded print that Tom's father had placed there when he first opened the shop.

Sundials can measure the hours in the day and reservoirs every drop of water. But no one has ever invented an instrument to quantify love.

For Jack, it was an immeasurable calculation.

CHAPTER 26

Bảo never shared the reason why he had run away from the motherhouse. It wasn't that the Sisters hadn't cared for him or fed him properly. In fact, they had been kind and patient with him ever since he'd arrived. But Bảo didn't think anyone else would understand, as none of the others had been as fascinated with the electric box as he had, the one the Sisters called "the television." He kept his reason for leaving a secret because he needed to keep his plan intact.

His desire to leave came only after he experienced the wonder of TV. The same way he had once heard voices trapped inside his father's radio, he was now amazed to witness men and women springing to life within this special contraption. One show in particular enthralled Bảo. It featured teenage twins, a boy and a girl, who were dressed in matching uniforms of deep violet and black and able to achieve incredible and mystifying feats. Once their fists interlocked, their powers intensified. Zan, the brother, could transform into any form of water, and Jayna, his sister, could morph into any animal. Together, there was nothing they couldn't accomplish, like the warrior Giong with his iron sword and horse. So every afternoon at four o'clock, magic washed over him as he sat glued in front of the box and waited for them to appear. Bảo thought that if he could somehow find these mythical spirits, they could use their powers to retrieve his parents from the ocean and bring them back to life.

The woman who had found him on the street had been so kind, he thought initially she might be taking him to meet Zan and Jayna and that perhaps she was sent by one of his ancestral spirits to help with his plan. But she had only brought him back to a house that was cold and foreign to him. There were no fruit trees or ceremonial shrines. He scanned the house to see if he could find anything that might be familiar to him but discovered nothing. The woman too was wholly unlike the colorful spirits on TV. And her two daughters—nothing was magical about them at all.

CHAPTER 27

Vietnam, 1969

THE MEN WERE ALL EAGERLY ANTICIPATING STANLEY'S BIRTH-day. "PFC Coates is finally turning eighteen." Larini grinned. "Feels like our young marine is about to grow up," he joked with the others. "We've got that boy a present he's going to remember."

"One that's going make him into a full-fledged man," Flannery agreed.

Stanley stood steps away from the other men, one knee bent, the other hand digging the ground with a small shovel.

"What's he up to over there?" one of the men asked while looking over toward him. Stanley still wore the helmet that said *Kong Killer*, but beneath its visor, his skin had remained oddly unburnished by the sun.

"He found a dead monkey this morning." Chief filled them in. "Lying just steps away from his foxhole." His gaze narrowed. "The Vietnamese believe the monkey spirit brings good luck."

"What about a dead monkey?" Larini joked. He lit a cigarette between his lips and took a long drag.

"Not so much," answered Chief.

The men stood in a cluster, watching Stanley bury the animal. Soon his shovel tapped the ground, and he seemed to mumble something over the small burial mound.

"You've got to be kidding me," Flannery said with palpable disbelief. "Is he really praying over that dead monkey?"

Larini burst out laughing. "He's going to go apeshit after he's done with the mother of all birthday presents we got for him tonight. We're going to surprise him with a woman. . . . Going to bring her in after sundown. He'll be sleeping in a tent tonight, not a damn foxhole, because we got Bates to take him off perimeter watch for his birthday."

Jack had cringed when they had written *Kong Killer* on Stanley's helmet a few months back. There was something pure about this young man he wanted to protect, he seemed like the only constant in the jungle. Every morning, he could be seen hunkered over his Bible, reading a passage to himself. During any other spare moment, Jack saw him writing letters home.

"You sure he's gonna want that?"

Flannery looked at him, perplexed. "Well, shit, *Hollywood*— who wouldn't want a birthday present like that? You think maybe we should call in a bird to drop in a Carvel ice cream cake? Come on, do you think he'd like that more?"

Jack didn't answer. The truth was he thought Stanley just might.

That night, two of Gomez's squad snuck the pretty, young Vietnamese girl into the perimeter. Jack first caught sight of her as she passed through the barbwire, a slender form in silk pajamas, her long black hair sleek in a long ponytail that went halfway down her back.

She dipped into the tent as the other men laughed and slapped each other on the shoulder.

It wasn't that Jack was a prude. He had been with a few girls before Becky, and even the ones he didn't love had certainly provided him with pleasure. But even though Stanley chose to go to Vietnam to become a man, Jack strongly doubted he had even considered sex as part of the equation. After all, the kid blushed every time one of the other guys mentioned the word *tits*.

Doc shared Jack's skepticism. "I don't like this." He shook his head. "And I can't help thinking that girl in there might be a child herself."

Minutes passed and Jack continued to look over at the tent. But the tarp flap remained closed. He had to admit that he was surprised that the girl hadn't been tossed out as soon as she arrived. Jack couldn't conceive that Stanley would have accepted her offer, especially knowing it had been the result of money being exchanged. But as time passed, he looked over at Doc and shrugged.

"Guess we were wrong. Seems like Stanley is enjoying his present."

A little over an hour later, the girl emerged. She dipped her head out from the tent with a smile on her face. Before she left, she whispered back to thank Stanley.

"How'd my boy do?" Flannery asked, hoping to get a full report from the girl.

She took a pack of cards out of her pocket and showed them to Flannery. "He no want boom boom," she answered. "He say . . . lucky boy . . . he play cards with pretty girl."

CHAPTER 28

Long Island, 1979

THE ROOM THE SISTERS PROVIDED FOR THEM WAS SPACIOUS AND contained two bunk beds. Anh had only seen beds like these once before, when she and Bảo had been on the vessel that rescued them when their first boat ran out of fuel in the middle of the South China Sea. The sailors on board, most of them French, had shown Bảo where they slept, and he'd been enamored with the prospect of sleeping on a bed that nearly touched the ceiling of the cabin.

Now they shared the room with another young family, a couple who had a little daughter who slept nestled against her mother while the husband slept in the bed above.

Anh spent much of each night unable to sleep. Aside from the husband's snoring, she found herself reflecting on the newfound responsibility of taking care of her nephew who had witnessed the trauma of seeing both his parents swallowed up by the ocean. Every time she saw the scar on his wrist, it pulled her back to that terrible night. Yet she had promised herself from the moment she held Bảo in her arms as he dipped in and out of consciousness, she would protect him and care for him as though he was her own.

Although she had no medical knowledge, she had cleansed his wound with salt water to stave off infection after they exhausted the betel leaves. But even with her diligent efforts, a pink scar still remained, a permanent reminder of the pain and sacrifice of their journey.

Sorrow often soaked through her bedclothes, perspiration from her sleeplessness. There were too many sounds in the communal bedroom that were hard to shut out. The couple's little girl often cried, despite her mother's best efforts to pacify her with lullabies that reminded Anh of what her own mother had sung to her as a child. She would also hear Bảo sometimes whimpering in his sleep. She didn't dare allow herself to contribute to this symphony of grief.

While she knew Bảo had witnessed the drowning of his parents, his arm a gravestone of his father's last moments, the nightmare of seeing Minh beaten to death also never left her.

Anh worried deeply about having abandoned him—leaving his grave untended—for it was a Vietnamese custom that a husband and wife be buried side by side so they would be reunited in the afterlife. Having left Minh behind for America, would she ever be returned to him? The thought of spending her eternity alone was even more frightening than this new life in America.

And yet, Anh recognized she was not, in fact, alone in this world. She, a childless mother, and Bảo, a motherless child, were now forever entwined, and she would do her best to honor her sister's spirit. Despite Bảo's being withdrawn and distant with her, she would try hard to find a way to build a life with him in this new, unfamiliar country.

There was an architecture to love. The first bricks of foundation were always how you honored your family.

CHAPTER 29

Vietnam, 1969

THREE MONTHS INTO HIS TOUR, JACK AND TWELVE MEN FROM his platoon were airlifted by helicopter into a wet world of dense jungle, biting insects and fear, thirty miles southwest of Hue. Their mission was a five-day recon patrol of the area to confirm and investigate possible Vietcong presence in the mountains west of Phú Lộc.

The men carried everything on their backs: the rolled ponchos, the canteens of water, the belts of ammunition, and their rifles. None had slept more than a couple of hours each day, and their bodies were worn down and hungry.

As they walked, a thick mist enveloped the foliage, and the earthen floor transformed into thick tracks of mud.

Most of the marines had jungle rot on their feet. Endless rain and too many days and nights treading through the tropical rain forest had left their skin with painful, pus-filled red blisters. Doc spent most of his time trying to ensure these ulcers didn't get infected, for that could lead to more serious complications.

Jack no longer had any dry socks in his pack, and he worried that he, too, might find himself with the dreaded jungle rot. His feet were already pruned and raw from wearing wet boots for days. The radio had also been malfunctioning recently, and he had spent the first hours of that morning drying the connections and replacing the battery to keep it alive. The last thing he wanted was Lieutenant Bates giving him shit about the radio not working. For most of the mission, it seemed as if they had been trekking through steam. It was certainly plausible that the intense humidity, even more extreme than usual, had caused the battery to malfunction. Luckily, the new battery seemed to rectify the problem, and soon communication was restored.

For several hours, the men had been slowly advancing toward Razorback. Corporal Gomez, the squad leader, made sure that Chief alternated positions with Flannery, the two of them taking turns going from the front of the patrol to the back to keep the point man alert.

Chief had discovered a booby trap that morning. While walking up the mountain—as the point man, his knife slicing through ropes of thick vines and brush—he sensed something amiss. He stopped suddenly and jerked his hand up in the halt position, one leg lifted above a low pile of brush. Without speaking a word, he waved for Larini, who was in charge of diffusing explosives, to come and inspect the suspicious covering.

They all stopped and dropped for cover. Above, a large-winged falcon circled over the treetops.

Larini got down on his knees and carefully lifted the thick carpet of leaves. Beneath them was a thin lattice work of twigs. He removed that, too, as the others kept their eyes peeled in surveillance. Underneath the covering was a deep well with a grenade propped in the side wall. One step farther would have ignited the fuse and blown Chief's leg off.

Larini worked slowly and carefully to disarm the grenade, and then he lay it off to the side. "Fucking hell," Flannery cursed, peering over at the trap when it was all over. "Chief, thank God you caught that one."

"I just had a feeling about it. . . ." His voice was solemn.

Stanley stepped back and steadied himself against a tree. He had been limping all morning and was two men ahead of Jack. His body was sagging underneath the weight of his flak jacket and pack. He'd thrown up near the stream hours earlier when they went to refill their canteens. His pale skin had grown even paler from his bout of sickness, and his lips had started to look a little blue.

Just after the booby trap incident, Doc had called him aside to see if he was drinking enough water. "You're overheating, Stan. Keep yourself hydrated." Doc gave a playful smack on his helmet, causing the words *Kong Killer* to dip over Stanley's large blue eyes.

"I'm okay, Doc," he answered politely. "I'm no hotter than everyone else."

"Do me a favor and finish your canteen. Then go over and refill it like *everyone else*."

"Okay, Doc."

"Still never had a beer, have you?" Doc smiled.

"Nope." A wide grin emerged on Stanley's face. "I'm going to wait and save it for the last day of my tour."

Doc tried to mask his cynicism. "Is that really wise, Private?"

"Yes, sir. I believe it is."

"You're a strange kid, Stanley," he remarked and pushed him toward the stream. "In the meantime, drink more water, will you?"

Stanley knelt by the stream and filled his two canteens, then unbuckled his helmet strap and scooped up some water into his helmet and dumped it over his blond head.

He shook off the water, sending droplets through the air that landed on Flannery. They were so damn hot, any water on their bodies, aside from their feet, was a welcome relief.

"Saddle up," Lieutenant Bates ordered. He rolled up his map inside his pack, checked his compass from his belt, and signaled for the squad to move out. The men inspected their M16 rifles, making sure they were locked and loaded. Jack hoisted the radio onto his back. Slowly, like a line of ants, they began to move again up the hill.

Chief and Flannery were walking point when they heard the first enemy gunshot.

Within seconds, the men opened fire in the direction of the attack.

"Corpsman up! Corpsman up!" Larini cried out. It was Murphy, who had been hit in the leg. Doc ran to attend to the wounded man as the firefight continued.

On his belly, Jack was manning the radio as Bates held the handset to his mouth and began shouting in their location and calling for backup. The jungle, once dark and green, was now illuminated in a thousand rays of orange and red.

The spray of bullets seemed to stretch for hours, but in reality, the exchange only lasted a few minutes. Two Vietcong were shot dead, and Murphy appeared to be the only man wounded, until Chief noticed that the Stanley wasn't behind him as he originally thought.

"No!" Flannery yelled when he came across Stanley's body a few yards away from the others. He was lying on his back, his blue eyes staring up at the sky.

Doc came running and ripped open Stanley's jacket. "You're okay, man. You're okay," he repeated as his hands became soaked in Stanley's blood. The bullet had entered in the worst possible place, right through his chest, rupturing his aorta. Doc immediately tried to stymie the bleeding with some thick gauze.

Stanley was gurgling now, trying to say something that Doc couldn't understand. He was choking on his own blood as he struggled to get out his words.

It was Jack who realized what he was trying to say with his last breaths. "He's asking for his Bible, man. His Bible." Jack worked quickly. He pulled the pack off his dying friend's shoulders, digging his hands into its interior until he found the small leather-bound book he'd seen Stanley read from every morning of his tour.

"Here you go, buddy. Here it is. . . ." Jack took Stanley's arm that was struggling to move and helped adjust it just as Doc gave him a dose of morphine to ease his pain.

Jack had placed the Bible on top of his chest. The last thing Stanley did was cover the book with his hand.

Silence enveloped the squad when they all realized Stanley was dead. Jack and Flannery helped wrap his body in his poncho, his blood staining their hands and clothes. The smell of death already filled the air.

"Fuck, this smells like hell," Flannery cursed as they wrapped up Stanley's bloody corpse.

Jack had been wanting to retch since seeing Stanley's vacant eyes and shattered chest but had fought it off. "Just shut up and do it," he snapped.

When the two were finished, Chief then lifted Stanley's body into his strong arms, first to his chest and then slung over his shoulder.

For the next hour, he climbed the mountain to reach the ridge where the helicopter was due to land to take Murphy and Stanley away.

Chief refused to let anyone else carry the body. He told the others that night when they set up camp that carrying Stanley's 150-pound body was not a burden, it was an honor.

"One of us would have helped you," Larini insisted as Lieutenant Bates handed out warm beers. After his platoon had returned to camp, he snagged a case of beer in honor of Stanley's memory.

"That boy was better than all of us." Chief turned his head and looked away. "I didn't want even his head to touch the ground . . . not a single part of him to graze the dirt. Couldn't trust anyone to do that but me."

Jack reached for a beer. He still could not erase the last image of Stanley from his mind. Due to the poor visibility, the chopper had to send a special piercing instrument to penetrate the fog. When the stretcher finally emerged through the clouds, it dangled as though it had been delivered from the heavens.

He watched as Chief lifted Stanley's enshrouded body from his shoulder and laid it down on the stretcher like an offering. Slowly, it was then carried back up through the mists.

Now, as they all drank beer in Stanley's honor, Jack realized the squad had lost something that had made them unique from the others. They had lost their innocent. The purity of Stanley was gone.

CHAPTER 30

Long Island, 1979

BUDDY, AN ONLY CHILD, HAD SPENT COUNTLESS HOURS WON-dering what it would be like to have a band of brothers to bond with. He glorified the masculine energy he searched for in his *Soldiers of Fortune* magazines, the war movies he absorbed on the television.

So, four days after school had ended, while most of the families in Bellegrove were spending their summer days ferrying their children into their spacious American cars to the beaches or pool clubs, toting picnic baskets packed with tuna fish and egg salad sandwiches and thermoses of sweetened iced tea, Buddy began seeking other ways to pass time. He found himself up to no good, stealing pen knives and packages of gum, even the odd cigarette pack from the five-and-dime store next to Kepler's Market. His partner in crime was Clayton Mavis, Bellegrove's new kid, who had arrived mid–school year from East Texas after his father was transferred for his job in the oil business and found East Coast suburban life just as stifling as Buddy did. Although Clayton had regaled him with stories of shooting beer cans and squirrels with a hunting rifle, Buddy had piqued his new friend's interest by suggesting they build a fortress-style bunker in the old woods near the reservoir, an idea that he had been contemplating for some time.

Just the thought of it enthralled Buddy. A place to call his own, one constructed with his two bare hands. A refuge far away from his overbearing mother. He first imagined it one afternoon as he lay in his bedroom. The sound of his mother vacuuming downstairs, the motor churning as she thrust all her energy into long angry strokes against the carpet. Adele had caught him eating potato chips in the living room and had unleashed a torrent of fury on him. "We eat in the kitchen in this house, young man! WE EAT IN THE KITCHEN!" Appearances were everything to his mother. She had lost her brother in the war, but she would now make her parents proud by being the pinnacle of perfection. Adele maintained the polished appearance of every room in the house with enviable vigor. From the moment his mother woke up each day, she had a rigid order she adhered to: she put on her makeup, zipped herself into a freshly washed dress (she loathed those women who spent the morning in their bathrobes), made breakfast for her husband and son, and then set out to make sure her home on Byron Lane gleamed from the inside out. Even the flowerpots by the front door were bursting with a rotation of flowers during the different seasons, and the porch swing was painted a sunny yellow.

Buddy often wondered what her friends at her church meetings would think about his mother if they saw how she transformed from her paper doll perfection into a tomato red–faced harpy who screamed at him behind closed doors. The sound of Adele's shrill voice radiated in his ears, and Buddy often felt a rage boil inside of him that he had to struggle to control. When he was little, she was always quick to defend him in public, but once she returned home, her maternal affection vanished. She never hit him. But she often said things that he knew would shock her close-knit circle of friends. His father, who traveled most of the week and was rarely at home, seemed to enjoy the tight ship his mother maintained.

That afternoon, when the idea of the fort first came to him, she had berated him over and over again, her eyes bulging from her head, her hand shaking the vacuum hose in his direction as if it were a dangerous weapon. Buddy escaped her ire by storming up the stairs to his bedroom. He slammed the door shut and flung himself on his bed.

Even his room didn't feel like his own. Adele had entered it while he had been out with Clayton and "sanitized" it, as she liked to say whenever she routinely invaded his space. She went through his desk drawers, collected all the stray pencils, and lined them up in neat little rows. She had taken his past issues of *Soldier of Fortune* magazine and stacked them in tall piles all in chronological order. She had even made his bed when he purposefully had left it unmade.

It even smelled differently. The scent of lemony disinfectant floated through the air, an aroma that he despised. He didn't understand why she hated the smell of gym socks so much; to him it was a comforting odor, like his favorite bologna-and-American-cheese sandwiches.

Buddy flipped off his shoes and let each one fall to the ground with a thud. He reached over, turned the radio on the loudest volume, and stared at the ceiling.

The idea of the fort came to him instinctively. He hated being alone in the house with his mother. Within seconds he had devised a plan. He would tell his mother he was at Clayton's so he could spend a few hours each day constructing the fort. He was sure his new friend would relish the opportunity. Still new to the town, Clayton was disappointed none of the kids owned a gun in Bellegrove and bemoaned how his recreational activities had become severely diminished.

Buddy was drawn to the outlaw-like quality of his new pal, and now he at least had someone to hang out with after school. The fortress would be a project they could labor over together and work up a real man's sweat for. He imagined it might have been something his uncle had even done in Vietnam, constructing a camouflaged hideout from which to scope out the enemy.

The woods behind the reservoir were thick with tall pine and balsam trees, pin oaks and juniper bushes. He and Clayton would harvest fallen sticks and branches and create a foundation they would build upward, layer by layer. They would use whatever they could find. They would use ingenuity and strength, just like his *Soldiers of Fortune* magazines touted on their covers. He felt the idea was a way of channeling his uncle, a man who he had never met, but to whom every pewter framed portrait in his home was buffed and polished lovingly by his mother. Dressed in his uniform, his face staring nobly from behind the glass.

CHAPTER 31

Vietnam, 1969

JACK WAS AT BASE CAMP WHEN THE TELEGRAM FROM THE RED
Cross arrived. It had been a difficult few days since Stanley's death and
most of the men couldn't believe he wasn't still with them, hiding out
somewhere clasping his Bible or begrudgingly putting on his helmet
with the offensive words scrawled on front.

But that morning Jack was resting for a few minutes outside the
exterior of his hooch, his utility shirt drying on the clothesline, a dark
green towel wrapped around his neck. He welcomed the beating sun,
after that fateful patrol where the rain had been relentless and the
leeches had been even worse than usual. The men had long since discovered that the thirsty bloodsuckers would crawl up their pant legs
and attach themselves to their chest and limbs, any place they could
reach. Jack's entire body was now a constellation of painful, open, slow-
healing, red sores, the only way to get the bastards off their skin was to
burn them with the end of a lit cigarette, cover them with salt, or douse
them with insect repellant. The men almost always opted for the torch
of a cigarette.

He still considered himself more fortunate than some of the others.
Chief, who had carried Stanley's body the whole way without any help,
looked exhausted. His eyes saddled with bags, his shoulders slumped.

He had not expected to suddenly see Lieutenant Bates standing in
front of him.

"Lance Corporal Grady . . ." His voice, which had always been
clipped and devoid of emotion, sounded strangely different in Jack's
ears. He held a thin envelope in his hand.

Years later, when Jack would think back on how he had first heard the news, he would recognize the unfamiliar tenor in Bates's voice to actually have been kindness.

Jack stood up. Half-naked, his pants low on his hips, his dog tags flat against his bare chest.

"This just came for you." Bates handed over the telegram to Jack. Printed on featherlight paper, the envelope fell out of his hand like a stone.

Jack took the telegram and pulled out the message.

We regret to inform you of the death of your mother, Eleanor Grady.... The death was reported this morning at 0700 hours. Transportation back home will be arranged by the Red Cross.... Two weeks' bereavement leave has been approved....

It took Jack several seconds to make sense of the words. He kept thinking he had misread them.

"My condolences, Lance Corporal Grady." Bates reached to squeeze Jack's shoulder.

For months, Jack had been living in a world that was full of discomfort and danger. He'd experienced the white-knuckle terror of rockets and grenades exploding just feet away from him and witnessed the senselessness of young men in body bags, their lives cut tragically short. But the one thing that Jack counted on was the knowledge that the two people he loved most were safe back at home.

After all, that was the natural order of things.

How many times had he imagined his mother receiving word of his own death? As soon as he learned he was drafted, Jack had envisioned two officers dressed in their military uniforms walking up the porch steps, solemnly saluting his mother, before offering her a neatly folded flag just as they did in the movies. It was a scene he had memorized because it was plausible under the circumstances.

But Jack had never imagined that he would be the one reading the telegram of his mother's passing. It was supposed to happen the other way around.

"The chopper will come in at thirteen hundred hours to pick you up and take you to the Da Nang airfield," Bates informed him.

Jack nodded blankly. He had been sweltering all day, but now he no longer felt the oppressive heat. His body felt cold, as if his veins were filled with ice.

News of Jack's mother's death spread quickly through the base camp. No one wanted to say they were envious that he was getting to go home on two weeks' leave. But still, the prospect of sleeping in a warm bed, eating food other than C-rations, and finding comfort in the arms of a girlfriend seemed to them an upside to the otherwise-heartbreaking news.

"Man, don't beat yourself up. I'm sure she was very proud of you." Doc was the first to go over to him and offer comforting words.

Flannery, too, tried to be positive. "At least you'll get to see your girl again, Hollywood."

Jack would be lying if he didn't admit Becky had flashed through his mind within seconds of learning the news about his mother.

But he was perplexed. Why was he only learning now that his mother had been ill? Why hadn't Becky mentioned to him that his mother's health was deteriorating in any of her letters?

Or had she, but he just hadn't taken notice of it? After all, she had written to him about his mother's cough, but he thought it was nothing more than a cold.

He opened his duffel and reached for the plastic bag where he stored all her letters and pulled out a handful of the most recent ones.

Your mother's cough is still quite bad. I brought her lemon loz-
enges from the drug store the other day. She told me the doctors
said it's nothing, but it does seem to take a lot out of her. I don't
get to visit as much as I'd like to with school making things so
busy for me. But when I do, we talk almost all about you. She
saves all of your letters, just like I do. . . .

And there was the last one, which had arrived at base camp only a couple of days ago.

Your mother looks weak to me. I made her Campbell's soup. She
was funny. I made the chicken and stars one. It was the only can
she had left in the cupboard. And your mom said something so
sweet. She said she was going to wish on one of the stars that you'd
come back home safe and sound. I only want to eat chicken and
stars soup now, Jack. I want to make the same wish on every one
until you get back home.

He knew the cigarettes she'd smoked since she was sixteen had made her voice permanently raspy and that she had a cough when he left for boot camp, but that was months ago. One thing he knew for certain was that his mother never once mentioned doctors or being sick. Rather, her letters read more like *TV Guide* manuals with detailed descriptions of the shows she was watching and the occasional reference to the lottery scratch-offs she was buying with her tips from the diner. *I'm going to win a million dollars and get an RV to take you across the country,* she wrote in her last letter to him, as if she were willing her dreams to life as she put pen to paper. *Make sure you're eating, Jack,* she'd remind him. *But most of all, don't do any-thing stupid,* she'd chide him, as if he were standing there in the living room and about to go out with friends. She had absolutely no idea of what his daily life in Vietnam was like, the weight of carrying that Prick-25 on his back, the sheer terror of not knowing if he'd be shot by enemy fire or blown to bits by stepping on a land mine. He would never write that to his mother because he wanted to spare her from the pain or the incessant worrying about things that were outside her, and his, control.

Perhaps he was guilty, just like her. He wanted her to think he was just fine when the truth was just the opposite.

He went into his hooch and packed his duffel quickly. He pulled down the clothes that were drying on the line, and then he threw in his kit, his journal, and the letters he kept from Becky, a thick stack tied with utility string.

He had imagined going home from the moment he first landed in Vietnam. When he packed sandbags or dug the latrines, he thought of home like it was an idealized place of perpetual Christmases. And although his home was never like a perfect Jimmy Stewart one on television, he began to reimagine it with softer edges and a lantern-like warmth. He edited his memory of the living room, erasing the thread-bare sofa or the chipped, mismatched dishes on which they ate their meals. He focused only on the good. He envisioned his mother making pancakes and link sausages in the frying pan. He saw her coming home from her job as a waitress at O'Hara's, pulling the crumpled bills from her purse and smoothing them on the countertop with a few quick sweeps of her hand.

How he loved it when he was just a little boy and she'd count out her tips and tell him they had enough extra for ice cream. Even now, the thought of the two of them walking down to the Dairy Queen to get soft serve cones, licking the ribbons of custard that dripped down the side, pulled him back to a place where he didn't have a care in the world.

So much had changed since then.

He recalled the photograph of the two of them his mother kept by her bedside. Her hair was pulled back in a high ponytail, and he was no older than four. He is nestled in her arms, his cheek pressed against hers, his head a crown of brown curls. In the photograph she is electric. Her hair is golden, her eyes Windex blue. But by the time he was in high school, her Kodak-color beauty had faded. Her eyes became cloudy. Her hair looked like straw. Her former luster had been lost to years of raising him on her own.

His mother was only twenty-two years old on the sunny afternoon that photograph was taken, the same age he is now as he packs his bag to bury her. Jack hoists his duffel over his shoulder and goes to wait for the chopper that will take him back to a motherless home.

In the two days that it took him to return to the States, Jack's thoughts bounced between the pain of losing his mother and the joy of being able to see Becky again.

His tour in Vietnam had made his body lean and taut; the hot sun turned his fair German Irish skin a deep chestnut brown. Dressed in his Class A uniform, he felt far more distinguished than he had when he left for boot camp only nine months earlier. His muscles filled out the chest and sleeves of his shirt. His belt accentuated his narrow waist. He could see his own reflection in the well-polished shine of his boots.

He was eager for Becky to see how much he had changed. He hoped she'd be impressed with how strong his body had become, and he couldn't wait to feel the weight of her in his arms. And yet, when he closed his eyes on the plane, the woman who appeared was not Becky at all. It was his mother. Her face young again and smooth. Her hands outstretched as if beckoning him to come closer to her with his first steps. Her laugh filling the air.

Changing planes in California, he had been surprised by the airline clerk who asked him if he was going to travel back to Pittsburgh in his uniform.

"There's a bathroom down the corridor. You can change out of your uniform in there if you'd like. . . . I've given you the military fare."

"No, ma'am," he answered. "That won't be necessary."

Jack took his ticket and hoisted his duffel over his shoulder and began to walk toward the gate. He had forty-five minutes until his plane boarded, and he was looking forward to getting a good old American burger at one of the restaurants before he took off.

But only minutes later, as he walked in the direction of one of the airport restaurants, he sensed footsteps behind him that seemed unnaturally close to his own. Jack instinctively slowed his pace, then turned around.

"May I help you?" He stood face-to-face with a young woman wearing overly large sunglasses on her pale, moon-shaped face. Long brown braids dangled from behind her ears.

"Back from Vietnam?" she sneered.

Jack had seen her type before. The long peasant skirt, the baggy T-shirt with no bra. He didn't hate the people in the peace movement before he left. Hell, he didn't want to go to Vietnam in the first place. But he didn't expect to be antagonized once he got back home either.

A freckled arm holding a tall drink extended out from her bright knit poncho. Stacks of dime-store bangles jangled on her wrist.

"I'm talking to you," she started again. Jack turned around to her, and that's when she pounced.

"Baby killer! Baby killer!" she shouted in his face, spit flying in the air. He was just about to push her out of the way when she hurled her drink in his face.

Jack stood there, frozen as the girl's ice-cold lemonade dripped down his cheeks and chest.

"What the hell?" he yelled back at her, his face pumping with blood. But she was already running down the hall, the back portion of her poncho fluttering behind her like a ridiculous cape.

Jack looked down at his soaked uniform. The sticky liquid had saturated his shirt and traveled down part of his pant leg.

Jet-lagged, exhausted, and in shock, he stood for several seconds, stunned.

"We'll be boarding flight 509 to Pittsburgh in ten minutes," a perfunctory voice announced over the PA system.

Had the woman really just called him a baby killer?

He had just spent five months with a radio strapped to his back, making him a bull's-eye for the enemy to kill him. He was scared for his life every second of the day. He had not killed a single Vietcong, and the idea of killing a baby was ludicrous. Yet he had come home to the country he was supposedly fighting for only to be unfairly accused of such abominable acts.

"There's a bathroom over there, son," an older gentleman said as he tapped Jack on the shoulder. He pulled out some paper napkins from his pocket and offered them to Jack. "She's just an ignorant hippie. Ignore her."

Jack took it and began to blot his wet chest. "Not the welcome I thought I'd get when I got back home."

"I imagine not." The man shook his head. "Do you have some clean clothes in that duffel?"

Jack nodded.

"Go change and clean yourself up. I'll make sure the plane doesn't leave without you."

Emotions swirled inside him, for the man was the only person to show him a gesture of kindness. "Thank you, sir. I appreciate it."

"Petty officer third class, United States Navy," the man said as he reached to shake Jack's still-wet hand.

CHAPTER 32

Long Island, 1979

THE MORNING THAT CLAYTON AND BUDDY SET OUT TO FIND the best place for their fort, they crossed paths with Katie Golden, who was en route and excited to be beginning her first day of work at her lifeguard job. Dressed in a terry white pullover, her red bathing suit concealed underneath, she still caught the boys' attention as she pedaled down Main Street.

It was Clayton who shouted out first to her. "Hey, hot stuff, you'd better slow down!" A smirk spread over his face like spilled kerosene.

Katie had seen the boys out of the corner of her eye and had tried to avoid them. She had never liked Buddy, but she had known him since they were toddlers, and he was like a pesky mosquito who irritated her more than anything. But since he had started hanging out with Clayton, she sensed something more menacing growing in him. The two of them had become inseparable, and she suspected what they were up to couldn't be anything good.

Buddy had always loved stirring the pot, but this new boy, Clayton, really had given her the willies. His pale eyes narrowed looking at her. Like he was hunting her.

They surprised her at the intersection of Main and Blythe streets. They clearly thought it would be amusing to take a shortcut and then reappear.

"Hey, Katie, what are you up to today? Hope you have something on under that cover up." Buddy grinned. "You're a lot prettier than that old bike of yours."

She was repulsed. "You're just gross. Why don't the two of you just get lost?" She hated every ounce of them. Buddy's wiry neck. His vampire-white skin and red hair.

"What did you say? I didn't hear you." Clayton mocked her. He stepped forward and put a hand in the center of her handlebars. "I like it when I get you mad. Your nose crinkles up like a little ferret."

She told them to buzz off. "You're both pathetic, you know that?"

Clayton came in closer, his face now only inches from hers. "I'll tell you again. I like it when you're mad." He snickered.

"Well, then, you're going to really like this," she announced before kicking him firmly in his shin.

Clayton fell back in pain, shouting expletives in her direction. But Katie hardly heard him. She'd already taken off toward the pool. She had worked far too hard to get the lifeguarding job that summer. It was the most coveted summer job in town, a stepping stone to high school popularity. Nothing was going to stop her. No one, not even a bunch of annoying boys, was going to threaten to take that away from her.

CHAPTER 33

THE BOYS FOUND THE SITE FOR THEIR FORT AFTER SURVEYING the woods for nearly an hour. Clayton wanted to pick a place that was slightly elevated, and Buddy wanted one that was built into a part of recessed earth. Both agreed that it couldn't be too near the entrance, where it might be seen by people in the parking lot, nor could it be too close to the reservoir, in case it ever overflowed.

In the end, Buddy deferred to Clayton for instruction, as he had never built anything like this before. He welcomed the architecture to his afternoons, the structure to have something to do in his endless free hours that summer that set him apart from his classmates. But perhaps even more enticing to Buddy was the fact that the fortress was his and Clayton's shared secret.

Over the course of the afternoon, they would bring saws and cut the trees into logs and begin layering the branches to start creating the structure.

"We'll bring a radio," Clayton announced, "so we can listen to any music we want."

"Too bad we can't sleep here," Buddy lamented. "I'd do anything to spend a night away from my house."

"Agreed," Clayton muttered as he pulled out a handsaw from his rucksack, the silver teeth reflecting in the low forest light. He'd taken a few of his father's tools, ones he'd yet to unpack from the boxes in their shed, knowing they'd hardly be missed. "We just need to put the work into it, and we'll finish soon enough. He slid the saw into a tree and moved the blade back and forth. Buddy watched as Clayton's face intensified as he worked.

"Don't just stand there, you lazy ass," he ordered, looking up after cutting three logs. "Go make yourself useful." So Buddy went to collect more branches and various odds-and-ends materials that were left in the woods. He found a piece of plywood and some discarded Coke bottles and stacked them in a pile with sticky pine branches and other dried twigs.

At one point, Buddy felt tired. He wasn't used to so much exercise. The back of his T-shirt was sweaty; his face was streaked with dirt. His skin glimmered with an impressive clamminess. Unable to keep up with Clayton's endurance (he had already cut seven long straight logs for the foundation), he sat down on one of the tree stumps to catch his breath.

Clayton approached and went over to size up the branches Buddy had found. "Good job. If we can't find a tarp, maybe we use these for a roof," he said, appraising the bounty. "We'll want to make sure we have our privacy."

They walked out of the forest smellier and dirtier than they had been since either of them could remember, and they savored every bit of what they knew their mothers would want them to scrub clean. Buddy's T-shirt was ripped in the back from where the thin material had come into contact with a low-hanging branch. They had leaves and small twigs in their hair, and their faces were smeared with soil.

The heat lifting off the asphalt parking lot made the air ripple, and the boys watched the shoppers come and go as if they were viewing them through thick lead-paned glass.

"When do you want to meet next?" Clayton asked as he lifted a freckled arm and wiped the perspiration from his brow.

"How about tomorrow?" Buddy grinned.

Clayton took a branch and started drawing in the ground. "I'm thinking we should give ourselves a name, like a secret society or something."

Buddy pondered the idea for a moment. "How about the Wolf Pack or the Dragon Teeth?"

"Those sound pretty stupid." Clayton shut him down quickly. "How about the Viper Squad? That sounds pretty intimidating, if you ask me."

Buddy shook his head. "Yeah . . . we could carve the initials 'VS' above the entrance of the fort."

"Cool," Clayton said. "This beats that dumb pool any day."

CHAPTER 34

GRACE FELT SHE HAD A NEW SENSE OF PURPOSE EVER SINCE SHE started visiting the motherhouse and tutoring there once a week. And for the first time since she'd become a parent, she'd even discovered the positive impact of television. She could see how Bảo was learning English far more quickly than many of the others because of his obsession with watching Saturday-morning cartoons.

"The middle school is arranging for a proper ESL teacher to start coming by soon," Sister Mary Alice updated Grace. "We're hoping the children will be able to start there in September, and the ESL will help bring them up to grade level. It's more the adults we don't want left behind." She looked at Grace. "So, I was hoping you could help Anh more with her conversational English. She's the one we're all concerned about, since she'll basically be a single mother to Bảo once the official adoption gets worked out. She'll have to go out into the work world to support the two of them."

"Of course," Grace said. "But I'm thinking it might be better to make things a little more hands-on for her. Maybe I could take her out for the day . . . like a trip to the grocery store so she could learn how one asks for things or hear a typical exchange with the cashier. You know, simple exchanges . . . but stuff we all have to do during our day."

"An excellent idea!" Sister Mary Alice chirped. Soon Grace found herself with a weekly appointment with Anh. Every Tuesday, she'd remind Katie that Molly would be at the pool club with the Connor family, but that she should routinely check on her younger sister when she was not perched on her lifeguard tower. Katie reluctantly agreed.

In the beginning, Anh remained quiet as she shadowed Grace in her daily errands, merely nodding as Grace went about her routine.

"Do you have change for a ten-dollar bill?" Grace asked the cashier when she went to pay for her items. She wanted Anh to hear the conversation so that soon she'd have the confidence to do it on her own.

The next time they were scheduled to go out together, Grace found Anh waiting in the common room, all dressed up for their excursion. Anh was wearing a yellow cotton sundress with little white daisies embroidered into the fabric that Grace had given her along with some other hand-me-downs from her closet. The dress, which was one of many that now no longer fit Grace, had once been one of her favorites, one she wore before she became pregnant with Katie. Now when she saw it on the younger Anh, she could hardly believe she'd ever been that thin. Had her waist really ever been that small?

"You look lovely, Anh. The yellow color really suits you."

"Thank you." Her eyes traveled over to her nephew, who was watching TV. "Okay if Bảo come today too?"

Grace was mad at herself. She'd been meaning to figure out a way to include Bảo on their excursions. It was on her list to see if she could take him and Anh to swim at the beach club.

"Of course. I should have thought of it myself. Molly has been asking if he can come to the beach club and go swimming. But today, let's all just go to the store."

Anh took the grocery list and focused on the items that Grace had carefully written in large, clear letters:

Eggs
Butter
Bread
Milk
Potato salad

"Let's see if you can find these things," Grace suggested as she lifted one of the plastic caddies and handed it to Anh. "If you can't find one of them, then you can ask him. . . ." She pointed to Karl, who was stocking the shelves with canned goods. "Okay?"

Anh nodded and looked at Bảo. "You help too," she said, practicing her English.

His eyes traveled across the shelves. Instead of answering, he dug his hands into the pockets of his shorts and shrugged.

"Well, okay, but stay close to us," Grace said.

The two women walked toward the deli counter. Behind the glass case, bowls of macaroni and potato salads, coleslaw, and bean salad were lined up in neat rows.

Fred smoothed his hands on his butcher's apron. "I see we have a new customer this morning."

"Yes, we do." Grace smiled. "Anh is practicing her English today. Just like I needed to practice speaking American when I first got here."

"Ah, yes." Fred laughed. "That brogue of yours still gets me confused every now and then. How can I help you ladies?"

Grace reached over and gently touched Anh's shoulder. "Go ahead," she said, when suddenly she heard a commotion coming from near the store's entrance.

"Hey, kid, put that back—you can't just take things," the cashier shouted.

"You little thief," another woman added. "We pay for things here in America."

Grace would recognize that voice anywhere.

It was Adele.

"I saw him steal it with my own two eyes!" Adele was standing next to Bảo, holding on to his wrist tightly. Her pink painted nails pressed into his skin, just above his scar.

"Let go of him," Grace said. "What is exactly going on here?"

"The boy took a Hershey's bar from the counter without paying. . . ."

Grace glared at Adele. "Please let go of him. He's with me."

Anh stood next to Grace, her fingers still clutching the shopping list. "Miss—Bảo good boy," she said to Adele. She reached into her purse for one of the bills she'd received from the Sisters. "Please . . . take . . . here." Her hand shook as she walked to the counter, put the money down, and pulled Bảo away from Adele.

"This is just a misunderstanding," Grace said, glaring at Adele. "I'm sure Bảo was going to put it with the rest of our groceries."

"Ma'am, he put it in his pocket. He was shoplifting." The cashier's chewing gum snapped like taffy in her mouth. "Mr. Kepler's noticed a lot of stuff's gone missing off the shelves lately."

"Well, if it has, it's not because of him," Grace protested. "Today's the first time he's even been to this store."

Fred came out behind the deli counter to try to sort everything out. "What's all the commotion about? Mrs. Golden was just in the back ordering some cold cuts with her friend here."

"Well, her *friend* should keep a better eye on her boy," Adele cut in.

Fred handed Grace the wrapped deli meat wrapped. "Let's all try to remain civil." His voice was measured. "It was actually on my fingertips to call you." His eyes met Adele's. "I saw your Buddy the other day with his friend. They were in the back trying to sneak out a couple beers."

"I find that hard to believe, Fred. You know my Buddy would never do something like that."

Fred turned to the cashier. "Tammy, you remember those two boys here the other day trying to nab some Pabst Blue Ribbons?"

"Yes," she said as she looked down at her fingers. "I do remember something like that."

"It must have been the other boy, then," Adele protested. "Anyway, Fred, I need some bologna and cheese. Can you help me with that, please?" She clutched her purse tightly to her side as she walked past Grace and Anh.

"We'll pay for this and the chocolate bar," Grace said, stepping up to the counter.

When they got outside, Anh began to apologize.

"He say his father told him before we left... Americans give chocolate bars for free."

Grace felt a lump in her throat. She had a memory of Jack once telling her about an incident involving a chocolate bar the GIs handed out.

"Here," she said, handing the candy bar to Bảo. "Better eat it before you get in the warm car." She pinched her fingers together. "Gets too hot, it'll melt all over your hands."

CHAPTER 35

Allentown, Pennsylvania, 1969

JACK SETTLED INTO THE SOFT SEAT OF THE AIRPLANE AND TRIED to close his eyes. In five and a half hours, if the trip went as planned, he'd be back in Pennsylvania and greeted by the only woman he now had in his life. Becky. The incident at the airport had unsettled him greatly and even after changing into a fresh set of clothes, he felt the woman's vitriol still clinging to his skin. She had made him feel dirty, and he hated her for it. As much as he tried to push the incident out of his mind, it felt slick and unctuous, as though she had somehow contaminated him with something ugly.

From the moment he arrived in boot camp, he had been trained to forcibly retaliate against anyone who attacked him. Had a man thrown a drink at him and called him a "baby killer," he wasn't sure he wouldn't have thrown him to the ground and then pounded his face in.

He had never been a fighter before his deployment. But now, as he floated in the skies above his own country, Jack realized that the military had somehow permanently altered him. And while he had initially only felt shock and confusion when the woman accosted him, he since had developed a delayed sense of rage.

"Can I offer you a drink, sir?" The stewardess's kind voice pulled him back.

He ordered a rum and Coke and let the sweet liquid run through him and soften the steely edges he thought he had left back in Vietnam. He reminded himself that he only had two weeks of leave, and most of that he'd also get to sleep in a warm bed next to his Becky. They'd wake up and eat pancakes with maple syrup, and then they'd go back to bed. When they finally rose for the day, she'd take him to her school and show him her new life so he'd have something beautiful to take back with him when he returned to his tour.

He didn't want to think of the other things he'd have to do once he got home, like bury his mother. He still struggled to comprehend that she was actually gone. His mind could easily conjure her sitting in her big comfy chair, the ashtray beside her as she raised one of her Camel cigarettes to her lips. He could easily recall her deep, throaty laugh and the sounds of her puttering around the kitchen late at night when she came home from work. Part of him wondered if he shouldn't have come back to bury her, because it was easier to pretend she was still alive while he was back in Vietnam, waiting alongside Becky for him to come home.

As he stepped into the arrival hall at the Pittsburgh airport, he spotted her immediately. She was a beacon of white light amid a sea of shadows. Becky stood in the front of the crowd, her brown hair even longer than he recalled and brushed to a perfect shine. She wasn't wearing scruffy dungarees and T-shirts like so many of the others in the crowd but was dressed in a lawn-green dress with a matching headband. In one hand she clutched a bouquet of white daisies, and in the other, a handwritten sign that said *Welcome Home!*

One of the things he loved most about Becky was her stillness. That afternoon, she brought him back to the apartment that she shared with another student off campus, and after he had showered, she pulled him to her bed and kissed him deeply before letting him just hold her.

He breathed her in. He inhaled her sweet fragrance and savored the softness of her skin against his own. She placed her hands on either side of his face and stared a moment before kissing him. "I'm so sorry

about your mother, baby," she whispered before kissing him again.
And it was only then, in the safety of her embrace, did he find himself
releasing all the pain he'd tried to push deep down inside him. He wept
openly in her arms.

CHAPTER 36

Long Island, 1979

WHEN GRACE RETURNED HOME FROM HER OUTING WITH ANH and Bảo that afternoon, she was still shaken by Adele's behavior. The woman had been so quick to condemn an innocent child whose only mistake was believing what his father had told him.

But he hadn't even wanted to eat the candy afterward. After she drove them back to Our Lady Queen of Martyrs, she noticed the candy bar was still in the rear seat and left unopened. When she went to take it out, she could feel how soft it was beneath the wrapper.

Her heart sank. Adele had ruined what was meant to be a happy excursion outside the motherhouse.

It had begun on such a positive note. She'd put the radio on, and the station wagon became flooded with the latest tunes of summer. "Music Box Dancer" by Frank Mills filled the air, and she caught sight of Bảo smiling in the rearview window. As they stepped into Kepler's, Anh stopped in front of the fruit section. Pyramids of peaches and plums were laid out in front. Plastic baskets of strawberries were arranged on a long wooden table, as well as other fruits in season. Anh reached out and picked up a mango and lifted it to her face. She took two deep breaths and inhaled, searching for its rich fragrance.

"Not ripe," Anh had simply said as she smiled at Grace. The two of them had then walked toward the deli counter, the first step in getting Anh to use her English with a stranger.

They were in the middle of ordering when the commotion with Bảo began.

Grace replayed the incident again in her head, then pulled down a glass from the cabinet and filled it with some tap water. She looked at the clock. In another hour, she'd head over to the beach club and pick up Katie and Molly. Outside, the flower boxes were parched, and the lawn had just sprouted some unwanted dandelions. She couldn't help but feel a bit melancholy. Had she bitten off too much, only to fail, despite her best intentions? Should she have taken Adele to task more for her terrible behavior? She sat down and finished her drink. Next time, they'd all go swimming at the club. Grace painted the scene in her head, the splashing, the laughter. She wanted to erase the memory of today and replace it with something better.

She heard her late father-in-law's voice in her head and reminded herself that time didn't move backward. Rather, it was the opposite. The future expanded with each passing minute. And there was plenty of room to get things right the next time.

CHAPTER 37

Anh walked into the motherhouse, avoiding eye contact with the Sisters. She knew they would ask her how the excursion had gone, and she didn't have the words nor the heart to try and explain what had happened. Bảo had already found his favorite spot in front of the television, his sneakers pulled off and his feet curled beneath him. She could see his was already trying to forget the uncomfortable incident, escaping into the storyline of his favorite program.

She had hoped the outing with Grace would help with the homesickness she'd been feeling since she'd arrived. She missed so much about Vietnam. Not just the comfort of their once-tight-knit family, the closeness with her sister, the warmth of her husband beside her. But also the canopy of trees, the scent of the frangipani flowers, and the food. In this strange country, the fruits had no smell or even taste. She had initially thought it might just be the fruit that the sisters served them at the motherhouse. But a trip out with the kind woman, Grace, had cemented her suspicions. This was a country where the fruit simply had no sweetness.

She longed for her former life, or the parts free of hardship or danger. Where were the succulent mangoes? The sweet longans and juicy pomelos? It was a terrible waste to eat a fruit that was picked too early. The taste, it seemed, had been left abandoned on the vine.

In America, they ate whatever was put in front of them, never pondering what was missing. But Anh knew she wasn't the only one who noticed this difference. Bảo had left the blueberries floating in the milk of his cereal that morning. Dinh, a single man in his late twenties who had been so severely beaten during an interrogation by the North Vietnamese Army that he still walked with a limp, had similarly made a comment over breakfast about how he wished he could start an orchard in the extensive backyard of the motherhouse because he so missed eating fruit that had fully ripened as it should.

"How sad these Americans must be to eat food with no flavor," he lamented as he ate the white toast and jam that the nuns took for themselves with their tea each morning. "What I'd do for some congee and pickled vegetables. . . ."

Anh laughed. She, too, missed her typical morning breakfast, the quiet ritual of preparing the rice gruel and flavoring it with fresh herbs and roasted peanuts. Her appetite had diminished since she arrived in America, a fact that amazed her because they had spent nearly every hour on the fishing boat dreaming of all the food they would have once they were rescued. Even in the refugee camp, where they had stayed before they heard the wonderful news that an American Catholic church would be sponsoring them, they had eaten a diet similar to what they had eaten at home, mostly rice and stewed vegetables. So the tasteless cornflakes or spongy bread that was now offered each morning had little appeal, as did the bland chicken or beef they would have at dinner.

There were also medicinal properties to their diet back home, the ones Linh had always been quick to recommend: ginger to fight off nausea or infection, chilies that gave one energy and kept one's bones strong. Anh had been so fatigued since she arrived, and she suspected it was from the change in her diet.

The upsetting episode at Kepler's had upturned everything for the rest of the afternoon. She had been hoping to buy a chicken and bring it back to the motherhouse to cook. Sister Mary Alice had given her twenty dollars to buy some ingredients, knowing that Anh enjoyed making things in the small kitchenette. Anh had been planning what

she would make even before getting in Grace's car. She'd boil the
chicken that night for supper, bones and all, and make a simple stock
that would give both she and Bảo the strength they had been lacking.

But the second stop never happened after they were at Kepler's.

"We can go to the butcher, if you'd like?" Grace was kind enough
to still offer. But Anh had just shaken her head.

"Not today, miss," she said. She could tell by Bảo's expression he
just wanted to go back to the motherhouse. Even she could still hear
the accusing tone of the woman with the pink fingernails and powdered face rattling around in her head. Sadly, Anh had wanted to go
back too.

She was sorry to have cut the day short. Earlier that morning,
before Grace arrived, she'd summoned up Linh's voice in her head,
reminding her to be less shy, to have courage, and to use the afternoon
to practice her English. Anh wanted to become more comfortable in
this new country, to learn its customs and language, but it did not
come that easy to her.

Dinh, on the other hand, had been quite forthcoming with the
sisters of Our Lady Queen of Martyrs. His easy smile and quick
laugh had helped make an instant connection with the women, and
they often relied on him to corral the others when they needed them
all to help with the general housekeeping. Looking at how quickly he
was to help scrub the floors or clean the dishes, he became a house
favorite.

There was something about him that reminded her of her late husband. Perhaps it was his eagerness to always pitch in and help. Her husband had been the same way, particularly early on in their courtship
when he wanted to show her parents that he was a good match. Anh
remembered fondly how he came over to her house and chopped firewood for her parents or did other tasks that were difficult for an aging
couple, like helping repair the tin roof when it leaked.

So many times, Anh had thought back to their wedding night, when he'd outdone himself with the most chivalrous act. It was the first time they'd made love, and much to her distress, she did not bleed on the marital sheet. The custom was to display proof of her virginity the next morning to her in-laws, but there were no red droplets to be seen.

"Don't worry, my beautiful bride," Minh had whispered, careful that no ears outside the wedding chamber could hear them. She watched as he stood up to retrieve a small knife on the shelf and quickly pricked his finger, squeezing some blood into the center.

"No one will know but us," he promised, kissing her again.

Now, for the first time since her husband's death, Anh felt aware of the kindness of another man toward her. She especially appreciated how Dinh enjoyed being playful with Bảo too, affectionately calling him by the nickname "Bi," which meant "little marble." He took scraps of paper and made origami little soldiers, sometimes piercing the paper with wooden toothpicks so they looked as if they were holding tiny swords.

When Anh had awakened to discover Bảo missing that dreadful morning during their first week with the sisters, it had been Dinh, who had consoled her in their native tongue as the sisters squawked around, throwing their hands in the air and speaking feverishly in fast sentences that she didn't understand.

And while Dinh had reassured her, kneeling next to her as she held her head in her hands and wept and telling her that Bảo would soon be found unharmed, it was Grace who'd actually brought him back safely.

Anh had a vague memory of seeing Grace at the police station, but she had been so distraught when Bảo finally stepped into the room, that she barely glanced at her, focusing only on her nephew.

When Grace appeared the next day at the motherhouse, a panic swept over her. Did this woman want to take him from her? Did she think it was something she had done to make him run away?

She soon learned Grace only wanted to help. She brought new books to practice English with and even some clothes.

When Grace arrived with a shopping bag full of dresses, Anh proved lucky enough to fit perfectly into the garments. The two other Vietnamese women were not as tall as Anh was and would need them hemmed. Not wanting to seem too greedy, Anh offered to alter one for each of them. There was a simple red one that was easy enough to take in from the bottom and sew two darts into the bodice; another was a prairie dress that she could shorten as well. After Anh spent several hours working on them so the other two women could also have something special to wear, Dinh had whispered to her with a kind smile, "They would both look so much prettier on you."

While Anh was only recently growing more confident using her English, Dinh had been the first of the adults to start speaking to the Sisters from the moment they arrived at the motherhouse. Later, he'd confided with her that he'd hope to set a precedent and show he was willing to make mistakes in order to learn. After he had mastered the basic phrases such as "I am hungry; I want to eat," he brought up what everyone was thinking. "I want to work. I want . . ." He made a gesture with his fingers. "I want money."

Anh was grateful that Dinh had brought up what was on all their minds. How would they ever come to be self-sufficient in this new country? They needed to work. They needed to earn their own money. None of them wanted to live under the Sisters' roof forever. When the social worker came to visit the next time, Dinh asked the questions for the group. They welcomed having a leader. They looked to Dinh to ensure there was a plan in place to help them find their way.

CHAPTER 38

Pittsburgh, 1969

JACK DIDN'T SLEEP AS PEACEFULLY AS HE THOUGHT HE WOULD that first night at Becky's apartment. He woke up with night sweats, his heart pounding. The noise outside her window, which was just harmless college students tossing a couple of beer bottles on the street, set off all the adrenaline in his body. He found himself bolting forward in Becky's bed, his eyes wide open and his hands instinctively grabbing for a rifle that, of course, wasn't there.

"What's wrong, baby?" Becky asked him as she sat up and rubbed his back. Naked from the waist down, her silhouette in the moonlight brought him back to reality.

"Nothing, just a bad dream." He rubbed his eyes.

She tried to pull him back to her, but his body hadn't quite settled yet. A thin blanket of perspiration covered his skin. Becky had left the window half-open and the early-autumn breeze entering the room sent a chill over him.

Jack left the bed and went to the bathroom, returning a few minutes later with a glass of water that he put down on the nightstand, next to a portrait the two of them taken when they were in Atlantic City right before he left for Camp Pendleton. He settled back in bed, facing the photograph, remembering that afternoon when they held hands on the boardwalk and had eaten cotton candy, how he later kissed her on the pier, Becky's hair whipping in the salt air.

The boy in the photograph now looked like a stranger to him.

"Try to get some sleep," she repeated, this time wrapping her arms around him. "You'll need your rest for tomorrow."

He lay motionless and Becky curled into him, her warm breath on his neck. He was surprised how much he wanted to wiggle away from her. He had craved the chance to be intimate with her again, but now he felt restless. Although he knew he was safe in her apartment, his body struggled to relax. His body could not relinquish its adrenaline, its need to constantly be on high alert. When a car rumbled, he thought it was a possible mortar shelling. When the radiator hissed, he imagined a VC under the bed. He wanted his rifle next to him because it had become like another limb for him. Without it, he felt unprotected and unsafe, despite him knowing full well he was in a sleepy college town outside Pittsburgh, as far away from Vietnam as one could be.

To calm himself he tried staring at the photograph of the two of them, the wide smiles on their faces. He couldn't help but notice how his eyes looked in the picture. People had always told him that he had beautiful eyes. Pale blue with flecks of gold, Becky used to say that was what first caught her attention when they were back in high school. "They glint," she told him. "Like they're smiling at me." She looked at him deeply and touched his face that first time they kissed behind the bleachers. "And with those thick curls," she said, her fingers running through his hair.

"I'm the one supposed to be doing the complimenting," he answered sweetly as he dipped in for another kiss.

"Can't a girl tell a man he's good-looking?" She giggled.

He'd spend the rest of the night contemplating the boy he saw in that portrait by her bedside. The difference in his expression is what now haunted him the most. He envied the carefreeness, the levity in his expression. And he couldn't help but wonder if he'd ever feel that way again.

He buried his mother in a graveside ceremony. The mourners consisted of just he, Becky, and a handful of her friends, and those who knew her from the diner. She had waitressed there for as long as he could remember, but he had no idea she was so well loved by her customers. The woman with the permanent smile who pours you coffee and remembers if you like your toast with extra butter or with strawberry jam holds a special spot for some people, especially the lonely ones who breakfasted at a counter each morning rather than at home with a family. His mother's boss, Walter, who had always been kind to both of them over the years and generous with a Christmas bonus or an envelope of extra money on her birthday, also came to pay his respects.

"Your mother was a good woman." Walter opened his arms and gave Jack a hug. "Don't you look smart in your uniform, son. She'd have been so proud."

Jack had dressed in his full Marine Corps regalia for the funeral. The blue-and-red jacket with his new medals, the blood stripe pants and white rimmed cap. As he buttoned his jacket and looked at himself in the mirror, he felt the full weight of the uniform. The protective shield that enabled him to put up a barrier between his grief and his responsibilities as a son.

He'd bury his mother with his shoulders back and without letting his emotions take over him. Like the marine he now truly was.

That afternoon, as he watched his mother's coffin be lowered into the ground, he couldn't think about all the other things that were being buried along with her. Her voice, her laugh, her concern for his well-being. He had always wanted to be the son who looked out for his mother, to protect her as she had for him. For almost all his life it had just been the two of them.

Becky, in a simple black dress and gloves, had driven them to the cemetery. Her bright orange VW Bug puttered through his childhood town, the streets familiar and unchanged. Jack didn't have the urge to speak, and Becky let the silence wash over them, her hand every now and then reaching over to touch his cheek when they idled at a traffic light.

At the intersection of Main Street and Hanson Avenue, he looked outside the window of the passenger seat and felt his throat tighten at the site of the Dairy Queen, where his mother used to buy him a soft serve cone with the few extra dollars she had from her tips. He almost made Becky stop the car so he could do something that threaded his heart to her before he said goodbye. It was silly, an ice cream cone . . . but somehow it symbolized everything to him. All her devotion and her personal sacrifices.

Had he thanked her all those times? He wasn't so sure now. He knew he told her he loved her, but had he actually ever sat down and thanked her for how she raised him on almost nothing? He knew grief was part of burying a loved one, but was guilt also? He suddenly felt like he had been a terrible son.

Becky, sensing Jack was lost in thoughts of his mother, gripped his hand and squeezed it.

Her quiet was one more thing he loved about her. Silence was its own form of language. And Becky sensed this. Her touch was a comfort. It replaced the need for words.

CHAPTER 39

JUST WHEN JACK HAD FINALLY BEGUN TO SOFTEN AT THE END OF those two weeks home, just as he was getting used to taking a cold beer out of a refrigerator and listening to records with Becky after they made love between her classes, and after he let her paint a picture of what their life would be like when he got home—"I'll finish up my teacher's degree, we'll get married, then, in a couple years, we'll start having kids"—he knew he'd soon be thrown back to that living hell, digging fighting holes and wondering if he'd survive the war.

The last two days with Becky had been the hardest. Over the weekend, she helped him pack up his childhood home. The landlord hadn't been as sympathetic as Jack hoped, and he was forced to spend his last days of leave clearing the whole place out. What he couldn't box away and put into storage, they lined up in the yard and sold for a few dollars.

The most difficult thing was going through his mother's belongings. She had never been a spendthrift, and her closet was filled with only two cotton dresses, a few blouses, a couple pairs of pants, and, of course, her waitress uniforms. But on the top shelf, he found several photographs from when he was little and trinkets she must have felt attached to. A Mickey Mouse hat, his cherished Evel Knievel doll, and a few paper cards he made for her when he was in grade school.

Two weeks earlier, when he first went to the funeral home, the manager had given him an envelope containing her watch and earrings.

"I thought you'd want these," he said, offering the items to Jack.

Jack didn't recognize the silver clip earrings, but the watch was special. He had bought it—a simple Timex watch with a thin leather strap and white dial for her thirty-fifth birthday—using the money he had saved from his modest allowance and what he had earned shoveling the neighbors' driveways when it snowed. Given that his mother was always running late to pick him up or when they were trying to get out the door, he had thought it would be a fitting gift for her special birthday that year.

She never took it off after that. It made her so proud that he had bought her something with his own money. She showed it off at the diner to all her customers, beaming with pride.

"I raised a good boy," she said as she hugged him. He was fifteen years old then, already significantly taller than his mother.

"No more running late, Ma," he joked with her.

Now, when he fingered the worn leather band, her smile flashed in his memory. He looked at the dial and saw it was still keeping good time. "Thank you," he said softly. "I appreciate your returning it to me."

That last night, after Becky and he arrived at her apartment and she put on her favorite Joni Mitchell record, he gave her his mother's watch. They had just finished eating a dinner she had made for his last night, a grilled steak he knew she had probably saved up to buy just for the occasion and creamed spinach, his favorite.

He took it out of the white envelope and held it for a moment between his fingers. It wasn't worth a lot of money, but at that moment, it seemed like the most priceless thing he had in his possession.

"Keep it safe for me," he whispered as he leaned in to kiss her. He wrapped it around her wrist and buckled it. "I bought it for my mom when I was just a kid. There's something special knowing it's still being worn by someone I love."

CHAPTER 40

Long Island, 1979

LOVE AND SADNESS TWISTED TOGETHER FOR GRACE. SHE FELT lucky she had married Tom. They had two healthy daughters and a home she was proud of. And yet, sometimes at night she'd find herself back at the river behind her childhood home, the waves crashing over the rocks, not loud enough to mute the sound of her mother crying in the bedroom.

She hated when these bouts of depression hit her. It felt like her heart was being strangled, obfuscating everything she knew to be good in her life. She became sullen and moody and snapped more at the girls than they deserved, and when Tom reached for her in the night, she pushed him away.

On some of those nights, she would do math in her head, calculating how old Bridey would be had she gone on to live and how many things had died when she drowned. As a child, she'd only seen it from her perspective, the change in her parents' marriage, the gray veil that came over her mother's eyes, her father's sadness that he wore like the rain jacket he wrapped his baby girl in when they pulled her from the river. But now, as a mother and a wife, Grace mourned her sister's death in another way. That Bridey never had the chance to marry and fall in love or to have children. Everything that had brought Grace joy later in life seemed tinged with a bittersweetness, knowing her sister had been robbed of also experiencing it. And although she knew as an adult that it was wrong to blame herself for a tragic accident, especially when she had only been a child herself when it happened, the fact that she had been making daisy chains when her sister fell into the river still haunted her.

Her daughters knew so little about her sister. Grace didn't want to burden the children with the pain of knowing how she drowned. She had waffled during her first pregnancy to name Katie after Bridey if the baby was born a girl, and then again with Molly. After much contemplation, though, she decided against it, thinking it too much of a weight to put upon a child. But she didn't anticipate the deep emotions it would continue to stir in her as the years passed. Molly was now several years older than her sister had been when she died, and there was so much of her daughter that reminded Grace of her sister. The laugh, the curiosity, even the love of animals. Grace had been seriously considering getting the girls a dog next year. They all loved Hendrix, Jack's black Labrador who came into the shop when he worked at night. He was such a gentle animal, she thought perhaps if they had a dog of their own, it would knit the girls closer together.

She'd have to make the decision sooner or later; after all, Katie was only home another two years before she would go off to college. Time was going by too fast. She needed to remind herself that it was not good for her be pulled back to the sadness of her past. Her father-in-law's favorite words circled inside her. "Time must move forward." It really was the only way to survive.

CHAPTER 41

Vietnam, 1969

AFTER JACK RETURNED FROM HIS TWO-WEEK LEAVE TO BURY HIS mother, he was slapped into the harsh reality of combat duty. The comfort of a real bed and Becky's soft skin was now cruelly replaced by the reality of sleeping in a foxhole with the radio headpiece in his ear and one of the men in company patrol keeping vigilant watch beside him.

Flannery was the first to welcome him back. He came over and slapped Jack on the back. "It's good to have you back, Hollywood. . . . They made me carry that damn radio when you were gone. Man, that thing's a bitch." He kicked the ground. "And I'm real sorry about your mom."

Jack tossed his head back. "Now you get why they call it a Prick-25."

"Yeah, no shit. Carrying thirty pounds in this heat is bad enough. Adding another twenty-five on your back. . . . Shit, man . . ." Flannery shook his head. "That's a fucking bad deal."

The men were just as he had left them: hungry, wet, and tired. Doc had just returned from Cam Ranh Bay for Rosh Hashana. None of them had ever heard of this holiday before, but the military had decided to make a conscientious effort to see that the Jews in the military would celebrate their New Year and Passover. So they flew the enlisted men out to an idyllic spot where a chaplain oversaw a service for the hundred or so Jewish men. According to Doc, three Jewish women were also there, one with a particularly good sense of humor who took a Polaroid to send home to her mother with an inscription on the back: *Who knew I had to go to Vietnam to meet a nice Jewish boy?*

There was something quirky but lovable about Doc. Perhaps it was the fact that he didn't appear as hardened as the rest of the men in the squad. He almost never swore, which was an anomaly. The others punctuated every other sentence with a curse. While the training and life in Vietnam had beaten every ounce of softness out of the men, he still had a boyish sensitivity in him that made him seem younger than his years.

It seemed strange to Jack that a corpsman like Doc, whose mother still sent him care packages of M&M's, would have enlisted on the day before his eighteenth birthday to be a field medic.

He knew that Navy corpsmen who served as medics had to first do extensive training at corps school, learning basic emergency first aid medical training and triage before they were even sent out into the field. Volunteering for the role involved a minimum three-year commitment.

"Why didn't you just go to college and medical school if your number wasn't even called, Mike? I just don't get it." Jack shook his head in disbelief. "You can't really like this shit? Can you?"

"I grew up hearing stories from my dad and my uncle about World War II." Doc tried to find the words to explain. "I idealized both of these guys. . . . Dad was a medic and so proud of serving in Patton's army as they tore through France." In the moonlight he looked pensive as he remembered the family lore, the very stories that had inspired him to enlist. "But it was my uncle's story, about a six-foot-three medic named Tex who saved him during the invasion of Peleliu, that I think really ultimately drew me to the corps." He closed his eyes and the story fell from his lips, the oral history that he had heard from his uncle that was a part of him. "Tex was patching up Uncle Nate from a shrapnel wound and then fell down on top of him during heavy fire to protect him, like a human shield—the medic just gave his own life, just like that," explained Doc. "Hearing stuff like that growing up as a kid just made me want to do my part, I guess."

Jack had not grown up hearing glorified War World II stories that had fed so many of his fellow marines' souls. Almost all of them were sons of vets, and it gave them a foundation of purpose that was missing for him. But perhaps it was for the best. He didn't want to burst any of their bubbles, but he knew firsthand from the incident in the airport that there wasn't going to be a ticker tape parade for them like their dads received when they returned home.

"You wanna be a doctor when you get back to the States, though, right?" Jack could easily imagine Doc sitting behind a wooden desk, talking gently to his patients. He had just that kind of demeanor that fit into the image of a typical television show about a devoted small-town physician.

"I think a pediatrician. I love kids."

"You'd be great. I wanna have five kids with my girlfriend." Jack slid back and laughed.

"You're just thinking about *making* five kids," Doc ribbed him.

"You're right, man," answered Jack before the conversation turned toward food, Doc dreaming of his mother's pot roast, Jack, a Philly cheese steak. Hunger manifested itself in so many ways.

CHAPTER 42

Long Island, 1979

JACK'S KITCHEN CONTAINED ONLY ONE POT AND ONE FRYING pan. In his refrigerator he only ever kept a handful of things: eggs for breakfast, cream for his coffee, and a few slices of cold cuts for his sandwiches, along with a tin of wet dog food for Hendrix. He had learned to keep his needs to a minimum, allowing him to avoid the large A&P to spare himself the painful stares of young children and their mothers who hushed them into silence. At Kepler's small store, he could go in quickly and purchase the few provisions he needed before any other customers noticed him. He knew exactly where the boxes of Kraft Macaroni & Cheese and Ritz crackers were located, and the jars of Welch's jelly and Wonder Bread. He felt lucky that Fred, who worked behind the deli counter, kept an eye out for him and often began slicing the roast beef and provolone cheese before he'd even reached the counter.

Food as others knew and enjoyed it was different for him. He ate to live, just to sustain himself, not for any kind of pleasure.

In Vietnam, they all tried to push their hunger away, the C-rations never proving adequate. Yet, despite their own famished bellies, the men often saved part of their food to give to the children who came begging for whatever the men were willing to share.

One afternoon, shortly after he returned from burying his mother, he found himself out traveling with a few battalion scouts in a transport truck. As the vehicle bumped over the rocky path, the men jostled against each other, their shoulders touching, rifles clutched to their chest. At one point, four small children came running out of the woods.

One of them, Jack remembered, was a little girl wearing a white cotton dress, her long brown legs exposed as she ran expertly over the uneven terrain with the other three boys. "Candy! Candy! Cigarettes!" the children cried with their hands outstretched. They already knew the words for food they liked or the cigarettes they could barter with back at their village.

Jack had some C-rations on him, and Doc had a tropical bar, a kind of chocolate that Hershey's had created to withstand the intense Southeast Asian heat. The scouts tossed the food and candy to the children. Flannery laughed and fumbled for a tin of lima beans he would never eat. Gomez threw a couple cigarettes. But the little girl in the white dress caught the most coveted prize, the chocolate bar. In that moment when her hands grasped the treasure wrapped in shiny silver foil, her face beamed in joy. It was so pure, so full of innocence, it made Jack reach down to his gear and see if he might have another one buried in a pocket somewhere, knowing it would have been worth it to see the same expression on another child's face.

The girl couldn't have been more than eight years old, but with the chocolate clutched in one hand, she ran unbridled and flew far ahead of the others. Her black hair whipping behind her and her thin legs coltish as they flew over the blades of grass and wildflowers.

Candy! Candy! Cigarettes!

Jack heard the boys' peals for more handouts ringing in his ears as the little girl ran ahead on the dirt path along the road. Doc and he both looked out the side of the vehicle, admiring her speed as she bounded ahead of the others and ran to overtake the truck, her white dress billowing with every stride. But as the driver slowed down so as not to strike her, the girl's foot hit a trip wire for a buried mine. There, right in front of all of them, a small but deadly explosion ignited. Instantly, the girl and her three friends were engulfed in a burst of fiery orange flames and ripped apart by shrapnel.

Sometimes when Jack flipped on his television and a commercial came across the screen for Hershey's chocolate, he filled with nausea. That something so sweet, so innocent, could turn into such a brutal memory. The memory of the girl's face was seared into his mind, her delight just before being eviscerated in front of him. How could one erase such a memory? Once, when he was cleaning up a classroom at Foxton Elementary, he came across a crumpled Hershey's wrapper, and when he picked it up to throw it into the large waste bin on his trolley, he found himself sobbing like a baby. He shut the door and hid his face in his palms and wept.

He wasn't sure if it was the Hershey's wrapper or the index card on the little brown desk, the one that had the name written in neat black letters: *Stanley*.

CHAPTER 43

THE SUMMER HEAT INDEX WAS SOARING. KATIE HAD BEEN working at the pool club for three weeks when her mother came up with the great idea to invite Bảo along to swim with Molly there for the day. The temperatures in Bellegrove had risen to close to ninety, and Grace thought the boy would enjoy an afternoon cooling off with another child his own age and she could spend some time with Anh poolside.

"You don't mind, honey, do you?" she questioned Molly over breakfast as she flipped two more pancakes onto the girl's plate.

"No, Mommy. I'd love to go swimming with him." She took the bottle of maple syrup and poured it over the pancakes.

"Thank you, honey. And maybe you can introduce him to some of your friends. The more conversational English he hears, the easier it will become for him. And he'll probably be at school with you next year, too."

Katie glowered and pushed what remained of her soggy pancakes to the side. "Does he have to come to the club, Mom? Why don't they just hang out here together and you can put the sprinkler on in the back?" Her voice was bristly, like worn rope. "I'm sure he'd like that better than the crowded pool."

"Do you always have to be so mean, Katherine Rose?" Grace shook her head, disgusted with her daughter's selfishness. "How does this have anything to do with you? I've asked Molly to spend time with Bảo, not you."

Katie slumped in her chair, her face distorted in a scowl. Why did her mother always need to be so saintly? Couldn't she just concentrate on her own family and leave the rest of the world's freaks outside their front door?

"I'm going to pick Anh and Bảo up at noon."

Katie smiled. She'd be on her lunch break then, and she made a mental note to be as far away from the pool as possible when her mother arrived with her embarrassing entourage.

As a result of Katie having her first job, Molly's summer had been uneventful and a bit lonely. Unlike her sister, who always seemed to have a gaggle of friends around her, Molly often found herself struggling to find someone to sit with at the school cafeteria or hang out with during recess.

While her sister had inherited Grace's blond hair and athletic build that instantly marked her for the popular crowd, Molly had been forced to wear thick glasses for her myopia, and her brown hair fell limp around her ears. The recent addition of braces on her teeth only intensified her awkwardness, and on top of it all, she wasn't good in gym class. Every afternoon, she was the last one picked when they made up teams. So when her mother suggested inviting Bảo to the pool club, she welcomed the idea. Though Molly only had a vague memory of the little boy in the Hulk T-shirt who she had briefly seen standing in their kitchen that afternoon a few months earlier, after her mother discovered him on the street.

Grace let her sit up front on the way to pick up Bảo at Lady Queen of Martyrs. "I appreciate you doing this, sweetie," she said, tapping Molly's leg with her soft hand. "You're such a good girl."

Molly smiled. Her lips were cut raw on the inside from those sharp little bits of metal. She pulled some wax out of her bag and put it on one of the brackets.

"Do you think he can go on the diving board?"

The car drove through the winding driveway and finally pulled to a stop. Grace suddenly had a pit in her stomach. Did he even know how to swim?

The kiddie pool was awash with toddlers with neon inflatable floating devices on their arms, mothers holding their babies in swollen diapers, and Molly and Bảo standing in water up to their ankles. Molly had chosen to wear her Wonder Woman bathing suit that day, her favorite purchase of the season because she thought it made her look like she was wearing the superhero's red-blue-and-gold uniform. She was happy to see Bảo's face light up when she took off her terry cloth coverup.

At first, Molly thought she had misheard Bảo when he made a fist and exclaimed, "Wonder Twins powers acti . . . v . . ."

"Activate?" Molly laughed. "You got the wrong superhero, Bảo. But that's very cool."

His feet shifted from side to side making small ripples in the pool.

"I'm Wonder Woman—well, not really, but I'm dressed like her. . . ." She knelt down in the water and gave one of the little kids a splash. The water was tepid, far warmer than the big pool. She wondered if they were actually standing in pee.

"You want to get something to eat? I'm hungry."

Bảo nodded.

When they went to the lounge chairs, she noticed that Bảo didn't wrap the towel around his waist. Instead, he wore it like it was a cape. He, too, fashioned himself like a superhero and walked next to her, smiling.

Anh sat quietly with the tall glass of lemonade under the umbrella. Grace had found a spot in the corner of the club for them, away from the crowded tables nearer to the two pools.

"I thought it would be nice for you and Bảo to come here . . . to get a little change of scenery."

Anh smiled. Every day the world seemed to grow larger for her. She thought about how previously she had foolishly thought that America was just another body of land, only a short distance from Vietnam, one they could float toward in a few short hours. She had no idea that it was on the other side of the world and the hardship they'd have to endure just to make it here. The first tragedy had been the loss of Bảo's parents, but the suffering would continue long after.

They would soon run out of fuel, the captain also guilty of failing to anticipate the correct length of the journey. Soon their supplies would be depleted. They would eventually find themselves adrift, floating for days without food and having to ration out a few spoonfuls of water between them. They shared a single lemon, biting the sour fruit and sucking the juice between them each day. She had tried to forgo her share of what remained and give it to Bảo, who had fallen in and out of consciousness for most of the trip. When the French tanker finally found them, they had been on the brink of death, all of them dehydrated and starving. After nearly ten days, the ship sprang out of the waters like a mirage, and when they lifted Bảo's body onto the lifeboat that hoisted them aboard, his sunburned skin was covered in sores.

The little boy walking with the makeshift cape floats past Anh. He does not blend in with the sea of white bodies in their Technicolor bathing suits and their plastic flip-flops that snap against the wet concrete floor. But the girl with the Wonder Woman one-piece, the thick glasses, and the ropes of wet brown hair does not either. Together they walk toward the canteen. And Anh sees Bảo smile—bright and uninhibited—not the kind he does to just signal to her he's okay, but one that comes from true joy. She takes a long sip of lemonade from the straw, and when Grace asks her if she needs anything else, she thinks hard and long about what the right answer should be in English. Then she answers politely, "No, miss. But thank you."

CHAPTER 44

Bảo does not have the words yet in English to tell the girl in the red-and-blue bathing suit with its gold belt of stars that the one thing about America that he knows to be good and reaffirming is the magic wooden box in the living room at the motherhouse. He counts the minutes each day until four o'clock, when the Sisters break from their English lessons with the others and they let him turn the switch on the television and settle into the large, roomy chair. Then all the animated figures spring to life.

So his face automatically ignited in a smile when she, too, knew the words "Wonder Twin powers, activate." Perhaps she knows Jayna and Zan. He recalls the last time they had appeared, when Jayna transformed from a girl into a dolphin and Zan from a man into a bucket of water. If one of them can become water and the other can travel into its depths, couldn't they find his parents on the bottom of the sea?

But despite the obstacle of not yet sharing a language, Molly's gestures serve as another form of communication. He follows her toward the canteen, his wet feet leaving dark footprints on the concrete. She orders two sandwiches on spongy white bread for them, one made with fish, the other egg, and no money passes between her and the teenage boy behind the counter. He has hair the color of sun-bleached wheat and a milky-white face.

He doesn't even look in Molly's direction as he writes down her family name on the chit. The boy with the black eyes and hair is merely an invisible shadow to him.

"Do you want to go sit over there?" Molly points to a white plastic table with a large yellow umbrella rising from its center. "It will be cooler, I think."

Båo sits down, peering at the white bread sandwich she's placed in front of him. He picks it up, takes a bite of the tuna salad, and sinks down in the chair.

Around them, children squeal, the diving board bounces up and down, and the girls do twirls and backflips off its edge, their mothers reminding them to be careful. The smell of chlorine in the water is thick in the air. He eyes one of Katie's friends taking lemon wedges from her mother's drink and squeezing them over her scalp and blond locks.

He is puzzled by the ritual of the lemon juice being applied to the already golden hair. The sight of the lemons triggers something in his memory, the face of a woman leaning over him, a small wedge of lemon between her fingers, her voice soft, asking him to open his mouth. And the juice, only a few droplets, sliding down his throat as their crowded wooden boat drifts aimlessly in the sea.

CHAPTER 45

IT'S 2:00 A.M., AND JACK PLACES A RECORD ONTO THE TURNTA-
ble as music fills the air. He does the same night after night, after he
has walked Hendrix through the reservoir, left his muddy boots by the
door, showered, and changed out of his clothes. Yet despite all these
rituals, his mind is still desperate for peace.

He looks at his bed—not as an invitation for sleep, but rather a
place where his ghosts come to visit each night. Part of him doesn't
want to see the faces from his past, but he doesn't want to forget them,
either. So he lets the song on the player lift off the vinyl and ease his
transition into the world of dreams. And then, as his eyes close, he is
instantly there again, suffocating in the hot, humid air with his buddies hovering around him.

They are so young and impossibly immortal in the haze of sunlight. Flannery's dog tags glimmer in the heat, his chest wet with perspiration, a cigarette dangling from his lips. Flannery is cleaning his
gun, and Doc is carefully checking his medical bag. Stanley is gone but
remains an angel even to the nonbelievers.

In his mind's eye, Jack can see Chief, strong and tall as a redwood,
telling him over breakfast, "The blackbird visited me last night." Chief's
massive hands clasp a cup of watered-downed coffee, warmed by a
burning heating tablet that fills the air with an acrid smoke.

Jack and the whole platoon knew that Chief was sensitive to
bad omens, dreams, and visions of all kinds, but a blackbird could be a
helicopter, couldn't it?

"Maybe you're just dreaming of Huey's, Chief," Flannery joked with him. He flung his cigarette to the ground. "Hey, the sky here is always full of blackbirds. . . ."

Chief's face is eerily placid; his dark eyes glassy with a wisdom so ancient that it transcends words.

He returns Flannery's gaze with silence, and Jack finds himself unnerved. He doesn't believe in prophecies or bad luck, does he? Every day they're in danger, so what difference does a dream about a blackbird mean to any of them? He wants to believe he doesn't believe in good luck or bad luck, yet he's still full of his own superstitions. All of them are.

He still keeps a letter from Becky in the lining of his helmet. His perspiration has long since caused the black ink to run, and the neatly folded paper is now so worn and delicate that when he unfolds it, it nearly falls apart in his hands. The others tease him for holding on to a letter that he can no longer read, but he carries it anyway, as a talisman, and the words are already memorized in his heart and mind.

During a briefing that morning, after Lieutenant Bates announces he's taking a reinforced squad of sixteen men to do a recon patrol on one of the nearby mountains, he, too, tries to shrug off the dark bird in Chief's dream.

Lieutenant Bates doesn't tell the men that battalion intelligence suspects there might be North Vietnamese Army up on that mountain or hidden arsenals buried in the bush. Jack learned months ago, even before Stanley's death, that he will never be told anything more than he needs to know.

"Get the radio and get it ready, Jack," Bates says. In a matter of minutes, he and the other men are saddled up and set to go.

Their flak jackets are on, their rifles are cleaned and loaded, their ammo belts are draped around their chest. Their steel helmets are a dark rainbow of words and mantras to keep them bold, just like *Kong*

Killer had adorned their fallen friend's. *Born to Kill*, reads one, while another one has a peace sign with a dagger protruding *Kill for Peace*. Flannery has written in large black letters, *From Texas with Mother-fucking Love*.

They don't share what they've tucked secretly within their pockets, like rabbit-foot charms from their younger brothers back home. Good luck comes in a thousand forms, and they all cling to the comfort of their magical thinking to help them survive. Gomez carries a small canvas pouch containing seventeen Vietnamese coins that symbolize the seventeen days he has left on his tour. His plan was to toss a lucky coin over his shoulder every morning until he's on his way home.

"Gomez, you shitbird short-timer," Jack ribs him. "Can't believe they're taking you out again." He shakes his head and places his fingers in his pocket. He leaves the camp weighted down by one less coin.

The column marches north.

Chief doesn't mention the blackbird again as he takes point. He is the man they trust to cut the path, the way in and the way out of death. He carries a Lakota hatchet given to him when he was twelve, and as he slices through the thick bamboo and jungle brush, gripping its well-oiled wooden handle, he believes his ancestors live on within the polished blade.

As the first in line, he is the eyes and ears for everything that is in front of them. He tucks the hatchet back into its belt and points his rifle forward. Every one of them listens to every sound, every monkey screech, every animal that scurries over a tree branch, as each step could land them in a leg trap.

Corporal Gomez is secretly hating on Lieutenant Bates. *Couldn't he have let me stay back?* he thinks to himself. He has a twenty-two-year-old wife waiting for him back home and a younger sister who writes him letters saying their mother prays every night for his safe return. He hates this goddamn place with all his heart, and all he wants now is to return home to homemade tortillas and ice-cold beer.

But Bates can't care that Gomez has less than three weeks left of his tour. He's one of his best rifle men, and he needs him.

Their boots sink into the mud. The canopy of green leaves is pierced by long beams of white. Unearthly light, Chief thinks as he pushes forward, as if they are entering a place they are not meant to tread.

They continue to walk uphill. Sweat tracking their faces, adrenaline lifting off their skin.

The radio remains strapped to Jack's back. At one point, the lieutenant stops and studies his compass and frowns.

An hour later, they take five at a clear running stream to refill their canteens and burn some of the leeches off their bodies. Some take their helmet and scoop up the water, pouring it over their heads to cool themselves off.

Chief is cleaning his knife with a piece of parachute silk, and the new kid, Danny Donovan, is singing the lyrics to the song "White Bird" under his breath, so low that almost no one but Chief can hear him.

"Not funny, man," Chief hisses. He turns his back and walks several feet away to distance him from the man he now thinks is a fool.

Lieutenant Bates checks his watch, looks up at the sky, and realizes they have no more than four more hours of sunlight. They are behind schedule, the men having moved slower than he would have liked. He eyes Jack, his gaze looking at the radio as if he is contemplating using it to call back to command, but decides against it. "Saddle up," he says. "Move out. . . . Chief, on point." His face is now taut, his energy agitated.

They follow the streambed up the mountain, preferring the tumbled rocks to the jungle bush. After three more hours of hiking, the air changes. Long strips of mist hover in the distance, and Jack hears Gomez mumble, "Hell, we're walking into the clouds."

Then something besides the air shifts. Chief comes to a halt.

He senses something before the rest of them do. The jungle has become too silent. He lifts his rifle. Gomez stops behind him and does the same.

It is then that Chief sees the camouflaged face of a North Vietnamese soldier, his helmet covered in leaves, his rifle pointed straight at him. Chief opens fire.

These are the things Jack remembers from that moment:

The explosion of bullets are ripping the air and shredding the leaves over his helmet. He hits the ground hard, the radio coming off his back, Lieutenant Bates yelling into the receiver that they are being ambushed by an NVA unit.

Jack is on his belly, his head lifting from the wet earth when he sees Chief and Flannery returning fire from their rifles.

They are surrounded by incoming grenades.

"Corpsman up! Corpsman up!" It is Flannery's voice hollering above the mayhem. "Man down! Gomez's been hit!"

The jungle is now roaring with gunfire and men screaming at the top of their lungs with terror and rage. Doc runs through the firestorm, clutching his M-1 bag between white-knuckled fingers, until he reaches Gomez, who is on his back, his eyes looking straight up at the sky.

"I'm here, man," Doc reassures him. His eyes are wide and full of fear. "I got you, man. Talk to me."

Gomez is mumbling about his wife and "all those fucking coins that didn't work." Doc does just as he's been trained: he tears through Gomez's flak jacket and shirt to see if he can get down to the wound and discover the entrance and exit path of the bullet. He finds it above Gomez's abdomen and works quickly placing a compression bandage on it. He takes out a small tube of morphine with the preexisting needle and shoots it into Gomez's arm; then, as medical protocol dictates, he wets a finger with Gomez's blood and draws an *M* on his forehead so the doctors back in the medical battalion will know he's already received a dose.

Lieutenant Bates is face down in the dirt next to Jack, the radio's receiver pressed to his ear. He's called in the coordinates, screaming them into the headset, requesting artillery backup and medical evacuation while Jack prays the radio connection doesn't break.

Hiding in the bush nearby, a young, heavily camouflaged NVA soldier holds a grenade he was issued a few days before. He has no idea it's Willie Pete, a white phosphorous grenade that burns with such intensity that it cuts through anything in its path and won't be extinguished with water—only through the elimination of oxygen.

He pulls the pin and hurls it at Bates, who is still on the radio. It explodes in a ball of flames and sets him ablaze. Jack, who, as always, is less than two feet away from his lieutenant, is also partially engulfed in the searing white flames.

The grenade brings with it five thousand degrees Fahrenheit of heat, and its force is so extreme that it incinerates Bates and burns part of Jack's face off, blinding him in his left eye and taking with it a portion of his scalp and hair. His skin melts through every muscle, down to the bone.

Jack does not remember Doc hurtling toward him, his friend's hands rushing to unbutton his own flak jacket and then pulling it off his body to smother the fire burning Jack's scalp and face. He will never recall the steps Doc takes to administer morphine and to seal off his wounds with Vaseline strips, or how his friend realized there was no place left on his head to write the letter *M*.

The helicopters are already circling above, laying down heavy fire to wipe out the enemy. One of them is lowering to retrieve the wounded and dead. Nobody knows what to do with Lieutenant Bates, who is no longer recognizable, like a ball of melted wax.

Chief and Doc are making stretchers out of the dead men's ponchos to carry them toward the chopper. Chief slings Flannery over his back and hurries to get him on board.

"There's one more man down," a voice calls out, and Doc hurries to find who it is.

"It's Danny," someone yells.

Exhausted and following the code of the corpsmen, Doc searches through the dead to find him.

Little Danny Donovan is only eighteen years old, a fresh recruit who came only a few weeks before to replace Stanley. He's crying that he thinks he's going to die, but Doc can see it's just a painful, but not fatal, shoulder wound.

"You're going to be okay, Danny. You're going to be okay."

He is wrapping Danny's shoulder as Chief and the other men help carry the remaining wounded and dead to the chopper. They won't leave a single body behind.

"Doc, am I dying?" Danny's eyes are wet with fear.

"You've got a long life ahead of you, you're going home," Doc assures him as he sees the crew chief on the chopper gesturing that they have to hurry and get the hell out of there.

He reaches to help pull Private Donovan up, hoping to rush him to the chopper, when out of nowhere, an NVA soldier who has been lying on the ground and thought by the others to be dead pulls himself up and shoots Doc in the head.

CHAPTER 46

KATIE'S MORNING HAD STARTED OFF POORLY. EVEN BEFORE SHE stepped outside the house, she sensed it was going to be a really, *really* bad day. Her mother had broken the yolk on her fried egg and refused to make her a fresh one, instead calling Katie wasteful and ungrateful. Plates were angrily slammed on the table, and no one lifted their glasses of orange juice to drink. Molly looked down at her bowl of cereal as though she was silently in prayer. Minutes later, Katie's father swept in, downed a cup of coffee, oblivious to the tension between his wife and eldest daughter, blithely kissing all three cheeks before heading out the door.

The slain egg now lay untouched. A sloppy white-and-yellow amorphous mass. Katie knew she'd soon be engaged in battle over whether that egg would end up in her stomach or in the waste bin. Clearly, it was going to be just that kind of day.

Grace looked over at her daughter and felt herself reaching her tipping point. All week Katie had been frustrating her, and now she found herself beyond exasperated with her eldest daughter. Katie had slipped her red swimsuit into the washing machine, instead of washing it in cold water in the sink, and subsequently ruined an entire load of everyone's clothes. "Katie Rose, I expect you to finish that egg," uttered Grace between gritted teeth.

Katie rolled her eyes and stabbed at the egg before moving it around the plate. Something happened between the two girls because suddenly Molly cried out, "Stop kicking me!"

Why did everything always have to be a battle with her eldest daughter?

The noise of the children bickering was the worst sound of all. Grace threw the pan into the sink. "Next time, Katie you can make your own breakfast! I was making meals for my sister and brother from the time I was seven years old." Her face flamed red. She was glad Tom had left already so he didn't have to witness her coming undone like this. Her fingers gripped into little balled fists. Would it be so terrible to reach for the rolling pin just to make Katie realize how angry she was? She reached for the drawer, but the inside was jammed with spatulas and slotted spoons. A single can opener. Where was that rolling pin when she really needed it?

"Mom, I'll eat the egg." Molly pulled the plate to her corner of the table. In a few minutes it was gone.

With her mother's palpable irritation in the air, Katie got up from the table and slyly hit her sister on the side of her arm. She did it just because she could, and somehow it made her feel slightly better. And while she knew it was juvenile on her part, if she were going to be cast as the bad daughter, she might as well go all out.

She was tired of having such a Goody Two-shoes for a younger sister, particularly as she had her own problems that no one else seemed to care about. Her period had arrived two days early and that had been just one more thing to put her in a bad mood. She loathed putting a bulky pad in her swimsuit and then having to cover it up with a baggy pair of shorts. The weather report had predicted temperatures above ninety degrees for that afternoon and she already felt sticky thinking about herself roasting outside on the lifeguard tower. Feeling bloated and irritable, Katie stormed off to the garage to retrieve her bicycle, only to find that the chain was dangling off the rear.

She fiddled with the chain, but, after several minutes, couldn't get it back on the tracking despite her best efforts. A wave of frustration rose inside her and Katie gave the bicycle a little shove. As it fell, the sound of the metal hitting the garage floor was loud enough for everyone in the Golden household to hear.

"What is it now?" Grace asked as Katie emerged in the kitchen. She had been scrubbing a frying pan in the sink and enjoying a few minutes of calm. She turned off the faucet and looked at her daughter standing blankly by the mudroom door.

"Mom—my bike's broken!" Katie's voice was a painful mixture of teenage anger and selfish desperation.

"What happened to it? You didn't mention anything yesterday when you got home. . . ." Grace looked up at the wall clock. It was already seven thirty and Katie was supposed to be at the club by eight. She knew what was coming even before her daughter said it.

"Can you drive me?" She heaved herself over the counter, pleading to Grace with great dramatic affect.

Grace wanted to tell her no. Her anger had dissipated, but it was still there. Like an oven that was still warm, even after the heat had been turned off.

"I *can't* be late, Mom. Janet already wants to take me off the Wednesday shift and give it to her niece!"

Grace pulled off her dishwashing gloves. "I'm very sorry this happened to your bike, but putting the word 'please' in front of your request would really go a long way."

Katie's eyes rolled. "Fine, Mom. *Please . . .*"

Grace shook her head in disgust. Every day her daughter grew more insolent. She had refused to even come over to say hello to Bảo and Anh the other day when Grace brought them to the club. Katie's focus seemed only to be on making enough pocket money to be able to go out with her friends or to save up for a pair of designer jeans that insulted Grace with their ridiculous price tag.

What was next? Katie asking her for a new bike? Grace had already firmly made up her mind that she was going to tell Katie that they expected her to put some of the money she'd earned toward a newer model if she didn't want to keep having to repair the old one. The girl needed to realize how lucky she was to have the life she enjoyed. The last time Grace went to the motherhouse and brought some homemade muffins, despite their very limited grasp of English, every one of the Vietnamese refugees already knew the words *please* and *thank you.* Was it so much to ask that her daughter to do the same?

Grace pulled a dishcloth off the hook and began drying the frying pan. She could feel Katie's impatience rising off her skin like steam.

She waited for a beat. Then another.

"Mom!"

"If you wait a second and change your tone, young lady, I'll throw on some clothes and drive you."

"I'm sorry, Mom, please!"

There were more than enough clocks in the Golden household for Grace to realize she needed to move quickly so Katie wouldn't be late.

CHAPTER 47

THERE ARE FRACTURES IN JACK'S MEMORY, TINY FAULT LINES that absorb moments he can't remember clearly. His mind's a constellation of jumbled images and words that he isn't sure actually happened or he imagined under a cloud of morphine. He has spent years trying to decipher whether the recurring dream he experiences nearly every night actually happened—or whether he has dreamt the scenario so often that he now believes it to be fact. But whether it is a memory he has conjured or something he had lived through, it continues to haunt him. In the dream, he's on the evac chopper, minutes after Doc has put out the fire on his head. Chief is loading Gomez's stretcher on board. Jack hears a voice saying, *He's not going to make it,* but there is a third nameless marine who is crouched next to him. He reaches for Jack's hand and squeezes it feeling the faintest bit of life still in his fingers. "He's alive," he tells the others, and the helicopter lifts off.

The rest would be a haze to him as he is transported to a field hospital where he is intubated and the Vaseline bandages that Doc had wrapped his face in are removed. The nurses have coated him in a thick paste of Silvadene and wrapped his face with gauze.

"If he makes it through the night, we have to get him on the next plane to Japan," someone says. "We can't do anything for him here."

Within twenty-four hours, Jack is on a hospital plane to Okinawa, where he remains heavily sedated until they can get him to the best military burn unit in the States, Brooke Army Medical Hospital in San Antonio, Texas.

He does not hear the doctors and nurses questioning whether they are reading his file correctly, his Record of Emergency Data form only has a single name listed: his mother, Eleanor Grady. Within the hour, they will learn she is deceased.

"Are you saying this marine has no living relative? Not a single other person listed on his form?" The doctor's voice is incredulous.

"Yes," the nurse answers. Her voice is steeped in sadness as she looks over to Jack, still under sedation in the hospital bed, his face is wrapped in layers of white gauze bandages that make him look like a mummy.

"He whimpers at night," she adds. "It's terrible to hear."

"There's nothing more painful than a burn . . . and this—Jesus Christ . . . the white phosphorous burned half his face down to nearly the bone." The surgeon sucks in his breath. "It's really a miracle that this man is still alive."

Over the next few days, Jack's face and scalp is debrided of any remaining dead tissue and he receives his first skin graft. The surgical team takes skin from his buttocks and thighs, and then reattach it piece by piece to where he's been wounded. They cannot restore his vision in his left eye, but they do their best to create a flap to create the allusion of an eyelid.

When he awakens from the long and intensive surgery, Jack can be heard swearing and screaming. In his delirium, he believes his face is still on fire. He repeatedly begs the nurses and doctors to let him die.

He floats in and out of consciousness and is only vaguely aware that a handful of nurses, after learning he has no remaining family now, come sit by his bedside and hold his hand. One of them plays music from a small transistor radio that she puts on the bedside table, next to the pitcher of water, a box of tissues, and a stack of plastic cups.

"What's your name?" he manages to ask her as the words struggle to emerge from his dry lips. Although he is still wrapped like a mummy, he can just about make out her face from one his one good eye.

"Barbara," she replies softly. "Barbara Starr."

She leans over toward the radio and adjusts the antenna until the sound shifts from static to song.

Blind Faith's "Can't Find My Way Home" filled the room and the music, so quietly sung, roused something inside him. Emotions that had been numbed by the enormity of his trauma and by the pain medicine bubbled forth.

Jack's eyes moistened with tears.

Barbara pulled some tissues from the bedside and dabbed both his eyes. Beneath the white coverlet, Jack's chest lifted and deflated with each deep breath.

"It's weird. I can't see out of my left eye, but can still cry from it?" He was struck by the strange poignancy of his eye's inability to fulfill its primary function, yet it could still emit emotion.

"I guess the lacrimal gland wasn't damaged too badly," she added gently. "Well, that's some good news, right?"

Jack remained silent. He could count the times in his life he had cried on one hand. Even as a little boy, he hardly showed emotion when he was upset. He knew his mother had enough on her shoulders, and he tried not to burden her with whatever troubled him.

It was a small mercy that she had not lived to see him burned like this. That was really the only good news he could admit to. Not the fact that a gland inside his eye could still shed tears.

The music on the radio now shifted to a breaking news report about a special air force raid on a prison north of Hanoi.

Barbara's hand lifted off the blanket and turned the radio off.

"You should be getting some rest now."

He knew she didn't want him becoming agitated by hearing any news about the war. But in reality, it was the music that had stirred something inside him, not the news.

The song's lyrics had penetrated even his thickest burns. The words of the song felt like they were written for him.

There were no mirrors in the burn unit at Brooke Army Hospital. "We just want you to concentrate on your healing," Jack was told when he asked the nurses when he'd be given a chance to see his new reflection once the bandages were removed.

He knew he would never again look anything like his former self. After all, the doctor had told him several times before the first surgery that he shouldn't expect his healing to be complete. But he still wondered, would he ever again even look normal?

The doctors and nurses did not know that Jack Grady had been voted "most handsome" in high school or that his buddies in his platoon called him "Hollywood." And they certainly had no idea that across the country, there was a girl named Becky, who had not the slightest inkling as to why she hadn't received an answer from Jack to her most recent letters.

The head plastic surgeon attempts to prepare Jack the best he can. In his softest voice, he speaks of the possibilities of additional surgeries to promote future skin growth. "Jack, it's important to realize that what you see in the mirror will not be the end result. We will continue to be vigilant about scar tissue and constriction. We'll make sure to do further grafting to ensure you have the best results we can give you, so you can go on to have a full life."

Full life. Jack hears the words and instantly thinks such a thing will never be possible.

He will not tell them about Becky Dougherty, the girl with the chestnut-brown hair whose letter he had carried in his helmet throughout his entire tour, before they were lost in an explosion in the jungle of Vietnam. Instead, he remains silent, and pushes the thought of her far down inside of him. Safely sheltered in a small college town, he only hopes Becky is moving on from him, and that because of his silence, she has given up and believes him to be dead.

The doctor unwraps his bandages slowly. The air on his wounds is painful. The rawness of his skin still overwhelms him, and he thinks to himself what he chooses not to say aloud, that he wishes he hadn't survived. "The good news is that the surgery was a success, and there is no sign of infection," the doctor informs him.

"You're still very swollen, Jack, so just remember what I said that this will all look a lot better in a few weeks."

"Doc, why didn't you do everyone a favor and shoot me up with too much morphine when I was under and just call it accident?"

"Jack . . ." The doctor's voice has lowered even further. "I'm a doctor. . . . I've taken an oath to save life, not extinguish it."

The quiet that follows is a pain in itself.

"I would like to see my reflection," Jack pushes.

"Not yet," the surgeon insists. "You need to heal more, then we can make a decision about when to bring in a mirror."

He remains in the burn unit for several more weeks. He will surrender to having his nurses gently cleanse his new skin and to change his dressings to prevent infection. He will wear a collar to ensure his skin doesn't constrict as it heals, and he will eventually be weaned from his pain medication.

And during this time, he will write not a single letter, nor make one phone call.

Jack is with his platoon in the jungle. Chief and Flannery. Stanley and Doc. Sometimes he will have conversations in his head with them. He will see Gomez's eyes flash with mischief as he pulls out a deck of cards from his pocket, or Stanley hunched over his Bible reciting a passage or uttering the comforting words of a psalm.

On the nights when the ward is enveloped in a silent darkness, except for the rolling wheels of the medicine cart, Jack will try to banish his memories of Chief walking up the mountain in the rain, holding Stanley's body wrapped in a blood-soaked poncho, his muscles straining to hold him, to ensure Stanley's head does not touch the ground.

When Jack's surgeon finally tells him he's ready to be discharged, he asks again for a mirror.

"I'd like to see myself before I leave, Doc," he tells him. "It only seems fair I get to do that before anyone else outside the hospital walls does. Doesn't it?"

The doctor takes a deep breath. "We usually wait for that to happen when the patient's back with his family, Jack." He pauses for a moment and considers his words. "But I'll have one of the nurses see if she can arrange something."

Jack nods and feels as if he has won a small victory. He needs to know how others will see him so he can figure out how to reconcile the loss of his former physical appearance with his current reality.

Later that afternoon, Barbara appears and hands Jack a small plastic handled mirror that she pulls out from the pocket of her scrubs. Out of respect, she lowers her eyes as Jack brings the mirror up to his face.

He lifts his finger and traces all the new valleys and bumps of skin on what was once his cheek and forehead. The left side of his face is enlarged and red, the topography of his pain and trauma read like braille. The hairline is irregular with the front portion of his black curls now completely gone. There is still a considerable amount of swelling where his left eyelid once was, and he looks like one of the villains he used to read about in comic books as a little kid, like Two-Face from *Batman*, or worse, an ogre from a Grimms' fairy tale.

"Fucking hell," he utters. "I don't even look human."

On the afternoon he is to be discharged, Barbara Starr tells him something special is planned for his departure.

"I don't want anything," he tells her. The very thought of some sort of farewell gesture makes him feel uncomfortable.

"You deserve *something*," she says gently. "Please, Jack. It's all been arranged."

An hour later, after he's been examined one last time by his doctor, five marines in their dress blue uniforms enter his room. Each one of them with their hat tucked beneath their arm.

"Lance Corporal Jack Grady," the honor guard announces. "On behalf of a grateful nation, we are here to present you with this Purple Heart. . . ." He begins to read from a citation letter describing Jack's injury and his service to his country.

While serving as a radio man, Lance Corporal Grady was engaging the enemy in Quang Tri Province and was severely wounded on November 27, 1969. . . . The entire nation is indebted for his service. . . .

The Gunnery Sergeant opens up a small brown box to reveal a purple ribbon with the gilding metal heart attached, the image of George Washington in its center.

With no family members to witness the Purple Heart presentation ceremony, three of his nurses and two of his doctors instead crowd the back of Jack's small hospital room. But it is Nurse Starr who is crying as the honor guard salutes her patient and pins the medal on his chest.

When he moves into a small apartment not far from the hospital, Jack puts the medal in a cardboard box on the top of his closet shelf, along with the Vietnam Campaign ribbon, the Marine Corps Combat Action ribbon, and his Presidential Unit Citation. For him, they mean nothing. A ribbon can't bring any of his friends back. A medal can't resurrect a life or heal his wounds.

He hears Walter Cronkite on the television reporting about the strengthening tides of the Vietnam Veterans Against the War. These men were nothing like the hippie who'd thrown a drink on him at the airport. Rather, they were guys like him who'd been in country and knew firsthand the insanity of it all—the lack of any clear directive or cogent reason to be there. With so much anger inside him, Jack wished he could join them. He'd lost everything. His friends. His future. And half his face. But how could he go out and raise a fist into the air, join their protesting? The cameramen would have a field day zooming in on his scars. Jack knew they'd make him the poster child of the god-damn war.

For the next ten months, he lives on his disability payments. He buries the thoughts of Becky along with the memories of the friends he left back on the battlefield.

He curses the doctors and nurses who neglected to ever inform him how painful scar tissue and the excision surgeries to remove it would be. He rages when he remembers one of the grunts asking an officer just before they shipped off, "What are we fighting for?" and the major revealing the hollowness of it all: "We've lost too many good men to turn back now."

The anger boils.

There will be nights when he has consumed too much whiskey that he picks up the phone to call Becky. But he counts the months she's been studying for her teacher's degree and realizes she would have graduated the month before.

But one afternoon, after he has numbed himself with two glasses of Jack Daniels, he calls her number, only to find it has been disconnected.

He then calls information and receives three different possible numbers for a Rebecca Dougherty in western Pennsylvania. Finally, he hears her voice on the other side, and its very sweetness causes his heart to constrict painfully in his chest.

"Becky?" The tenor of his voice sounds as fragile as glass.

Silence engulfs the line.

"It's me . . . Jack."

Again, there is only silence, and Jack's entire body grows rigid in the stinging quiet.

Becky's stomach is in the back of her throat. "I thought you were . . ." Her voice cracks, but after a few seconds, she has regained a stoic sense of composure. "Jack, I thought you were dead. I tried everywhere to get more information, but no one would tell me anything."

He has concocted an excuse, practiced in his mind over the course of several nights, one where he can test the waters before committing himself to the pain of her seeing him with his disfigurement.

"I'm at a hospital in Texas, I have a friend with me whose face is so badly damaged. Jeez, it's just the worst thing to see." He sucks in his breath and closes his eyes.

"He's being discharged in a few days, and he's got no family, Becky. That's why I went missing. I had to stay with him." He adjusts the receiver to his ear. "My buddy doesn't have a place to go, and I was wondering . . . I know it's been a long time since I saw you, and it was really shitty I stopped writing to you. But do you think we could come over, and the two of us could hang at your place a while?" He takes a hard swallow. "You gotta know how much I missed you. . . ."

A few seconds of silence swim between them. She is so overwhelmed. She has waited for him and wondered what had happened for nearly fourteen months and spent countless nights lying in her bed crying for someone she didn't know was dead or alive. She more than missed him . . . she had grieved for him.

"Can I just see you alone first, Jack? Let me see you and then we can talk about your friend. I haven't seen you or that beautiful face of yours in so long. . . ."

He doesn't hear any of her words except "that beautiful face."

She doesn't know that he has made up the story about his friend to test her. To gauge her response in order to protect himself from being hurt any further than he's already suffered.

The line falls mute.

"Jack?"

He hangs up the phone and tells himself he has the answers he needs. But this time it is not his one good eye and blind one leaking tears. It's his heart. Opening like a raw wound, weeping inside his chest.

CHAPTER 48

Since he left San Antonio and his doctors at Brooke Army Medical, Jack had developed a weakness for broken things. Over time, he'd come to learn that there were two types of people in the world: those who threw things away once they stopped working, and those who tried to salvage them. Jack belonged to the latter group. His friend, Tom Golden, did as well. That was one of the many things that bound the two men together, adding another layer of meaning to their work at the Golden Hours. How often had Tom relayed how a customer had come into the store heartbroken that her great-uncle's pocket watch no longer ran or that wristwatch, gifted from a parent at graduation, had stopped keeping the proper time. Tom would hold the timepiece in his hand and show it to Jack. "We need to fix this one," he'd announce firmly. Being able to breathe new life into these heirlooms had made Jack still feel useful and gave him a sense of purpose after his injury.

He had felt a similar sense of calling when he worked at Foxton Elementary School. Despite having abandoned any dreams of marriage or having children of his own, the close proximity of hope and possibility that were nurtured in the classrooms had breathed a quiet optimism in him. When the door on classroom 8 changed from paper autumn leaves to jagged cut snowflakes, his heart lifted, and he felt the parts of him that had hardened from his injury soften and thaw.

Hendrix had also helped with Jack's healing. He'd gotten the black Labrador shortly after he moved above the store. He was told that the dog had been abused by its last owner and had arrived at the shelter emaciated, and with an injury to his hind leg. He was on the list to be euthanized when Jack noticed him in the cage, his sad eyes searching Jack's for kindness.

Hendrix had been overlooked by all the families, who peered into the metal cages with their children in tow, falling in love with the animals that didn't carry their scars up front. The ones that didn't have open wounds on their coat or who shrunk to the corner of their cages.

Jack felt an immediate kinship with Hendrix. He saw his neglect as an invitation for love. He saw past the unsightly open sore on his leg and the carriage that had no meat on its bones. Jack brought Hendrix home and the animal, wounded and scared, kept his distance, always walking toward the farthest corner of the small apartment and curling into a ball, as if trying to take up as little space as possible. Even when Jack placed a bowl of food and fresh water down, the dog wouldn't approach them until Jack had left the room. With only a small galley kitchen and a one-room living space, it meant Jack having to retreat to his bed or the small sofa that was positioned across from the television whenever Hendrix ate.

The two would finally get to know each other better once Jack started taking the dog out on his nightly walks. They would set out around 10:00 p.m. for their long walks in the wooded acreage that bordered the reservoir. For Jack, those outings were meditative. As he walked beneath the canopy of trees, he heard the sound of his drill instructors "calling cadence" back in Parris Island, chanting, "Left. Right. Left. Right. Left, *easy day*, second platoon, *easy day* . . ." He experienced something cathartic as his body moved on and his mind surrendered to the task.

Hendrix, it seemed, also enjoyed these long treks and soon learned to trot along Jack's side. He filled out, and where there had once been only a rack of ribs, thinly veiled by a dry black coat of fur, muscle and even a little fat now appeared.

"Come on, boy," Jack would whisper after they would close up and lock the shop door behind them. He'd attach the long red leash and start walking toward the Ace Hardware Shopping Center. They'd pass the now empty lot, free of cars and pedestrians at this late hour, and navigate the area behind the hardware store where huge empty cartons were piled on top of dumpsters. When the concrete curb soon merged with the soft, dry earth, they would begin to forge ahead.

Left. Right. Left.

Hendrix with his long, black snout sniffed the ground, eager to experience the rich scents of the forest. Patches of moist soil, fragrant with the smell of fungi and pine. His eyes lifted toward the branches where squirrels darted up and down the boughs with acorns clenched between their teeth.

It took them nearly forty minutes to reach the cusp where the tree line ended and the water shimmered in the reservoir.

Jack sat down and Hendrix kneeled beside him. He stroked the animal's back, feeling the length of his spine, his hand falling to the tail that was now luxuriant and silky from an improved diet. He felt Hendrix soften at his touch, and the dog returned his affection by licking the edge of Jack's hand. Jack felt a quiet perfection in these moments between the two of them. They had come a long way together since they first laid eyes on each other in the animal shelter nearly four years before. He was now his best friend.

CHAPTER 49

IT HAD BEEN A LONG AFTERNOON FOR KATIE AT THE POOL AND she was counting the hours until her shift ended. Buddy had brought Clayton to the club as his guest and the two of them thought it would be a great idea to bring toy water pistols to the kiddie pool and start shooting them at the children. They knew they'd only have a few minutes to spray the kids until someone shut them down. Today, that job fell on Katie, who blew her whistle loud and clear, halting their ridiculous prank.

Buddy threw his gun on the ground and looked up at her in the tower. To him, she looked like a Valkyrie, a Norse goddess ready to choose who she'd let into her realm and who she'd throw out. Buddy was happy to be thrown out if it gave him even the slightest chance to look down her bathing suit.

"Next time, you're banished from swimming here at all," she said, squinting and pointing her finger at them. She enjoyed the power and would have liked nothing less to make sure neither of them ever showed their face again at the pool. Buddy was a pest, but Clayton looked at her in a way that made her blood grow cold.

"We're sorry, Your Majesty," Buddy mocked, trying to impress his friend. "Please don't banish us from your kingdom."

"Cut it out," she answered back quickly. "Why are the two of you such jerks?"

Clayton made an obscene gesture to her, which she answered by giving him the finger. As soon as she had done it, she regretted it because she knew if one of the adults caught her behaving like that, she'd be fired.

So when Buddy hollered something back at her, she chose to ignore him this time. One thing was certain: neither of them was worth her losing her job over.

CHAPTER 50

JACK'S APARTMENT HAD NO PAINTINGS OR DECORATION. THE white walls were monastic. He maintained a telephone line, though almost no one except Tom ever called him. And he hardly ever went out, except for groceries, laundry, the occasional slice of pizza at Nino's, and to the Sunday dinner invitation he accepted from Grace once a month.

He loved those dinners more than he cared to admit. The house smelled like warm biscuits and childhood. Aside from the scent of crackling meat and roasted potatoes in the kitchen, the family room smelled of pencils freshly sharpened for Monday morning, loose leaf paper and highlighter pens. It brought him back to his days at Foxton Elementary and also even further back to the Sunday meals his mother used to make on her day off. His mother wasn't the cook Grace was. She'd never in her life made a standing roast seasoned with paprika and garlic powder, or maple-glazed carrots. But she had mastered the art of breaded chicken cutlets, and the two of them had been known to polish off a tray of Pillsbury crescent rolls, torn open and smeared with butter.

The first time he came for dinner at the Goldens' he had spent most of that Sunday afternoon fraught with anxiety. How would the children be able to enjoy their supper with him sitting next to them at the table? He considered wearing a baseball cap to create a shadow across his face, but then thought it might be considered disrespectful to wear one at Grace's dinner table.

"The girls would love to meet you," Tom had told him with such kindness it was hard to refuse. Yes, even with the skin grafts finally behind him, he knew he'd be a scary sight for the children. His skin was red and bumpy. His left eyelid drooped over his bad eye. There was a patch of hair near his forehead that had never fully grown back. He remembered the first time he stroked Hendrix and saw the bare patches of white, scaly skin, it was as though his fingers were also touching a side of himself.

His face had healed considerably over the years. He had been wholly unprepared for that initial moment at the hospital in Texas, when they unwrapped the bandages. His reflection could have been Mars for all intents and purposes, as there was nothing he remembered of his former self. The skin was mottled and his face, once bronzed from the sun in Vietnam, the cheeks that Becky had caressed and kissed, had all been burned to an unrecognizable canvas. But now the skin, although damaged and half of his face was clearly deformed, was hardly as bad as it had been when he'd first arrived at the hospital.

He hated thinking of his former self. The photographs he had from his younger days had been put away, though he did still have that single photograph of Becky and him beside his bed. He would hold it between his hands sometimes when he was feeling especially bad about things. On those nights time stood still in a different way from his night terrors or memories of Vietnam. It was like peeking into a time capsule of another life, its jagged edges softened like sea glass in his palm. He could peer into it and remember what it was like to be touched. To be loved.

Oddly enough, his face had actually helped another veteran heal, or at least enabled an old man to finally put a painful memory to rest. Jack came to consider their brief interaction together sacred, for not only had it between two people who knew the horrors of war, but the man was also Tom's father.

He met the senior Golden early on in his friendship with Tom. In the weeks that followed after he had lost his job at Foxton, he offered to visit Harry at the veterans home while Tom was busy at the store. He was happy to make himself useful with so much extra time on his hands.

"You'd really pay him a visit? Maybe read to him or something?"

"It'll be my pleasure," he told Tom. "I don't have much else to keep me busy these days."

That afternoon he went to visit Harry, Jack tried to make himself look halfway decent. He wore a pair of khaki pants and a button-down shirt he had bought for himself at the Salvation Army. He brought the most recent copy of *National Geographic*, thinking Harry might enjoy hearing about the Aboriginal people in Australia. He thought the photographs of the warriors with their hunting spears and native jewelry might spark some interesting conversation.

He knew the layout of the veterans hospital very well, having gone for countless appointments to appraise his scar tissue and healing.

Harry's room was at the end of the corridor, number 707, as Tom had written down for him.

But when he entered Harry's room, Jack found a man who had no interest in the magazine underneath his arm.

Harry, tucked underneath a yellow blanket with pillows propped behind his head, turned to greet him. An old Bulova military watch was strapped to his wrist as he waved hello.

"Jim? Jimmy Connelly? Hell, is that you?" Harry piped up, a flash of excitement washed over the old man's face. "Why, I thought you didn't make it.... All I saw was that pant leg and boot after your jeep exploded...." He squinted at Jack, tears pooling in his eyes.

"Jesus Christ." Harry shook his head. "You have no idea how happy it makes me to see you survived."

Jack stood near his bed, frozen, not sure whether he should tell Harry that he wasn't his old friend Jimmy or instead allow the man a chance to revisit someone he clearly cared about and kept trapped in memory all these years.

"Guess you got wounded pretty bad, though." He touched his face and looked sympathetically at the man standing across from him.

"Yeah, I did," Jack answered honestly.

"Sit down." Harry patted his bed. "I don't get many visitors who've been through what we've been through. The only people who stop by are my son and his family."

Jack shook his head. "I know it's tough to find someone who gets what we've been through."

"Yes," Harry nodded. "It really is. I'm always waking my wife, Rosie, with my bad dreams, but I'd never tell her what they're about. Why upset her? Right?"

"Uh-huh." Jack knew far too well what it was like to wake up screaming in the middle of the night. Even if he did have someone to share his bed with, he was sure he'd never burden another soul with what was inside of him.

"I brought you a magazine, I could read it to you if you want. . . ." he offered, trying to bring something more lighthearted into the conversation. He lifted the cover so Harry could see. "Thought the photographs looked pretty interesting. . . ."

Harry peered over and shrugged. "I'm just happy to see you're still alive, Jimmy. Can't tell you how much I've thought about you over the years." His eyes narrowed as he looked at Jack more closely. "That burn seems pretty bad." He lowered his voice. "I'm real sorry about that. No one gets the war out here. . . ." He tapped his head. "But you have it written all over your face. . . ."

Jack's eyes fell. Harry's mental deterioration had put him beyond polite small talk, but ironically it enabled him to speak the truth more freely.

"It's not easy, that's for sure," Jack answered.

"Yeah. I get the worst nightmares sometimes. I wake up thinking I'm standing in front of corpses. Still got that smell in my nose." Harry touched the edge of his nostrils. "You know that stench of death."

"Yes," Jack said. It wasn't something one could ever forget.

"And, God, I saw you go up in flames. . . . I didn't know how you'd ever survive that. . . ."

Jack felt his stomach flip.

"It wasn't easy. A lot of surgeries. A lot of rehabilitation."

"I can imagine," Harry sympathized.

"But, hey, at least you're not dead, right?" Harry grinned.

Jack laughed. There was a part of him that enjoyed black humor. "Yeah, that's the one upside to being stuck with a face like this. . . ."

He adjusted himself in the chair, looked around at the small room with the pitcher of water on the bedside, next to the array of photographs of Tom with Grace and their children.

"I'm sure glad you came to visit me, Jimmy," Harry said as he looked out toward the window. "I'm relieved I don't have to imagine your parents burying you like I did so many times after I came home."

"Thank you," Jack said softly. "I'm glad I came too."

Harry nodded. "You ever think about time, Jimmy?"

"Time?"

"Yeah, like how we spent our time over there counting the days until we could get home. And now, I don't know about you, but I spend my days just trying to fill the hours. The days seem so damn slow. . . ."

"I know what you mean," Jack said.

"My son, Tom, he's just a teenager, but he doesn't understand. . . . The young people today . . ."

"Hard for them to understand if they didn't live it," Jack said.

"Yes, and I wouldn't wish that on anyone," Harry said. "I feel bad, but I think I need to cut this visit short, Jimmy. I'm getting tired now."

"No problem, I'll come again."

"That would be great." Harry started to nod off.

Jack stood up and placed the magazine by Harry's bedside, next to one of the many framed photographs of the Golden family. He noticed one of Tom, no older than ten, perched on the seat of a red bicycle. He smiled. It was the first time he noticed Katie had Tom's eyes.

CHAPTER 51

TOM HOISTED THE BICYCLE INTO THE BACK OF GRACE'S STATION wagon, reassuring his daughter that it was an easy fix to repair the chain.

"Randall will take care of it one-two-three, honey." Katie forced a smile, her eyes drifted down to her sneakers. She'd been working six days a week and had clocked in fifty hours at $3 an hour, which brought her about $150, and she had already researched and knew Randall's bike store was selling a new Schwinn with racing-bar handles for $110. Katie really wanted to tell her dad not to spend the money to fix it. Instead, she wanted to use her newly earned salary on getting a new bike.

She wasn't sure how to stop the repair though, since her father had been so sweet about it. She also knew that asking her parents for a new bike would be out of the question, especially since she was supposed to be pulling more of her weight on things that weren't really in the household budget. Her dad made a decent enough living, but it was modest compared to a lot of her friends' parents.

"Dad?" Her voice rose inside her, taking even her a little by surprise. "Do you think I can come with you?"

Tom's face lit up. It had felt like an eternity since Katie had asked to spend time with him.

"Are you kidding, baby girl? Of course!"

She slid into the saddle-colored seats, the leather cracking beneath her, and as Tom glanced over at his teenage daughter, his heart nearly exploded because it had been months since she had even deigned to look at him. From the time she hit high school last year, Katie's world seemed to revolve around her friends and he and Grace were planets she had banished to another orbit.

"Do you want to choose the music?"

She reached over and turned the radio dial to one of the popular stations. Blondie, a group he only knew because she had played their latest record over and over, so often that Grace and he wanted to break it in half, was playing. With the music now filling the air, Katie smiled as she looked out the window.

"We'll get that track fixed, probably while we wait," he said trying to coax her into conversation.

She didn't say anything until they hit the traffic light on Salisbury Road. "You know, Dad . . . I've already earned over a hundred dollars this summer . . . and I'm thinking maybe I should just buy a new bike. . . ."

The traffic light changed to red. "That's awfully responsible of you, Kat . . . but don't you think it would be more prudent to save the money for something else? I really don't think it's going to cost a lot to repair the one you have now."

She didn't answer.

There was something very noisy about the silence of a teenager. Tom felt he could have interpreted it in a hundred different ways. But he chose to take the simplest path, which was to just cherish having his daughter sitting next to him. It was a fifteen-minute drive. He intended to enjoy every second and not spoil it with words she didn't want to hear.

Randall's bike shop was much like the Golden Hours, a mom-and-pop shop that had been there for as long as anyone could remember. Tom had bought his first bike there from old Randall, who was now close to seventy-five years old. His son, Pete, worked in the front with sales, while the older man still insisted on doing all the repairs. It was bittersweet for Tom to walk inside, not just because the smell of rubber tires and metal made him nostalgic, but because it made him miss his own father as well. He hadn't truly appreciated those years having his father working in the back of the shop with him, and now it was too late.

"Hey, Tom," Pete greeted him from behind the cash register. Katie held the door as her father wheeled in her bike. "What can I do for you today?"

"We've got a dropped chain on this one...." Tom pointed to the problem.

Out of the corner of his eye, he saw Katie standing in the corner near a dolphin-blue Schwinn, with racing handlebars and ten speeds. The bike was a Cadillac compared with what she'd been riding for the past five years.

"That one's a beaut." Pete had apparently seen her looking at it too. "The metallic paint just sparkles in the sunlight."

Tom watched as Katie fingered the price tag.

"How much, honey?" he asked her.

"One hundred and eighty," she sighed. Her disappointment broke his heart.

"And how much for the repair?"

"Ten bucks. We can have it ready for you tomorrow."

He hated seeing his daughter look so forlornly at the new bike and he could still get the other one repaired and give it to Molly, who was close to outgrowing her bike anyway.

He looked over at Pete.

"Why don't you sit on it and see how it feels," Pete suggested, giving a discreet wink to Tom.

Katie kicked the stand up, moved it to the center of the store, and then mounted it, her tiptoes just grazing the floor. Tom saw her face transform in front of him, her somber mood suddenly lifted, and her face filled with light.

"I have nearly all the money, Dad. If I work just two more days, I'll have all of it."

"We can take ten percent off," Pete offered. "We like to keep those smiles on our customers' faces."

"How about we split the difference? I know your mom thinks it important we don't spoil you too much . . . but I think I can get away with telling her this is part of an early Christmas present."

Katie kicked the stand down and hopped off the bike. "Really, Dad?" She walked over and gave him something he hadn't had in quite a while from her. A hug.

The scent of her strawberry shampoo, her happiness, all of it lifted off her. And as Tom went to pull his wallet out of his pocket, he knew this was one of those moments he had to press into his mind and savor.

They brought the old bike in for repair and wheeled the new one out to the car, the two of them joining efforts to slide it into the trunk. When he again offered her the chance to tune the radio to her favorite station, she deferred to him.

"No, you choose, Dad."

He felt a pang in his heart. Now he understood what Grace had been talking about, feeling time slipping through her fingers too quickly. He only had three years left with Katie before she went off to college. It felt like only yesterday she was wrapped in pink bunting and he had been so surprised by just how powerful his emotions of being a young father had struck him. It wasn't just the new and overwhelming responsibility—it was the sheer awe of having created something so perfect with Grace. When he held Katie to his chest that first time, her little finger reaching to touch his, a sense of completeness washed over him that that struck him to his core.

His father was full of wisdom back in those early days. When he'd arrive bleary eyed from lack of sleep, trying to help Grace with at least one late-night bottle feeding as she recuperated from the delivery, Harry would tell him that this time of infancy-related struggles was finite. "Now you think of them as being babies for the rest of your life, but they're not."

He didn't really quite understand it back then, and even now he was trying to figure fatherhood out. No one had given him a map for parenthood, and he knew Grace was still struggling to find a way to navigate the emotions of having a teenager under their roof. But he also knew, even though they didn't say it aloud to each other, that the full house that Grace and he shared with the girls—with it its messes, the bickering, the constant bills for groceries and new clothes—would one day be over. This future quiet, its very stillness, flashed like a painful premonition.

At the next traffic light, Van Morrison's "Tupelo Honey" came on the radio, and Tom's heart opened in a way that only a good song could unlock. He belted out the lyrics, crooning off key, laughing as he sang.

"Come on, Dad. You're *so* corny."

They crossed over Delaney onto Main Street and paused at the stop sign. His eyes didn't notice Anh and Bảo walking toward Kepler's with a straw shopping basket, for Tom's gaze was focused on stealing another glance at Katie. As her giggle filled the chamber of the car, his heart soaked it up like sunshine.

CHAPTER 52

ANH HAD FINALLY MANAGED THE COURAGE TO VENTURE INTO town with Bảo by her side. It was now mid-July, and she knew it wasn't going to get any easier if she didn't put in the effort necessary to practice using English outside of the motherhouse. Bảo would be starting middle school in little over a month and he, too, would need to become more comfortable speaking to the outside world. As Dinh would constantly remind them when the Sisters had left the group to socialize by themselves, "We're not returning to Vietnam. Like saplings to new soil, we must put down roots and grow."

Anh often felt Dinh was talking specifically to her, even when she was surrounded by the others. His eyes focused on her when he spoke, and his smile was always full of hope.

When she confided in him that she was overwhelmed by her new-found responsibility to be Bảo's adoptive guardian, he reassured her that she would blossom under the role.

"You will find your way, *em,*" he'd promise and touch her gently on the wrist. The warmth of his touch, no matter how fleeting it was, always soothed her.

Aside from Dinh, she had trusted Grace too. Anh had expressed concern at first about Bảo's fascination with American cartoons, particularly the *Super Friends* episodes that always absorbed his attention. But Grace had assured her that the show was popular with lots of school-age children. Anh was relieved to see that when Bảo was with Grace's daughter, Molly, watching the show gave them something in common.

Bảo's language was now peppered with phrases that weren't in his practice workbook, like "Holy cow!" and "Sure thing!" which made the Sisters giggle when they worked on conversational English with all of them.

Today, however, was their first day out together by themselves, and Anh wanted to make sure everything went well. She'd been nervous when Sister Mary Alice drove them toward the heart of town, where lots of small shops lined the streets. The incident at Kepler's had been unsettling and she wanted to replace it with something more positive.

"Meet me back here at three o'clock," Sister Mary Alice instructed, showing three fingers and pointing to her watch. She then pointed to the large green clock on the side of the brick building that housed the Golden Hours.

Anh nodded and Bảo jumped out of the car.

In the crisp July sunlight, the two of them walked side by side. As they crossed the street, the Goldens' station wagon zoomed by. The window half-open, Anh heard, for a second, laughter in the breeze.

She reached out to hold Bảo's hand and for the first time since they arrived, he slipped his small fingers into her own.

"We'll get some mangoes today. I'll find you a sweet one, bé tí," she promised.

Anh pointed in the direction of Kepler's, but Bảo shook his head.

"I'll be quick," she said in Vietnamese. "I'll find the sweetest one for you and then we'll go back home."

But Bảo pulled her toward the store with the window full of clocks.

They walked closer, Bảo's steps increasing with speed, until they were standing directly in front of it.

Anh felt the same sense of curiosity as her nephew as she took in the dazzling array of timepieces. Two tall grandfather clocks flanked both sides of the display. One was sharp and rectangular and had a sun and moon in its golden center, the other was shaped like an hour-glass. On a pedestal table sat a white clock with painted flowers. But most intriguing was a chestnut-colored clock that had been carved to resemble a birdhouse. Just as the other clocks sounded the half hour, a tiny bird peeked out from a carved hole.

Bảo's finger pressed against the glass. She knew his father had some-times secretly taken him to the shed and shown him how the inside of a radio worked, now she could see that same curiosity sparked.

"Do you want to go inside?" she asked.

But when they went to the door it was locked.

On the front door there was a handmade sign that said CLOSED FOR THE DAY. She glanced at the green and gold painted letters above: THE GOLDEN HOURS. They were standing in front of Grace's family's store.

She bought the fruit and a few other provisions. "We'll go back to the clock store the next time," she promised. She took the mango she felt was the ripest and handed it to him, her heart filling with the memory of Linh.

Later that afternoon, Anh shared with Dinh how she had to sort through at least a dozen mangoes at Kepler's till she found three worthy of bringing back home. She cut the fruit up into slices in the kitchen area they all shared.

Dinh took the fruit between two fingers and dropped it into his mouth.

"We need to find a way to fill our bodies with sweetness in this new life . . . too much sadness otherwise." His face was full of hopeful-ness that moved something inside her.

"They pick the fruit before it has time to ripen, that's the problem," Dinh said as he sucked on his fingers. "We know the longer it stays on the vine the better." He smiled at her gently. "Like children, right?"

Her own child had not stayed too long on the vine, but she did not share that with him.

"Yes," she said softly. "Just like children."

"This Kepler's Market needs some help with their fruit, I think," he said with a grin. "And we need to help them."

Anh smiled. She imagined her village in better times with bamboo woven baskets filled with exotic varieties of fruit piled high.

"There is so much I miss," she added to the space between them. Her voice was full of longing. Anh closed her eyes and imagined the inside of her childhood home, the smell of cooking rice, her mother's papery hands cutting cilantro and radishes on a wooden board. The sounds of the laughing thrushes and greenfinches in the trees.

It pained her that she could not bring anything from the ancestral shrine with her. The incense. The tiny vase they used for flowers. The two framed photographs. All of that had been left behind.

"We could only bring so much, right?" she widened her eyes as she looked over to Dinh. "And almost everything I brought was either lost on the boat or in the refugee camp. I naively thought America was just a few hours' journey, not on the other side of the world."

"We all thought that, Anh," he replied. "I left with a friend who constructed our boat from the wood of an abandoned piano and a small motor. Even parts of the keyboard and the strings were used to make the small dinghy. Can you imagine?"

Dinh closed his eyes. "My friend discovered it in one of the abandoned halls of an old colonial hotel. He cut it apart with an axe and constructed it during the night when no one was looking. We thought it would keep us afloat for a couple days . . . which is how long he thought it would take to get to America."

"We all believed the same foolishness," Anh said softly. She reached for the last mango and took her paring knife, deftly peeling away the skin.

"My friend died after our tenth day adrift. Sometimes at night when I can't sleep, I still see him on his back, hollow eyes looking up at the sky. He's telling me in only a whisper of breath that he thinks we're really close ... that we're bound to see the horizon tomorrow. I hear his voice in my head, Anh, and then I see myself rolling his dead body into the sea."

CHAPTER 53

SUMMER WAS HURTLING TOWARD ITS LAST WEEKS, AND THE club was bouncing with children. Katie was enjoying her daily commute on her new, shiny wheels. Her bicycle, with its ten speeds and racer handlebars, made her feel like she was riding a Rolls-Royce.

Grace had found a new rhythm with the children being out of school and was finding great satisfaction in helping Anh practice her English. They had developed their own special rapport when they went out on errands together.

One day, after returning from Kepler's, it occurred to Grace that Anh might enjoy another way to practice her English.

"Maybe you'd like to cook a meal here one afternoon?" she mentioned casually as she pulled out some of the groceries and put them in the refrigerator. "I could share some of my recipes, and maybe you could show me some from Vietnam?"

Anh's face lit up. "Yes. Please."

They decided to make it a weekly date. In the beginning, Grace showed her how to make simple American dishes she knew her family savored, like breaded chicken cutlets or spaghetti and meatballs. But then one day, she asked Anh if she'd be interested in making something a little more time-consuming.

"It's a bit heavy for summer, but it brings back good memories of my late mother-in-law teaching me something from her family," Grace smiled. "It's called matzo ball soup, and I'm sure you've never tasted anything like it. It's soft and comforting when you're feeling down. I always make it for my children when they're sick."

Grace felt a wave of longing for her late mother-in-law, Rosie, when she brought up the soup. When asked what her secret recipe was that kept her dumplings so soft and fluffy, Rosie used to say: "A splash of club soda and a little bit of love . . ." Her words were now a warmth inside her.

Anh delighted in forming the round, soft balls in her hands and placing them in the boiling water until they floated on top. After they ladled them into bowls of chicken broth, Anh sat down and took a bite. "This so good," she said. "Taste like food . . . for here." She placed her hand over her heart. "Next time, I teach you to make Vietnamese soup called *phở*. So you learn, too."

The prospect of being able to expand her culinary expertise and learn from Anh excited Grace. Just as Rosie had taught her how to make matzo ball soup and brisket, dishes she had never heard of before she arrived in New York, Grace now relished the chance to learn something new under Anh's guidance. The cooking sessions were no longer just about Anh expanding her English vocabulary. They became more of an opportunity for two friends to work together to prepare a meal for the people they loved.

While the women cooked, Molly and Bảo hung out in the den together, most of the time watching television. Molly knew the Wonder Twins were Bảo's favorite, but he was still happy to just watch anything on the television.

"He really loves those superheroes," Grace commented casually to Anh one afternoon as she gently cleaned some mint leaves from the garden in a glass bowl. Their conversations had become more fluid over the past few weeks and the connection between them had strengthened. "It's funny how that's the thing he seems to love most here. . . ."

Anh looked up and tried to find the right words. "Miss, he think they help him find his parents."

Grace's face grew perplexed. "But they died, didn't they?"

"Yes . . . but he believe the cartoon boy and girl become water and find them in ocean. They have powers to . . . you know . . . help bring them back like special warrior with magic power."

Grace put down her knife. "That's heartbreaking, Anh." She looked over at Bảo stretched out on his belly on the carpet. He was completely entranced by what he saw on the screen.

"But by now, he must sense that what he's watching isn't real. . . ." Grace thought of herself in those moments after learning her sister had drowned. How she had thrown down the sun-bleached gull bone that she believed to have magical powers once she discovered it was useless to help her.

Anh shrugged. "I don't know, miss."

"Surely he understands that they're not coming back, though. . . ."

Anh looked out toward the window and noticed a small white bird perched on the sill, its beak pecking at something between its feet.

"In my country, we believe the dead are not really dead. That they are around us. Spirits of our ancestors. You know what I mean? They not really gone."

Grace grew quiet. She thought of her mother and father who had passed on. She thought about her sister, Bridey. She understood exactly what Anh meant. She often sensed their spirits hovering in the air.

"I feel my sister when it rains," Grace confided. "It's never faded even after all these years. I wake up and the dampness triggers everything about her. It used to be that I'd only remember the day of her drowning. I'd see her face framed with curls, clasping a sweet bun between her fingers, and then I see my father holding her lifeless in his arms before someone drapes a raincoat over her tiny body."

Anh closed her eyes. "I am sorry, miss. You had terrible pain, too."

"It's strange because when I was younger, before I had my daughters, I could only imagine the loss of her through my own ten-year-old eyes, as the girl who lost a sister. But now that I've had my own children, I also see it through the eyes of my mother." Grace took in a deep breath. "It's terrible beyond words."

The light changed in the kitchen as the sun shifted behind the clouds.

Anh grabbed one of the carrots from the bunch that Grace had peeled and washed for the soup they were going to prepare together. She picked up a knife and began chopping, but then paused. She turned and looked at Grace.

"I lost baby after husband was killed." Her voice trembled. "I believe his death the worst thing that could happen to me, but I force myself to get up . . . I get up and I eat a few spoonfuls of rice and I wipe my tears, because I have child I need to take care of." She put the knife down and lifted her hands to her eyes and began to weep. "But when that baby leaves my body, I feel I have nothing."

The sound of rain began to patter against the window.

Grace lifted her arms and wrapped them around Anh.

"Now I must be mother for Bảo," she acknowledged between her tears. "But how? I know so little."

"You know more than you think, Anh," Grace brought her close.

"You have been his guardian in getting him safely across the world and you will make a new life for yourselves here. I'm confident it will all work out for the best."

"Thank you," she said before pulling away from Grace's embrace. She turned to finish chopping the remaining carrots, regaining her composure.

Grace reached for the onion. As her knife slid into its layered center, she was grateful it provided her an excuse to wipe away her tears.

CHAPTER 54

Jack hesitated for more than a few seconds when Tom invited him to Sunday dinner. This time there would be two other guests besides him.

"Do you remember me telling you about that little boy, Bảo, that Grace found on Maple Street?" Tom mentioned casually. "Well, she's been volunteering at Our Lady Queen of Martyrs . . . helping him and his aunt learn English."

"That's kind of her. . . . Grace always tries to do the right thing."

Tom laughed. "That she does. . . . anyway, we wanted to extend the invite to you, too. She's making something called phở. Some kind of noodle soup, I think."

Jack put down his calipers on the watch he was working on, stalling for time while trying to come up with an excuse not to come.

Tom sensed Jack's discomfort.

"I know what you're thinking, but they're from the south part of Vietnam . . . so that makes them the good guys, right? That's why they were able to get sponsored here in the first place because they fought alongside the Americans."

Jack forced a smile. In the years since he returned home, he no longer thought about the war in such simple terms. He might have arrived in Vietnam thinking the war was like a John Wayne movie where it was easy to divide the good guys from the bad, but the war had been nothing more than a senseless and futile effort made by the government with far too many lives lost. The only thing Jack knew for certain was all the pain that still lingered. The North, the South, the American GIs, all of them had suffered.

"I get that, Tom . . . but you know it's more about this . . ." Jack lifted a finger toward his face. "It's kind hard to meet new people, if you know what I mean . . ."

"I understand, but Grace has been practicing making that soup with Anh and I think it would mean a lot to have you there."

"I've been in a more solitary mood than normal lately. . . . I'm just not sure I'm up to it this weekend."

Hendrix, curled up underneath the workshop table, lifted his snout and let out a little snort, as if to question whether his master was actually telling the truth.

"Well, think about it, Jack. You don't need to tell me today. Sleep on it and let me know in a day or two." Tom stood up and put his tools back in the drawer.

"I'll see you tomorrow." He bent down and gave Hendrix a rub.

Jack heard the door close behind Tom as he headed back home to his family, leaving him and Hendrix alone in the back workshop. He let out a deep sigh and Hendrix lifted his head, studied his master for a second, and then returned to his curled position on the floor.

"What do you want to hear, buddy?" He glanced over at the dog. "Don't got an answer? Guess it's left for me to decide . . ." Jack reached for a shoebox he kept full of his favorite cassettes. He pulled out a tape of Dobie Gray's album *Drift Away* and popped it into the small boom box on the worktable. The title song, with its hopeful lyrics, soon floated through the air. The music began to relax him, and the discomfort of the dinner invitation started to lessen with each note.

In front of him rested an old Elgin watch from the 1950s whose owner had brought in for a repair.

It was evident it had been a watch much loved. The cognac-colored leather band had been softened and creased with age; a less sentimental person would have replaced it years ago with a new one. The gold casing had acquired a lovely patina, too, and engraved on the back was an inscription that read simply *Love*, with scripted initials beneath.

Jack ran his finger over the engraving. He always relished reading the words that people chose to make permanent on a timepiece. It seemed almost sacred to him, the same way it felt when he would come across a tree during one of his late-night walks and see two sets of initials carved into the trunk, a fossilization of someone else's adoration.

The Elgin watch was a mechanical one, so it wasn't an easy repair that simply required a change in the quartz battery. He contemplated if perhaps it needed to have its gears stripped and cleaned. He pulled the magnifying visor down over his head and slowly began to unscrew the back of the case and then laid it on the table, revealing the insides of the watch.

The internal mechanisms of a watch were beautiful to him: the gear train, the escapement and balance wheel. All the working calipers, framed by the bridge, came together in an enviable harmony. Jack felt as if he was peering into a perfect world when he opened up a watch, one where one component fit perfectly into the next, where everything merged to make two linked hands move ahead.

He saw this beauty all through the lens of his one good eye. And even when a watch didn't work as it should, there was the expectation that it could still be resurrected with the proper care. But could a life be as well?

Nothing in his life had ever come together like the workings of a watch. But while the sadness and isolation of his life had gutted him prior to meeting Tom and his family, Jack had realized just this evening why he no longer saw his life as a tragedy. The invitation to Sunday night dinner was in fact not offered out of pity, as he once believed.

Instead, he had the impression that when Tom asked him to come, he wanted him there because he and Grace now considered him part of their family.

That Sunday evening, rather than the usual round roast or baked chicken, Grace set the table with large soup bowls and chopsticks collected from all the times they had ordered in Chinese food from Charlie Suey's. The house smelled of new flavors and scents. Hours earlier, she and Anh had taken the old station wagon to Queens, where she'd lived before marrying Tom. There she knew they could find all the ingredients they needed for Anh's recipe. Anh had written out her shopping list in Vietnamese.

"Remind me again what we're getting for tonight?" she'd asked.

"Rice noodle. Garlic. Coriander..." Ahn had practiced with Sister Mary the day before to remember the English translations for the ingredients.

Grace had smelled some of Anh's cooking at the motherhouse, and it always made her mouth water. "It all sounds wonderful," she said. "I can't wait to taste what you make tonight."

"I am happy to cook for you and your family," Anh grinned. She patted the shopping list with her hand.

She felt almost giddy with the windows rolled down, the breeze rippling through both their hair. Grace caught Anh smiling as she looked out at the changing scenery, the rows of suburban houses being replaced by two-family homes, redbrick apartment buildings and storefronts that reflected the neighborhood's rich immigrant community. Grace pointed to a pub next to an Indian restaurant that had an Irish flag in one of its windows. "I used to go there with my girlfriends," she laughed. "I'm glad ol' Malachy's is still around."

A few minutes later, Grace spotted the sign for Lo's Market. "Here we are." She slowed the car and pulled into a parking spot just in front.

Anh looked at the sign. "This store we go to, it owned by Vietnamese?"

"It's actually Chinese," Grace clarified. "But I called this morning, and they said they have your noodles and spices, too."

The two women got out of the car and walked inside. In the past, it was Grace who'd always taken charge whenever they stepped through the threshold of Kepler's. But now she walked behind Anh, who floated confidently through the store's narrow aisles, her fingers combing through the bushels of familiar produce and herbs. She smiled as she lifted a small knob of ginger root to her nose.

"This place very good," she told Grace as she eyed the stack of cellophane vermicelli noodles on the shelf. "We can make phở just like back home."

Now the Golden house was filled with the scents steaming off from the rich broth that Anh had showed Grace how to make when they'd returned from the Asian grocery store.

Jack was drinking a cold beer with Tom in the living room, and a few minutes later the doorbell rang. It was Anh, who had gone back to the motherhouse an hour earlier to get Bảo.

"We made pounded sweet bean and rice treats with the Sisters yesterday." Anh offered Grace a tin filled with the dessert. "We have full Vietnamese meal now," she said, smiling.

"That's so kind of you, Anh. Thank you," Grace said, taking the tin and walking her toward the living room where Tom and the others were waiting. Katie was still not back from her job, but Molly rushed over to greet Bảo.

"Well, you know our Molly . . . and Katie will be home soon." Grace pushed a cheeriness into her voice. "And this is our friend Jack. He works with Tom at the store."

Anh stepped forward and proudly offered a handshake. Her eyes did not react even when they registered the disfigurement on Jack's left side. She felt the warmth and strength in the man's grip flood through her.

Båo swiveled around after greeting Molly and seemed to ponder for a moment the man who stood rigid in the living room, staring out at him with one good eye and a face etched with scars. His eyes lifted from the ground and traced Jack's silhouette in its entirety.

"Hello, sir. It's nice to meet you," he articulated his words with careful, practiced diction. Dressed in a checked button-down shirt and khaki pants that hit him above the ankle, Båo extended his hand. Jack grasped it and shook it firmly.

"It is a pleasure, young man," Jack said softly. He was surprised how much emotion welled inside him from such a simple gesture. But there was something about seeing two children, both from two different worlds, standing next to each other and bonded in friendship, that filled Jack with an emotion he hadn't felt since he'd left Foxton Elementary: a beautiful feeling of hope.

The steaming bowls of broth brimming with ribbons of rice noodles, cilantro leaves, and thin slices of beef were placed down cheerily by Grace and Molly.

Jack sat down at the table. "It certainly smells delicious."

"Anh showed Mom how to do everything," Molly chirped. "We need some new dishes around here, right Dad?" She dipped her head closer and inhaled the scent of ginger, clove, and coriander wafting off the surface, then reached for the lime wedge to squeeze into the soup and a few bean sprouts. Anh had told her to add both before taking her first sip of the broth.

Tom settled into his chair. "Well, I'm excited. This will be my first time eating Vietnamese food."

"Please," Anh said now standing at the front of the table with Grace and smiling as she saw Molly take the lime and sprouts. "No good basil at store and beef not cut just right, but we make as good as we can."

Jack considered mentioning that he had been lucky enough to taste phở a few times but decided against it. Instead, he pulled his chopsticks apart and then looked over warmly at Grace, then Anh. "Thank you, ladies, for inviting me tonight. It looks like you both worked so hard. . . ." He glanced over at Katie's empty seat at the table. "I hope Katie isn't going to miss it."

"She's just running late. They had a lifeguard meeting at the club she had to go to," Tom answered. "Nothing to worry about. Unless we eat her share, right?" Tom looked over to his wife and smiled. "Really, honey, it looks and smells great."

The thing about Jack was that even with only one good eye, he still had a keen ability to pick up small details from other people's behavior. When Katie finally bounded into the room, he noticed she barely looked at anyone when she plopped down in her seat.

"I'm famished," she groaned as Grace got up to bring her a bowl of phở. Within seconds, she had taken her spoon (she remained the only one at the table who didn't even attempt to use the chopsticks Grace had provided). Tom had given up after a few awkward attempts to shovel the noodles in his mouth, but Molly and Grace were slowly getting the hang of it.

The little boy, however, had lifted his head several times from his bowl to look at Jack. It wasn't something that bothered Jack as much as it used to. As a matter of fact, part of him preferred people who were willing to lift their eyes toward him, rather than purposefully avert them.

"Will Bảo be in the same grade as you?" Jack asked.

"Yes," Molly answered before Båo could reply.

"They'll have tutoring at school," Grace added. "But he's already doing so well." She looked over at him and smiled. "I'd like to think it was meant to be that afternoon I found Båo." She glanced at the opposite of the table to where Anh was. "We wouldn't be having such a nice dinner like this, if I hadn't."

Jack caught sight of Katie rolling her eyes.

Grace noticed too, and he watched her face redden.

"Life's kinda like that, right?" Jack pushed into the conversation awkwardly. "Meeting Tom that day at the VA hospital, that sure made my life a whole lot better...."

"Aw, come on, now." Tom chuckled and lifted his beer in Jack's direction. "Let's not go overboard. I'm just happy to have you now as a buddy." He took a swig of his drink. "And let's not forget you can repair even the most pain-in-the-ass watch better than anyone I know."

Something in Båo's face flickered. Jack saw it like a recognition of something. It lit up the little boy's whole face.

He tapped his wrist. "You fix watch?"

Jack's eyes studied Båo.

"I do," he answered. "I work in Tom's shop."

Jack squinted at the boy's wrist and thought he saw a horseshoe-shaped scar, but he wasn't sure if it was a trick of his impaired vision.

"We saw it other day. We look in window." Anh smiled. "I learn later this is the Goldens' family shop. You have many beautiful things."

"You make them new again?" Curiosity spread on Båo's face.

"Well, actually, yes." He lifted a finger toward the bad side of his face. "I only have one good eye, but I can still see up close. And I use a magnifying glass, too." To better explain his words, he pretended to bring something imaginary up to his one good eye and squinted.

"Båo's father was good at fixing things, too," Anh added. "My husband no such much, but he was better farmer."

The boy smiled and nodded. "Radios. Not watch."

Jack's heart constricted in his chest.

Just the mention of Bảo's father working on radios back in Vietnam made him remember the radio he had carried strapped to his back, and the final moments of him taking the hand receiver from Lieutenant Bates just before the terrible explosion.

"You all right, Jack?" Tom looked concerned. "You're looking kind of pale...."

Jack took a few seconds to reply. When he finally looked up from his bowl of soup, Molly was beside him offering him a glass of water.

Jack accepted the glass and swallowed hard.

"Yeah," he answered. He felt the flashbacks begin to settle. "I was just thinking about how it takes a certain type of person to have the patience to fix things. Not everyone has that, you know? The desire to make what's broken right again."

Jack's words floated over the women at the table, none of them registering the sentiment. But Tom looked down, acknowledging them quietly, and the little boy also nodded, his eyes burning bright.

CHAPTER 55

WHEN CLAYTON GOT HOME, HE FOUND HIS FATHER SPLAYED out on the sofa drinking whiskey, the soft velour upholstery sinking beneath his wiry frame. His belt half unbuckled, Ross Mavis lifted the glass tumbler of Jack Daniels to his lips as he watched the evening news.

"Hey, boy," he spat, lifting up his glass to acknowledge his son. Clayton had spent the past several hours putting the finishing touches on his fort with Bobby. His body was sore and covered with patches of dirt. A thin coat of perspiration glistened on his skin.

His father lifted his thick wrist from his lap and looked at his watch. "You're late."

Clayton eyes narrowed. "I was busy with something," he answered curtly before he kicked off his shoes that were caked with mud and left them in the hall. "Jeez, I wish you'd just lay off. . . ."

"Don't you go talking to me like that or I'll shove some rocks down your throat to shut you up." The old man snorted and lifted his glass to his lips. The orange hairs of his mustache cupped the rim of his tumbler as he took another swig.

There was a time, perhaps even as little as three months ago, that Clayton would have quivered at his father's threats. But this time something has changed within him. His body has transformed over the past few weeks from sawing branches and constructing the fort with Buddy. Long, thick ropes of muscles have emerged on his once scrawny, freckled arms. So, as he pulls off his damp, sweaty T-shirt, revealing his stronger physique, he wants his father to take notice that he is no longer the little boy who had once been called a weakling and cowered in his shadow.

He stares at his father and considers if this should be the evening he finally knocks him down, and teaches him what it's like to be hit with a fist.

He has endured his old man's beatings for too many years. He's been fed on a diet of anger and belittling as long as he can remember. The first time his dad hit him, he couldn't have been older than four or five. He had no recollection of what he'd done to ignite his father's ire, but he remembered the consequence, the force of his large, pulpy hand striking him. The pain as it flooded through his body and made tears spring from his eyes.

There would be so many more that followed, a dance of anger between his glass of whiskey and his son.

While his mother shrank in the kitchen, her hands knotted between the cloth of a tea towel, he was forced to count the number of lashings he received. What first began with the back of his father's hand, soon expanded to include the strap of his leather belt. Recently his father had graduated to his clenched fist.

"You need to be punished, boy," his father liked to say before sliding his belt from the loops or cocking his fist up to his eye. But now Clayton wanted to do the same thing to his old man.

He wanted to punish his father.

Ross Mavis, six feet tall, with ginger hair and matching mustache, rose from the mustard-colored sofa. The ice in his drank jingled as he steadied himself and began walking toward the table.

"What are you looking at, Clayton?" he jeered as he came closer until they were only inches away from each other. Clayton could smell the alcohol on his breath.

His father had been in a foul mood for nearly the entire three-month period since he'd been transferred up to the Northeast. He disliked everything about Bellegrove—perhaps even more than Clayton did. He detested his commute on the train. He hated his neighbors, who lived in such close range that he could hear their television when the windows were open. In Texas, they had lived on several acres, and he could do or say as he pleased without worrying whether anyone was spying on his business.

Clayton's mother emerged from the kitchen. Pale and tiny as a church mouse, she lifted her hand to her mouth, but nothing came out. Over the years, Clayton had come to see his mother as one of those Russian nesting dolls. She had shrunk so many times into herself that one day he thought she might just disappear.

Clayton clenched his fingers to his side. His heart pulsed with adrenaline. His father had taught him many things, like how to shoot a deer, how to skin a squirrel, and how to clean the barrel of a shotgun. But he had also taught Clayton something he hadn't intended. He taught him how to inflict pain.

"Your father..." His mother finally spoke. Her words floated through the air like spun sugar, weightless and without substance. "Doesn't mean what he . . ."

Clayton lifted his arm back just as his father stepped closer, his menacing bloodshot eyes all too familiar to him. At the moment, his fist hit his father's cheek, he felt the thrill of the impact ricochet throughout his entire body. Ross fell backward and his drink flew out of his hand. The glass fell to the ground and shattered into dozens of dangerous, tiny shards.

"You fucking idiot," his father bellowed as he tried to raise himself from the ground.

Clayton threw his shoulders back and stared down at his old man as he struggled to regain his footing. Still drunk, and swearing incoherently, the left side of Ross's face was red and had begun to swell.

"Yeah," Clayton said as his mother scurried back into the kitchen to get the broom. "Tell me something you haven't already said before."

CHAPTER 56

GRACE OPENED THE DOOR OF THE STATION WAGON AND Båo
and Molly slid into the back seat. Anh was seated in the front, her legs
neatly folded in front of her, a straw bag lying flat on her lap. Molly had
asked if Båo could join them at the swimming pool again.

It was already mid-August, and Grace could count on one hand
how many days were left before school started again. It always amazed
her how fast summer went by. Once they hit the Fourth of July weekend, it all seemed to race toward the finish line.

Båo stepped out of the car with Molly, both of their feet squishing
in their flip-flops as they headed toward the pool area.

"Get us a few lounge chairs in the shade," Grace hollered out
to them as they ran ahead. She clutched a floppy pink hat between
her fingers.

The two women walked through the short pathway that led from
the parking lot to the pools. Already, Grace could see Katie on one of
the tallest towers. Her blond hair pulled back in a high ponytail, her
focus intense on the large and crowded pool below.

The air was filled with high-pitched squeals and laughter, along
with the patter of wet feet on the hot concrete.

Båo and Molly were closer to the kiddie pool where mothers still
hovered and wrapped their little ones in towels.

Grace paused over one of the lounge chairs Molly had secured and
pulled off her cover-up. Looking down at her legs, she winced. They
were as pale as they had been since summer began. Her thighs looked
like bread dough, soft and plump, small dimples dotting the surface.

She let out a deep sigh before spreading her towel on the chair and finding comfort in the warmth of the sun.

"It's nice the children enjoy being together. . . ." she said, stretching out. But Anh didn't seem to be listening to her. She stood rigid at the foot of the plastic lounge chair, watching as Molly was taking Bảo toward the main pool that was already crowded with swimmers. Women in bright floral bathing caps were doing laps in the two roped off lanes and teenagers were clowning around in clusters by the pool's edge.

She watched vigilantly as Molly led him toward the entrance of the shallow section. He took a step in, his ankles submerged in the pale blue water, his hand wrapped around the metal banister.

Molly, a few feet ahead of him, was already waist-deep in the water.

"Come a little deeper," she beckoned toward him with a wave of her hand. "I want to teach you a few strokes." She gestured the breaststroke with her two gangly arms.

Bảo's fingers gripped tighter around the railing at Molly's words. He hesitated for a moment before his body became stiff and he stood on the steps.

Above them, in her lifeguard tower, Katie held her whistle between her teeth and signaled to a group of boys to stop splashing, warning them they'd be pulled out of the pool if they didn't stop.

"You're okay," Molly encouraged Bảo as she came back to the steps and tried to coax him to take a few more strides into the pool.

Bảo stands frozen. He can see and hear the sounds of the other children enjoying the cool, refreshing comfort of the water. But for him, the idea of going more than ankle-deep, as he had done for many weeks in the kiddie pool, is terrifying.

The water is full of life. Children's laughter. Beach balls with rainbow stripes being thrown into the air. Toddlers with inflatable wings kicking toward their mother's open arms.

But to Bảo, the water draws him to that night he stood in the reeds with his mother and father beside him. His mother's hand in his own. He feels the memory overtake him. It penetrates his skin and snakes into every coil of his mind. He no longer inhales the chlorine from the pool, but the swampy humidity of the Vietnamese shoreline. The marshy silt underneath his feet.

"Bảo!" Molly laughs. "The water's only up to here!" She gestures toward her waistline.

Bảo takes another step, and the water comes up to his thigh.

He feels Anh's eyes watching him, her own self-imposed patrol. Both of them know far too well the danger of water.

Finally, after several minutes of Molly's coaxing, Bảo manages to release his hand completely from the banister and treads into the pool. The cold water envelops his legs, and he feels his mind cleave into two sections. One half sees his mother beside him and the other half, a new friend. Molly's arms are open, and she is smiling. Her braces catch the light as she opens up her mouth in a wide grin.

"You're halfway there," Molly encourages. Intuitively, she knows today is not the day to ask him to put his head into the water or to teach him how to turn his head and cup for breath.

Instead, she just splashes water at him. The two of them laugh as Katie shrieks her whistle and tells Molly she has been warned.

CHAPTER 57

INSIDE THE WALLS OF THE FORT, BEHIND THE PLASTIC TARP THE boys have used to mark the entrance, Clayton and Buddy are flat on their backs, their arms and legs stretched out on the dirt floor. Over the past three weeks, they have managed to build the structure using everything from the tiny saplings in the forest to discarded pieces of plywood and scavenged Coke cans. Intense satisfaction with themselves washes over them as only this morning they finished the final touches.

Clayton is immensely proud that he has successfully engineered a roof using an old boat tarp he found in his neighbor's weekly garbage heap. Now, with the plastic sheeting above their head and the dark soil underneath their backs, they breathe in their accomplishment.

"It's finally done," Buddy exhales, his chest rising and falling beneath his yellow T-shirt.

Clayton lets out a grunt. "It needs a feature to make it even cooler than this . . . like a firepit in the center or something rad like that."

He turns on his side, and his dungarees fall slightly around the nobs of his hips. Buddy notices a long, raised welt that snakes around past his waistband.

Clayton takes one of the remaining twigs and draws a circle between them. "We can build it right here. Dig out a hole in the center and mark the perimeter with small rocks."

Buddy is tired and only half listening, but Clayton is already pulling him up from the ground. "Come on, jerkoff . . . let's finish it. After we're done, we can steal some beers from my dad's fridge downstairs and celebrate we made a kick-ass castle for ourselves." He ran his fingers though his pale, corn silk hair. His eyes are as steely as they are blue.

"I want this whole damn thing done before school starts."

Buddy inches himself to the ground. "Can't we wait until tomorrow? I'm exhausted."

Clayton stands over Buddy with his arms folded. *"I said, GET UP!"* His voice is the edge of a knife. It slices through Buddy with cold precision. "What kind of viper are you, anyway?"

They collect every pebble they can find. Larger rocks, too, flinted with flecks of mica. Clayton thrusts his hands into the earth and digs out jagged pieces of quartz and smoother stones the color of the moon. They pull out the edge of their T-shirts and form a makeshift basket with the cloth to collect their bounty. Then, rock by rock, they make a perimeter around a pit that Clayton has shoveled several inches deep. What they have created now looks almost prehistoric. Like a small Stonehenge they've constructed with their two hands.

Crouched in one of the corners, Clayton grins with satisfaction. "If we ever make a fire, we'll have to create something to pull back the tarp to let the smoke out. But still—" he laughs. "Hell, we're pretty damn awesome."

Buddy wishes he could show someone else what they've made. After all, it's pretty astonishing they've managed to create something with four walls and a roof out of just salvaged materials they'd found.

"So do you think we can ever invite people to come out here?" Buddy is clearly the naïf between them. "I mean, it's a shame to waste it just on ourselves."

"Who else would you even want to bring here?"

Buddy shrugs. But secretly he knows exactly who he'd like to bring. Images of Katie Golden flash through his mind. With her perfect blonde ponytail, shapely physique, and her sharp tongue that somehow excites him. How many times has he fantasized about her in the solitude of his bedroom, that image of her high on her lifeguard tower, haughty as ever, looking down on him like a queen.

"Nobody . . . I just thought maybe one day we might . . ."

Clayton is already shutting him down. "Let's go get those beers," he smirks.

Buddy lets go of the idea of tasting Katie's lips for the first time, and instead allows his mind to drift to the idea of the alcohol. He feels older in Clayton's company and revels in their clandestine activities. With their fort finally actualized, he sees them no longer as boys. He believes that after all their hard work over the past few weeks, they can now call themselves men.

CHAPTER 58

THE LAST WEEK OF SUMMER WAS UPON THEM, AND EVERYTHING was pregnant with the "lasts," as Grace liked to say. The "last" barbecue, the "last" trip to the beach, the "last" week to sleep in late.

The weather had suddenly lifted too. The oppressive heat of early July and August had given way to the first whiff of autumn in the air. "Smells like school is coming." Grace raised her chin and sniffed the breeze. Behind her, Bảo and Molly waited for her to unlock the station wagon's back door so they could pile in and take up Tom's invitation to show Bảo all the different clocks and watches at the store.

"Oh, Mom, don't be so corny," Molly had said with a giggle. "You can't smell school."

There was a time not too long ago, perhaps even last year, that Molly would have indulged her and humored her playfulness. But with each day that passed, her youngest daughter was moving closer to being an adult and further away from being her baby. Just the other afternoon, Molly stood in the kitchen wearing a daisy-printed smocked top and green Danskin shorts. Her legs looked like they had grown two more inches over the break, and the shorts now barely covered her bottom.

"Those shorts won't be fitting you next summer," Grace appraised, in awe of how fast Molly was growing. "We should drop them off at the church thrift store before school starts."

Molly had agreed but hadn't pondered her mother's observation more than a minute before she was asking if she could bring Bảo to the Golden Hours. "I'd like to show him all the grandfather clocks Daddy has in his collection. Maybe even show him how to wind the clocks."

Grace had agreed, thinking it would be a lovely expedition for Bảo. Sister Mary Alice had mentioned that Anh and the other Vietnamese adults had started an ESL class at the local library. The visit to the store was a good way to keep the boy busy.

So today, Grace was making good on her promise, picking Bảo up early from the motherhouse so he could eat lunch with Molly before they ventured over to the store.

The Golden Hours had always been a magical place for the children when they were younger. They loved how there were so many clocks of assorted measure, how certain dials had the image of the sun and the moon while others had more delicate borders with tiny rosebuds or arabesques.

They also delighted in the sound of the varying chimes every hour and learned quickly how their father had created a system to ensure that the small, interior space didn't become a cacophony of competing sounds as each hour passed. Tom silenced some of the clocks on one week and released the chimes on others, so every one of them was subject to rotation, liberating its unique melody from its inner chamber.

"We're here," Grace hollered to the back as the three of them entered the store's interior.

Tom stepped out from behind the curtain and smiled.

"Dad, can I show Bảo how to crank the clocks?"

"Of course, honey."

It was hard to mask his pleasure at her request. Winding the clocks had been a ritual Tom had delighted in as a child himself, one that he had happily passed down to Katie and Molly. It had also been the first task he'd given Jack when he came to work at the store, before he started to introduce the more complicated repairs that he wasn't sure at that time Jack would ever be able to do.

He watched Molly go toward the corner to retrieve the stool the children always used to reach the crown of the clock, he felt he was finally able to see the big picture of what his father had always hoped the store would be.

"It's a legacy I'm passing down," his father said. "One day you'll understand that the only thing in the world you wish you had more of isn't money. It's time.

"None of us will know how much time we actually have on this earth," he added. "But I can assure you, son, your work here will make you appreciate how each minute pushes into the next and how quickly it moves, more than anyone else who does a different kind of job."

His father had affectionately squeezed his arm when he said it, and Tom now felt his late father's words soak into him. He didn't expect either of his daughters to want to take over the store after he was gone, but Tom hoped that if they had a sense of appreciating how quickly one's life sped forth, he still would have imparted something of value to them. And that was a legacy in itself.

Molly called out to Bảo to follow her.

"First you have to find the crank key," she instructed with an impressive air of confidence. "Every clock has its own one. Dad sells it with the clock." Tom always had a little envelope taped to the back of each clock with its key.

Molly led Bảo over to a tall clock carved out of walnut wood. Majestic and proud, it stood nearly eight feet tall. "This one has the Whittington chimes." She sounded like she was teaching a class in school, proud of the knowledge she could share.

"You can never let the chimes fall to the bottom, it's not good for the clock." She pointed to the brass pendulum suspended on gold chains in the glass window box.

She wasn't sure if Bảo understood everything she was saying, so she tried to speak slowly and point with her hands.

"Here it is." She took the key from the envelope taped in the back and handed it to Bảo. "Now we use the crank to lift up the bells that power the clock."

She climbed on top of the stool and pulled open the clock's top glass window that protected the dial. She inserted the little key and began to turn it clockwise until the right weighted pendulum lifted. Once it was fully suspended, she put the key in the left hole and did the same.

She then took her finger to the brass pendulum in the center and gave it a little push so it would initiate the ticking again.

Bảo took to the job instantly and was soon moving from clock to clock, making sure each one had been properly wound with its respective key.

"It's almost three o'clock," Grace announced, tapping her finger on her own wristwatch, the same one Tom had given to her years before on her late father-in-law's instruction.

Molly knitted her hands. "Oh, Bảo, you're going to love this."

She looked over at the tall presidential grandfather clock and waited until it was precisely three, when suddenly the space was filled with a symphony of chimes.

Bảo's smile was electric as the room exploded in melody.

"Isn't it wonderful?" Molly exclaimed with such glee in her voice. Seeing Bảo's reaction made her return to her own childhood memories of hearing the clock for the first time.

Tom approached Grace and put his arm around her.

"Did you hear I have 'Aura Lee' on the rotation this week, Gracie?" He gave her a flirtatious wink. "Do you remember that one, honey?"

Grace blushed in the children's company. How could she forget the first time her husband had whispered the words "I love you" to her?

They had gone back to the watch store after Tom's father had suggested his son pick out a watch for her. That evening, as she peered over the glass display case admiring the different antique timepieces, the melody of "Aura Lee" soon filled the air. Tom had pulled her to his chest as they began to dance to the clock's bells. He then whispered in her ear "Do you know the melody of 'Aura Lee' is the same as Elvis Presley's 'Love Me Tender'?" He began singing the words.

Even so, many years later she could still remember how he whispered "I love you" over the soft sound of the chimes and how he had lifted her fingertips to his lips and kissed them gently, one by one, before kissing her more deeply on the mouth.

Her whole body warmed at the memory.

For as long as she knew Tom, she was aware how much the Golden Hours had helped those who had made it their life's work. First her father-in-law, then her husband, and then Jack. Now she saw how her daughter was rediscovering its magic through showing Bảo how each minute pushed one of the clock's hands forward.

She smiled. What she wanted to tell Tom, but she'd wait until they were alone, was that his heart was the melody she loved most to hear. She listened to its beating against his chest every night, and it still filled her with wonder.

CHAPTER 59

AS THEIR ENGLISH LESSON CAME TO AN END, ANH TOOK HER marbleized composition book and neatly tucked it into her bag. Dinh studied her movements like a bird-watcher, every gesture of her hand, every quiet glance gave him pleasure.

He had always believed one had to harvest life's little joys where you could find them. A perfect noodle broth, or a smile from a stranger. When he came to this new country, not knowing a single soul, his mind still haunted by nightmares of his journey and the year and half spent in the refugee camp, the small piece of joy here had always been Anh.

On the days he could coax a smile from her, he felt as if he had won a mountain of gold. And on those few afternoons he managed to make her laugh, he felt like he had been crowned an emperor.

And now, after living under the same roof with her for three months at the motherhouse, he wished every day for one more brick of joy, so that eventually he could build her a house with all those blocks of happiness.

He imagined the three of them, Anh, Bảo and himself, underneath this imagined shelter, forging ahead to begin a new life in America.

A comfortable ease fell between them as they waited outside the library for Sister Mary Alice to pick them up. Dinh lifted his head and felt the warm caress of sunshine on his skin.

"How is Bảo enjoying his new bicycle?" Dinh asked, sinking his hands into his pockets.

Anh had told him days earlier how Grace had offered Bảo a spare bicycle that had once been Molly's.

"I'm concerned the color might bother him," Grace said, elaborating that the bike was a deep violet shade with a white leather seat embossed with flowers. "But it's in our garage for him if he'd like it."

When Grace rolled the bike out for Bảo to examine, he wasn't at all disappointed by the color, rather it delighted him. She had no idea that back in Vietnam he had learned to ride a bicycle on only wire frames.

Bảo ran his hand over the shiny metallic finish. A huge grin appeared on his face.

"Like Wonder Twins," he beamed, noticing the color was the exact same shade as the twins' uniform.

Bảo hopped on the bike and gripped its handles, paying no attention to the circle of embossed flowers beneath his seat.

"He loves it," Anh informed Dinh. An enormous smile now emerged on her face. The sight of her lips made Dinh forget all the mistakes he had made with their English tutor. It felt like another brick of happiness had been offered to him. And he accepted it greedily.

CHAPTER 60

SOON BẢO WAS RIDING NEARLY EVERYWHERE ON HIS NEW BIKE.
He had never experienced such a smooth ride, with the firm black tires
rolling beneath him. He rode down to the beach club and met Molly
for a game of shuffleboard. He accepted Sister Mary Alice's invitation to have a small basket put on the handlebars, and he began doing
errands for the motherhouse in exchange for pocket money, saving
every nickel and dime that he earned except for the occasional pack of
gum. But the best news was when Anh told him about the possibility
of working a few hours each week at the Golden Hours.

"Grace says you can help wind the clocks, and maybe also help
clean the tools and put them back in the drawers." She went over and
tousled Bảo's hair. "Jack said he'd be happy to show you how all the
timepieces work."

Bảo's shoulders straightened.

"I'll work hard."

"Yes, you will," Anh agreed.

"And I'll learn to fix watches, just like Dad fixed radios."

Anh looked at Bảo's expression, joy glinted in his eyes. Her nephew
never once mentioned the wounds on Jack's face. He only saw the possibility of learning something new from a person willing to share.

Bảo loved having the wind on his back, his bottom lifting off the
leather seat as he perched with his weight forward, coasting down the
winding hills toward the center of town. It was a thirty-minute ride to
the store, but he never felt tired.

When he arrived that first afternoon, Tom had just left for home and Jack was hunched over his latest repair.

He took off his magnifying visor. Beside him, Hendrix got to his feet and trotted over to greet the newest visitor.

"Hey, welcome," Jack said over the hum of his cassette tape. He quickly lowered the volume, Fleetwood Mac's "Landslide" faded into the background "I'm glad you were up to helping us out here."

Bảo smiled and bent down to rub Hendrix's fur. "I want to learn," he said as his eyes scanned the workshop.

"Do you remember how to wind the clocks like Molly showed you?" Jack pointed to the doorway that led to the showroom.

"Why don't you start in there? That's where Tom started me off, before I learned the bigger stuff."

"Okay," Bảo answered. "I start there." He gave Hendrix one last pat and then stepped into the next room, where he was greeted by the sound of a dozen minute hands ticking in perfect synchronicity.

Over the next few weeks, every time he arrived at the Golden Hours, Bảo tried hard to do his best work. He cleaned the tools in disinfectant and organized them with care. Sometimes when he laid things out at Tom or Jack's workstation, he thought about his mother—how she'd always tended to every object in their family altar with such tenderness and respect. In the same way she'd brought him up to honor his ancestors, he wanted to show his reverence for the two men who now made it possible for him to work at the store.

Sometimes, as he worked alongside Jack, he sensed a small ripple in the air, like a puff of breath on his shoulder. Bảo felt his father's voice whispering how proud he was of his boy. Though it was more of a sensation than a tangible experience, Bảo knew it was real. And when Jack showed him a few simple tasks like how to replace a worn leather wristband or a broken buckle, he felt one step closer to believing this new place could become his home.

But one afternoon as he rode toward the Golden Hours, two boys started heckling at him. Buddy and Clayton had just stepped into Kepler's to get two egg sandwiches to take back to their fort, when Bảo rode past them.

Bảo didn't understand what the word *faggot* meant when the one with the red hair shouted it at him. But he did understand the spitting and the venom with which the word was hurled into the air.

And when the lankier of the two figures, the one with the short, cropped blond hair, had taken a small rock and thrown it in his direction, he got that too. The rock missed Bảo's ankle by inches and ricocheted off the bike's metal fender.

"Who rides a friggin' purple bicycle?" Clayton muttered, tearing off a piece of the roll with his front teeth and swallowing it hard, his Adam's apple pulsating like a little toad trapped in his throat.

"A dumb gook, that's who," he sneered.

Clayton crumbled the wax paper from his sandwich into a tight ball and threw it at the metal waste bin, missing it by a foot.

"I bet my uncle killed a shitload of 'em when he was in 'Nam," Buddy boasted. He kicked the curb with the toe of his sneaker. "And now they're in our own backyard. My mom said a whole boatful of them came over and are staying up the road with some nuns."

In the sunlight, Clayton's eyes looked eerily transparent, as if the blue color had been drained liked pool water, leaving them nearly white. Buddy looked up at him in quiet awe. Everything about him appeared dangerous and cool: the dungarees that hung below his hips, the white T-shirt with the small tear at the hem, and the Puma sneakers. Even his Texas accent made him sound tough. As Bảo pedaled faster away from them, Buddy hung on to his friend's every word.

CHAPTER 61

ON THE KITCHEN TABLE OF THE GOLDENS' HOUSE, A SINGLE sheet of yellow paper announced the annual fundraising dance at the high school.

Katie lifted the paper and smiled. Last year, she'd gone on her mother's insistence and found herself standing alone awkwardly with her friend Millie, who was nice enough but wasn't much of a spark plug of fun. But just yesterday, Linda Atkinson, the most popular girl in her grade—who she'd managed to become friendly with at the beach club due to their overlapping lifeguard shifts—asked her if she was planning to go.

"I'm not sure," Katie answered, trying to sound cool. "Last year, it was a bit of a drag."

Linda rolled her eyes and blew a small pink bubble with her chewing gum, before snapping it back like a salamander catching a fly. "I know, right? But my mom's making me go and help her sell cupcakes as part of my punishment for coming back late from my curfew last week."

"That sucks."

"Yeah, tell me about it." Linda glanced at her wrist. "We have to be back on our shift in ten minutes. But think about coming, we could sell the cupcakes together then maybe go out for ice cream or whatever afterward." She stood up and stretched her long tan arms above her head and adjusted her blond ponytail. "Please try to come, Katie. It'd be so much better if I had a friend there."

Friend. Just the sound of being called Linda's friend was thrilling to her. She took the yellow paper and tacked it to the family's bulletin board before writing the word *Dance* on the wall calendar just as Grace came into the kitchen.

"What's that, honey?"

Katie swung around and smiled at her mother. "The PTA dance. Linda Atkinson asked if I wanted to sell cupcakes with her there. Her mother's baking them for the fundraiser."

"Shelby Atkinson's daughter? I didn't know you've become friendly with her." Grace was honestly a bit surprised, considering the girl had always rebuffed Kate's birthday invitations back when they were in elementary school. And Grace recalled how once Linda said no, an avalanche of other girls suddenly responded saying they couldn't attend either.

"Well, since we started lifeguarding, we've become friends," Katie said.

"Oh, that's a new development...." Grace responded, trying to contain her suspicions. She had an old-world sensibility bred into her which made her believe Linda's true nature had showed at a young age.

"It's just she wasn't that kind to you when you were back in—"

"Mom!" Katie cut her mother off. "That was ages ago, and why can't you just be happy she asked me to go with her?"

Grace's head ached. No one had told her parenting a teenager could be this relentless. She bit her tongue, trying to stop herself from saying things that she knew would only spiral into another fight with her eldest daughter. Didn't Katie understand she only wanted what was best for her? That she didn't want her to have her feelings hurt. She could almost anticipate the scene at the dance with Linda asking Katie to hang out with her until someone better and more socially advantageous came along.

What was it about American motherhood that seemed so paradoxically different from her own experience of being a daughter back home in Ireland? She would never have dared to speak back to her mother, even though there were times—many times—she had wanted to say something about a particular unfairness or frustration but held her tongue out of respect. Her childhood was filled with swallowed words and buried emotion. But here in America, children filled the air with their every thought and feeling. The space between her and Katie often felt so thick, she could barely breathe.

But before she could explain herself to her daughter, Katie had stormed out of the kitchen. Grace heard her daughter's feet stomping loudly on the stairwell as she headed toward her room. The door slammed and Grace looked at the clock. It wasn't even 10:00 a.m. yet, but she already felt weary.

As much as she longed for the laziness of summer break, she now craved school starting and the structure it brought with it.

Minutes later, when Molly stumbled into the kitchen in her pajamas, her face still drowsy with sleep, Grace tried to think of something that would make both of them happy.

"How about we go down to the drugstore for some new notebooks and pencils for school?" she suggested while pouring milk into a bowl of cornflakes.

"I need a new backpack too."

"Well, we can take a drive down to the Foxton Mall for that, and maybe some new shoes too . . ."

Molly perked up. "No saddle shoes this year, Mom, okay? I want penny loafers."

These were requests that were easy to fulfill. Grace stood in the kitchen and poured herself a mug of coffee, while upstairs she could still hear Katie's angry footsteps and the slamming of her bedroom drawers.

Bellegrove High School, with its brick facade and flat roof, was a testament to 1960s functional architecture. Gone were the neoclassical pillars that flanked many of the neighboring towns' schools that were

built in the 1930s or '40s. Through the heavy doors, past the rows
of metal lockers, and down the long corridor was the school gymnasium, where the PTA dance would be held. Even after the long summer break, the scent of school lunches and teammate perspiration still
clung to walls. Katie sprayed a little perfume on her wrist, hoping to fill
her nostrils with something more delicate than the scent of hamburger
and gym socks, before she headed out to the dance.

Grace had volunteered to help with decorations earlier that afternoon and had come home happy to report that the gym had been transformed into a Hawaiian oasis, replete with huge paper flowers made of
colorful streamers and fake tiki torches that someone had made from
old wrapping paper tubing.

Katie was just relieved her mother's volunteer work had ended
earlier that afternoon. There was nothing she wanted less than having
her mother hover around her while she and Linda sold the cupcakes.

She happily slid into the front seat of the family's Pontiac, her
father perched at the steering wheel listening to John Denver on
the radio.

"You look so grown-up, sweetheart." It was hard to see her walk
toward the car in her pink top and denim skirt. If he blinked, he could
have imagined Grace, twenty years earlier, though perhaps wearing a
longer hemline. He could smell she was wearing perfume too.

"Thanks," she answered matter-of-factly. She pulled the sun visor
down, glanced at herself in the mirror and reapplied her lip gloss.

"We should go, Dad. We don't want to be late."

Several blocks away, Clayton grabbed a clean T-shirt from his drawers
and pulled it over his chest. His father's breath, heavy with the scent
of Marlboro cigarettes and Jack Daniels, was still in his nostrils. He
couldn't believe he had actually agreed to go with Buddy to this ridiculous dance at the school. But he realized it wasn't the actual dance

his friend wanted to attend, it was the opportunity to get closer to Katie Golden.

Clayton, however, had no interest in spending one minute longer than he needed to in that dumbass high school. He hated every part of it. The dented lockers, the glass cases with the decades' old trophies, and the cafeteria with its pathetic long metal tables and benches.

But if he had to choose between spending the night at home with his old man and his whiskey breath and his insults, or the evening hanging out with Buddy to see if he could get to second base with that girl, he'd choose the latter.

After all, Buddy had promised him they'd leave after an hour and just head over to the fort.

"We should definitely have a few beers before we go," Buddy puffed, trying to sound cool.

Underneath his bed, in his utility bag, Clayton had already stashed four cans of Pabst Blue Ribbon beer. Buddy promised he'd bring four more.

He swiveled around, hoisted the bag onto his shoulders and headed out the door, his father cursing at him as he slammed the screen door shut.

CHAPTER 62

OUTSIDE, IN THE HIGH SCHOOL PARKING LOT, THE SCENT OF maple leaves fills the early September air. Katie lifts one of the Tupperware cases of frosted cupcakes from the back of a long brown Lincoln. Linda's mother turns off the ignition key, slides a hand into the neckline of her silky, polyester blouse and adjusts her bra strap, before checking her lipstick in the mirror.

"You got that, girls?" Mrs. Atkinson, with her clingy top and high-rise pants, wants to be at the dance probably as little as the girls do. But Adele has made sure all the women in the PTA participated in the annual fundraising dance.

"And don't stack them on top of each other. I don't want the frosting to get smudged. I spent hours redoing the ones that Linda tried to decorate."

Linda, her eyes lined in dark pencil, her lips swiped with lip gloss, makes a face.

"Come on, let's just go set up," she mutters under her breath. Katie beams, absorbing every word of her new friend, basking in her new-found popularity.

"Sure," she says, and her face is bright like the moon. "I'll follow you inside."

The gymnasium has been decorated with ropes of streamers. Electric-blue-and-white crepe paper twists and loops across the border of the room, where banners announce the championships Bellegrove High has won over the years. Outside the doors, the PTA committee has set up long tables where cans of soda and platters of homemade chocolate-chip cookies have already been placed. Linda and Katie set down the trays of cupcakes and pull off the plastic covers.

"Oh, now, don't those look delicious, girls," Adele says, peering down at the perfectly frosted tops. "Did you do all of this, Linda?"

Linda laughed. "Oh, no, my mom made them."

"Well, I'm sure you helped, honey," the voice of Shelby Atkinson interrupts. "Linda's always so helpful."

Adele smiles. "Just like my Buddy. He's always helping around the house."

Only hours before, Adele had asked Buddy to help her decorate the gymnasium with the other women on the committee, but he informed her bluntly that he had already made other plans.

He did not tell his mother that Clayton and he were going to buy beer at the local liquor store and get pounded before the dance. And he certainly didn't tell her the second part of his plan, which involved approaching Katie Golden and making it known he liked her.

"The other women aren't tall enough to hang all the streamers," Adele complained. "And no one is going to want to climb a ladder if they're wearing pumps. Can't you just come for an hour, Bud? You could bring Clayton."

He looked at her with an apathetic glace and shook his head no.

Adele glowered. "If my parents asked me to do the littlest thing, I'd jump to help them!" She sighed deeply to emphasize her annoyance. "And you, young man, can't do anything at all for me!"

But Buddy had learned long ago how to ignore his mother. He tied the laces of his new sneakers, pulled on his new denim jacket, and didn't even look over his shoulder as Adele sent dagger-like glares in his direction. He blithely walked out the door.

**

Clayton was already waiting for him behind the C&P Mini Mart when Buddy rode up and parked his bike near the dumpster. Dressed in a brown denim jacket and faded Wranglers, Clayton's bottom lip swelled from a marble-sized wad of chewing tobacco he had just stuck into the corner of his mouth.

"Hey," he said, before spitting brown juice onto the pavement. "I paid some old guy to get us a six-pack of Pabst."

"Cool." Buddy handed him a crumpled wad of one-dollar bills.

Clayton took the money and stuffed it into his back pocket. "I think we should chug some of them here before we head over."

"A mighty good plan," Buddy agreed and looked around to see if anyone was watching them.

"You sure you really wanna waste time at that stupid dance? I mean we could just get loaded and forget even going over there."

Buddy did his best to appear casual. "Let's just go for a bit."

"It's that girl. . . . You're hot for her, aren't you?" He spit out some more tobacco juice. "I thought she was a Jew."

Buddy flinched. "I just want to see who else is going to be there."

Clayton kicked the asphalt with his boot. He imagined being at the dance would be a lot like being stuck in a zoo, and he had no interest at all in it. He wanted to go back to Texas where the back of his house bordered a large, wild acreage. Where he could hunt and practice his shooting. Where he could skewer his fresh kill on a stick over an open firepit. He didn't want to be a caged animal. He wanted to unbridle himself, unleash all the dark corners of his mind and be free.

"There wasn't any change," the old man announced as he handed the six-pack in a brown paper bag to Clayton. "'Don't drink it all in one place," he advised them through a chipped tooth smile, before walking back to his car parked in the front lot.

Clayton reached into the bag and pulled out a beer for each of them.

"Guess we're not listening to him..." Buddy reached for the beer and pulled the tab open. Both of them drank down the first can in seconds.

Clayton swallowed hard, his wiry neck pulsating as the drink went down. "Man, I hate Pabst, but it's the cheapest."

Buddy felt the head rush fill him with lightness. "It does the trick."

He reached into the bag for his second can, popped it open and finished it even more quickly than the first.

Buzzed, Clayton and Buddy managed to ride their bikes to the high school, both of them searching out bits of garbage and stray cans to run over. When they walked into the gymnasium, the DJ was playing the Bee Gees and a group of girls, including Katie and Linda, were huddled beneath the basketball hoop nursing cans of Sunkist and root beer.

Buddy's eyes lock on Katie, dressed in a denim skirt and pink halter top, her face lit by the glow of party lights. He has slipped into the gymnasium with Clayton at his side, the two of them flushed by the alcohol burning in their veins. The beer has emboldened Buddy. It's made him confident in a way that thrills him. It makes him feel inches taller next to his friend, who moves through the gym like a lynx.

In the past few nights, they have spent hours huddled in their new fort, with a circle of pebbles between them. But while Clayton dreams of shooting squirrels and skinning them with his Swiss Army knife as a form of recreation, Buddy's mind has been full of fantasies about bringing Katie there without Clayton.

She has occupied every inch of his mind the whole summer, ever since he saw her that first week in her red bathing suit at the beach club. Buddy felt the same way looking at her as he did when his father took him to the mechanic to pick up his car and he spotted a poster of

Farrah Fawcett in her red swimsuit. Gone were her braids and braces, the Katie he had known his whole childhood. Every time he saw her now, he felt as if the wind had been sucked out of him, and his mind scattered in a thousand directions. He couldn't help but imagine what she might look like without her lifeguard swimsuit.

His heart pumps with adrenaline as he contemplates whether to ask her to dance (after all, there are three couples moving on the dance floor: Frank Lafferty has his hands stiffly placed on Jenny Rodano's hips, and she has her arms locked around his neck, while two other couples move in the same robotic way).

Buddy mimics his friend's stealthy, uninhibited movements in order to gain confidence. He envisions a coyote, the way Clayton described the animal to him during one of their nights out at the fort, when the moon shone through the cracks of the structure, and his friend detailed the circle of life as he imagined it: *The weak are hunted, so the strong can survive. They prowl silently, each step almost undetectable, before they strike their prey.*

He has stepped away from Clayton, who has retreated to a corner of the gym, and Buddy now hovers just behind Katie's circle of friends. Their laughter is a practiced language of popularity, their scent a powdery mixture of baby powder and chewing gum. He hears Linda Atkinson mention that Brian Flannigan has asked her to go to the movies over the weekend, and the other girls are all giggling and hanging on her every word.

"Hey," he says, pushing into the circle, penetrating the closed formation with a swagger he's practiced in his head for nearly the entire summer. "Katie, can I talk to you for a sec?"

Her face immediately transforms from an expression of polished coolness to a look bordering on personal mortification. "What do you want?" she mutters, clearly annoyed by his intrusion.

He remains undeterred, as the beer has made him feel invincible.

"Clayton and I have some extra beers, and we're wondering if you want to go and drink them with us." There is an awkward pause, but he ignores it. "Bring some of your friends, if you want. . . ."

She looks at him like he is out of his mind. Even worse, her face transforms into a look of disgust. "Are you kidding me, Buddy?" she hisses beneath her breath. She leans into him, and her mouth is only inches away from his ear. He can smell the scent of her strawberry shampoo. *"Can you please just leave me alone?"*

And then she adds something that really crushes him.

"Buddy, you—are—embarrassing me."

Outside the high school, Buddy finds Clayton crouching between their two bicycles and his fury at Katie drips off him like sweat.

"It was looking a little painful for you back there," Clayton mutters. "I thought it best to get some air."

Buddy tears at his cuticle, the sharp pain sending a strange sense of pleasure through him. "She's such a bitch."

Clayton's eyes glint like two sharpened arrowheads. "I was thinking about what we could do to get back at her if she rejected you. . . ."

He laughs and unzips the backpack. One of the two remaining Pabst cans is gone. "Sorry, I drank mine, man, but look what I stole from the supply closet." He reaches into the nylon bag and pulls out a can of white spray paint, the kind used to mark the lines on the school's football field.

"Thought we could have some fun with this."

He lifts the long, metal cylinder up in the moonlight like a grenade.

Buddy looks at the spray can, but first reaches for the remaining can of beer. He snaps it open and drinks it quickly before tossing it to the ground.

"Let's go over there." He points to the rear of the school, not far from the fire exit.

He grabs the spray can from Clayton, looking for a place to unleash his humiliation, which feels like a fresh wound.

"I'm going to do to her what she did to me," he snarls. "I'm going to embarrass the hell out of her."

CHAPTER 63

Bảo promised Anh and the Sisters of Our Lady Queen of Martyrs that he would be home by 8:00 p.m., before it got dark. His new job enabled him to spend a few hours each week at the Golden Hours winding the clocks, ensuring the hands kept moving forward, the brass pendulums kept swinging, and the bells kept ringing. He still found delight each time the various chimes sounded throughout the store, or whenever Jack called him over to teach him something new.

The generous six-dollar weekly salary he received made Bảo feel both useful and proud that he was working to earn his keep. It also gave him the sense that he was preparing for life outside of the motherhouse. Recently, he'd overheard Anh speaking with Sister Mary Alice about coming up with a way for her to earn an income so she could start saving up to rent an apartment. "Not a big place," she said slowly, "but two rooms. One for Bảo. One for me."

Theirs was a culture where the emotions of the heart were rarely expressed in words. His mother never said "I love you" to either him or his father. Instead, she displayed her love through a series of countless, silent gestures. His mother would show her affection through offering him a perfect mango she had peeled just for him, or by sacrificing her bowl of rice so he could eat it instead.

And whenever Bảo looked down at the scar from where his father had bitten him, he would ask himself whether that too had that been a gesture of parental love. That act, as painful as it was, saved Bảo's life by ensuring he wasn't also pulled down into the ocean that night.

He was fully aware that his aunt had been forced to become his caretaker due to tragic circumstances. She'd stoically cared for him from the moment he was orphaned at sea. His mind flashed to her cleansing his wound and wrapping it with strips from the bottom of her cotton shirt. He remembered her applying the betel leaves and later drizzling salt water on his wrist to prevent infection.

But more and more, her quiet, selfless gestures were starting to remind Bảo of the love his late parents had always shown him. He thought, too, about how Anh had helped him to get his job at the Golden Hours. And now, as Bảo overheard her speaking about preparing for a future for them—wanting to get a place of their own and seeking to find work to provide life's essentials for him—his heart now felt her actions deeply. They felt like a mother's love.

Every day, Anh spoke about her desire for independence and self-sufficiency. Bảo overheard his aunt's conversations with Dinh, how they would bolster each other's confidence to keep studying and practicing their English. He listened also to the talks she had with Grace and how eager Anh was to see if it was possible for her to start working part time as a stockgirl at Kepler's Market. She would stock the pyramids of fruit with the ripest ones on top, so that the customers were never disappointed. She would strive to bring joy to those who walked through the store, just as Dinh told her to harvest a bit of it each day for herself.

Bảo, on the other hand, loved spending time inside the watch store. When Jack put on the radio as he worked and strange, wonderful music by bands called the Beatles or the Rolling Stones filled the air. Their unusual names made him smile, for when translated into Vietnamese, the words meant something to him.

It also comforted him to be near Hendrix, to watch as the dog curled up next to Jack and tucked his paws beneath his chin. Looking at Hendrix, he couldn't help but think of Bibo back home and how the animal had been such a beloved companion to him.

But what he loved more than anything else was observing Jack hunched over the table in the workshop toiling on one of the watches that needed repair. It reminded him less about his father's skill with radios; now it simply reminded him of his father's joy.

One evening after Bảo had been coming to the store for a second week in a row, Jack motioned for him to come into the workshop. As Bảo entered the space, Jack pushed his magnifying visor up, the red and mottled left side of his face painfully visible, and announced, "I want to show you something I think you might find interesting."

Bảo inched closer.

Jack patted the work stool next to him and Bảo bounced up on it and sat down.

"Look at this, little fella . . ." Jack lifted a round glass disc from his left hand. Straight down its center was a thin crack. "You see this? The crystal is broken, and it needs to be replaced."

He passed the damaged pocket watch to Bảo.

Bảo took the crystal and began to carefully examine it, marveling how the broken glass still remained intact.

"Tom told me the owner came in and said he'd found the watch in his father's junk drawer. Wanted to know if it was worth anything."

Bảo handed the watch back to Jack and listened.

"When Tom told the man that the casing wasn't made of gold, the guy didn't want to dish out any money to repair it," he shook his head. "So here it is . . . now with us." Jack traced the fracture with his finger. "I learned from the Goldens that there's isn't a timepiece that's not worth saving." He paused, contemplating his words. "Tom gave the man a few dollars for it and once it's fixed, we'll find it a new owner who'll cherish it."

"You can make it work." Bảo beamed optimistically.

"Yes," Jack said. "That's the beauty of it. Fixing broken things . . . it kind of feels like medicine for me."

In the moonlit calm of the workshop, Jack pulled out a square paper envelope from one of the drawers and revealed a new, pristine crystal.

"We're going to make this old watch so spiffy that no one ever mistakes it for junk again."

The replacement glass rested in his palm.

"Now, let me show you how we do this." He pulled a watch case press from the shelf. Then, step by step, he showed Bảo how to slip the new crystal into the gasket.

"Next thing is getting it to keep time," he laughed. "That's the tricky part, Bảo."

He took out his set of tools, lining up the pliers and the small tweezers. "You have to imagine that the inside of a watch is like a human heart. When it's broken, you need to mend it with a lot of care."

The energy between the two of them shifts as they work side by side.

As Jack guides him, Bảo feels the same warmth he once experienced with his dad back in Vietnam. A wave of fascination and excitement washes over him, for he is eager to learn something new. He is grateful to Jack for sharing his wisdom.

Jack does not say how Bảo's presence in the store has helped him. He does not say that when they listen to the songs on the radio together, the music brings him back to another time, to a part of his history where men like Doc or Stanley are still alive beside him. Or Becky is nestled against him in bed.

It gives him great satisfaction that Bảo now considers the workshop a safe space to practice his English, that he asks if he can arrange the toolbox or wind the smaller timepieces in the display case, not just the larger ones displayed in the showroom. He is comforted by the boy's affection for Hendrix, his ability to be quiet and still when he is deep in concentration.

But what is unexpected—and what he's almost at a loss of words on how to express—is the realization that the child has made him feel like he has something of worth to offer.

"We fix it together," Bảo says. And Jack's heart nearly explodes within his chest for it's the same sweetness and innocence he saw at a distance when he cleaned desks at Foxton or when he sat beside Stanley with his Bible. It is so pure and bright, it lights up the room.

He realizes that the Golden Hours has become a sacred space for yet one more person. A refuge for the broken to heal.

CHAPTER 64

BUDDY SEIZES THE CAN OF WHITE SPRAY PAINT AND WALKS toward the back of the gym as the music pounds from inside. Queen's "We Are the Champions" is playing, and everyone is loudly chanting the lyrics.

He doesn't think about what he's going to write, but the humiliation and rage he feels toward Katie, combined with the beer, fuels him.

He takes the paint, holds the nozzle down with his forefinger, and scrawls in large white letters, *Katie Golden is a WHORE.*

Clayton grins as his friend steps away from the brick facade to reveal what he's written. He stares at the letters, watching with great titillation as their wet borders drip down the wall like the edges of an angry scar.

"We should probably get the hell out of here before we get caught," Buddy spits as he throws the can into the shrubs and casts a frenzied glare in Clayton's direction.

Neither of the boys saw Bảo riding past the school on his way back from the clock store. Just as he rolls his bike around the rear perimeter, he eyes Buddy stepping away from his hateful graffiti.

Bảo stares at the words. It takes him only seconds to recognizes Katie's name and the last name of the one family who has shown him and his aunt Anh kindness since they arrived. And although he does not know the exact meaning of the sentence, the fury and haste in which it has so obviously been written exudes a palpable aggression. He immediately senses that the menacing white strokes of spray paint are a slur against Katie.

He stands near the bushes, still perched on his bike, and considers saying something to the boys, but the words are caught in his throat.

But even so, as the boys hoist their legs over their bicycles and start to ride off, his desire to reprimand them and punish the villains, just like his favorite superheroes would, gets the better of him.

He pushes off pavement with his foot and begins to follow them.

As Bảo pedals behind them, still at a distance, the other boys don't yet take notice of him. In his mind, he is channeling the warrior spirits of Giong, Jayna, and Zan. He is thinking how he will correct a wrong that has been done to Molly's sister and make it right.

Clayton and Buddy continue to ride far ahead, inhaling air into their lungs enjoying the sensation of speed beneath them.

The tall lanky one rides on a dirt bike, his knees nearly up to the handlebars, the fat wheels veering *S* shapes as he pedals forth. He is laughing with his head thrown back, the hair on his head rising in the rush of autumn wind.

It isn't until they approach the Ace Hardware Shopping Center and steer toward the entrance that leads to the reservoir and their fort that Buddy senses they are being followed.

They coast toward the back of the hardware store and throw their bikes down on the curb. It is only then that Buddy turns around and sees Bảo staring at them with a look that transforms him from a boy wanting to be a hero to a boy now clearly afraid.

"What the fuck do you want?" Clayton is the first to break the quiet in the night. He takes a step closer to Bảo. "Fucking faggot with his purple bicycle!" he bellows, spitting to the ground.

"He's got flowers under his ass." Buddy points a finger to the leather seat.

"You wrote..." Bảo takes his hand and starts gesturing large sweeps of writing. "About Ka... tee. I will tell..."

Clayton's laughter suddenly stops. He lunges toward Bảo, throwing him to the pavement.

Bảo is featherlight; his body crashes to the asphalt with little effort from Clayton.

"He's going to rat us out," Clayton seethes.

Buddy's heart is pounding. He's the one who's going to get in trouble. He can instantly see his mother's face in front of him, furious that he's brought shame to their family.

He cannot have Bảo tell anyone about what he did, not the police, not the school, and most of all not Katie's family.

"You gonna be a snitch?" he mutters as he kicks Bảo over and over.

Bảo cries out in pain, his body buckling under the force of Buddy's foot. "Stop," he whimpers, and he lifts his hands up to protect his face.

The boys now don't talk to each other. As Bảo lies on the ground crying, Clayton hoists him up over his shoulder and heads toward their fort.

Anh stares at the dial of the mounted clock in the den of the motherhouse. It's nearly 9:00 p.m., and her heart is pounding because Bảo has not yet returned. The ride from the Golden Hours back to Our Lady Queen of Martyrs should not take him longer than thirty minutes. Fear seizes her heart.

She does not want to disturb the Sisters, but she worries if he might have run away again or even worse, hit by a car? She will give it five more minutes before she walks down the corridor to where Sister Mary Alice's room is and then she will knock.

But before that, she decides she will go to the room of the one person she knows she can freely share her worry with. She goes to the community kitchen where, just a few minutes before, she saw him with a cup of tea and practicing the exercises in his English workbook.

"What is wrong, *em*?" Dinh asks her in Vietnamese.

"It's Bảo," she explains. His name breaks in her throat, and she quickly covers her mouth with her hand because she thinks she might cry. "He's late. He's always been on time for the past two weeks. He never comes home a minute late." She taps her wrist. "I'm so worried." She begins to cry.

To Dinh, her coming to him now in her moment of distress is a sign she thinks more of him than the others they live with at the motherhouse.

"You and I will wait for him for a few more minutes . . . then we'll go find Sister Mary Alice. We won't wait too long, I promise." Dinh takes her hand, and the warmth penetrates his skin.

Jack has now finished his last repair for the evening and has no other chores to do, as Bảo wound up all the clocks before he left for the night. He glances at the pocket watch they worked on together and smiles, buffing it one more time with a cloth before placing it in the drawer. He then glances at the time. It's a couple hours earlier than he typically takes Hendrix for their long walk, but the dog is pacing around the room, restless to go out.

"What's wrong, boy? You want some exercise?" Jack bends down and pats Hendrix's black coat. The dog nuzzles his snout into the side of his hand and his eyes look up with pure adoration. The light in the store has shifted from twilight to nearly darkness and it strikes Jack that the long nights of summer have already shortened. He wonders if the stars will be particularly bright this evening as he walks Hendrix toward the reservoir.

He pulls the dog leash from the chair and snaps it onto Hendrix's collar.

After about twenty minutes into their walk, he arrives at the entrance of the reservoir where he finds himself startled by the sight of three bikes thrown to the ground, and one small sneaker turned on its side.

But it is the sight of the purple bicycle with the flowered leather seat that sends Jack into full panic. His body rushes with adrenaline and fear, a frightening combination he hasn't experienced since he was back in the jungles of Vietnam. His body becomes rigid, and his heart beats wildly inside his chest as he senses that something terrible has happened or is about to.

Hendrix must detect the changes rushing through him, the fear that's changing his body chemistry. He must smell it deep in his dark, wet nostrils and hear it in his ears that are now in high alert. Hendrix barks and rushes toward the long winding path, pulling Jack into the forest.

Less than thirty minutes before, the boys pounced on Bảo and began dragging him toward the fort.

Clayton's laugh is menacing, and Bảo is afraid. It suddenly hits him he has no actual superhero powers. He cannot transform himself like the Wonder Twin Zan into a powerful element of water, like a blizzard or a monsoon. He cannot vanquish these boys who threaten him and who have written bad things against Katie.

He weakens quicker than he wants to, as the tall one with the yellow hair is far too strong. His arm feels like a rope, the muscles sinewy and hard.

Bảo is breathing hard as Clayton throws him inside the shelter made of sticks, twigs, pieces of broken lumber and plastic tarp.

His body feels like it has been shot with arrows. The pain is intense and overwhelming. His face is streaked with tears.

"What are we going to do with him?" asks Buddy.

"We can't let him snitch on us." Clayton's eyes are fierce, and his bicep is locked beneath Bảo's chin. "I'm not getting in trouble for what *you* did back at the school."

Buddy only hears "what *you* did" and begins to panic.

He bites down hard on his lip, and the metallic taste of his own blood on his tongue surprises him. *"We need to make him shut up."*

Bảo begins to wrestle underneath Clayton's tightening grip. His face is darkening like a ripening plum.

It is then that Clayton's eyes flash toward the circle of small pebbles around the makeshift firepit. Small and smooth as tiny moons, he reaches for one of them and brings it slowly to Bảo's lips.

Bảo kicks the earth and desperately shakes his head no.

In the back of his mind, Clayton hears the words his father threatened him with earlier. "Here," Clayton hisses. "Swallow this, you little gook." He pushes the marble-sized rock into Bảo's mouth and orders him to swallow it.

CHAPTER 65

When Bảo still hasn't returned home by 10:00 p.m., Dinh urges Anh to tell Sister Mary Alice.

"She will be sleeping," Anh says nervously, but without any other options, Dinh and she rap on the sister's door.

The first thing that Sister Mary Alice does is tighten the sash of her bathrobe and then head to her desk to find her address book. In precise delicate penmanship she has two numbers written under Grace and Tom Golden, their home number and the number for the Golden Hours. She gestures for Anh to come inside her room, and they call the store first, hoping that Jack will just pick up and tell them that Bảo was only running a bit late.

But no one picks up at the store. So Sister Mary Alice calmly dials the Golden house.

"Grace, it's Sister Mary Alice," she begins slowly in a measured voice. "I'm sorry to be calling at this hour, but Anh is here with me, and she's concerned Bảo isn't home yet. She glances at the clock on the wall. "Anh says he's typically back home by eight on the nights he works at the store."

She hears a rustle on the other end of the line. "And Jack didn't answer the phone?" Grace inquires. "Tom says Jack usually works until ten or eleven some nights."

"No, I tried there first, but no one picked up."

"That's very strange," Grace says, her voice revealing her concern. "Tom says he's going to head down to the store just to check. It's not a problem."

"Are you sure?"

"Yes. I'd go with him, but I have to head over to the high school to pick up Katie."

Sister Mary Alice thanks them and hangs up the receiver. She turns to Anh and tells her that Tom is heading over to the Golden Hours. "Don't worry," she pats Anh's hand gently. "He'll be there in only a few minutes and I'm sure he's going to tell us everything is okay."

The Pontiac station wagon slowly pulls up to the entrance of Belle-grove High School, where strangely, Grace, doesn't seem to see any of the students congregating. As she drives toward the back, where she expects there will be open parking spots, she sees a huge crowd of students and even some parents amassed by the rear wall. She parks the car, grabs her handbag, and gets out.

"Oh, heavens, has something happened?" She catches Leslie Francis and her daughter Caroline's attention as they try to hurry to their car. Leslie's face turns white.

"What is it?" Grace leans in, concerned that a child might have been hurt. But there are no ambulances or paramedics by the crowd. "Is everything okay, Leslie? I hope no one's hurt. . . ."

Caroline is squirming next to her mother, her eyes unable to look up and meet Grace's.

"Well, we should be going," Leslie says quickly. "Good to see you, Grace."

Caroline follows her mother's lead and quickly heads in the direction of their car.

It is only when Grace is a few steps away from the crowd that her eyes land on the graffiti on the wall, where she sees her daughter's name scrawled in white paint. And then, most painful, the horrible word connected to it.

She feels the weight of stares on her, but she pushes past the crowd that has congregated with voyeuristic curiosity on how she'll react. But she doesn't care. Her first instinct is to find Katie.

Linda Atkinson's mother tells her she thinks Katie is inside. Grace sees Linda is standing with a bunch of other girls, but not with her daughter.

Inside the school, in a dimly lit corner, just outside the girls' bathroom, Grace finds Katie with one of her old friends from elementary school, Rachel, who is rubbing her back and holding another tissue out to Katie to wipe away her tears.

Katie looks up. Her expression is raw with vulnerability. "Mom . . ." she sobs, her expression falling, her cheeks streaked red from crying. She rushes toward her mother and falls into her open arms. She is heaving, trying to catch her breath.

Grace holds Katie tightly to her chest, her nose buried into her hair, and tries to calm her.

"Let's walk out the front entrance," she says gently. "You can wait there, and I'll get the car."

Her daughter looks like a little girl to her again, one grateful for her protection. She hates to think that a hateful teenage prank could bring them closer. But when Katie squeezes her hand, as if beseeching her not to leave her, Grace tightens her grip around her daughter's fingers, a silent language between them, letting her know that everything is going to be okay.

CHAPTER 66

As Tom enters the store, the place is completely dark, and neither Jack nor Bảo is there. He switches on the light, heads back to the workshop, and lifts the receiver off the phone to call Grace and let her know that no one else is there. But Molly has answered instead and tells him that Grace is still at the school.

"I'll call over to Jack's apartment. Maybe there's a chance he took Bảo there to show him something. . . ."

"But he never invites anyone up there," Molly reminds him. "I've always wanted to visit, but you told me how private he is, Daddy."

His daughter is right. "I know, honey, but it can't hurt to call. Tell Mommy I'll drive around a bit looking for them if he's not home." He keeps his words to a minimum, not wanting Molly to panic. He tries to convince himself that many things could have happened; perhaps Bảo was watching TV with Jack or out walking with him and Hendrix. He picks up the phone again to call Jack. But after several seconds with no answer, he hangs up the receiver, grabs his car keys, and heads out to find them.

Bảo manages to swallow the first pebble after Clayton orders Buddy to hold his arms back and he shoves the rock into his mouth. The second one is still pinched between Clayton's fingers when Buddy grows afraid.

"Come on man, that's enough," he cuts in as Bảo continues to wriggle beneath his grip. Clayton pushes the rock into Bảo's pursed lips.

Bảo tries to scream several times, but Clayton just pushes his hand over his mouth and threatens to suffocate him.

"He can't swallow all those stones." Buddy eyes the circle of rocks in the fort's center. "He'll suffocate, Clay. . . . He'll die. . . ."

Bảo is kicking now underneath Buddy's grip, grunting as Clayton tries to push the next stone down.

And then suddenly they all hear the sound of a dog barking.

"What the fuck?" Buddy says as he lets go of Bảo, who lunges forth and falls to his knees, gasping for breath.

Soon they also hear the sound of heavy footsteps, not just the barking and panting of a dog. Jack pulls away the flimsy shower curtain entrance and bends down to enter the fort.

"What's going on here?" his voice booms, as he spots Bảo curled in a ball on the dirt floor, his face mottled with cuts and emerging bruises, his body heaving, and his hand grasping his throat.

Buddy doesn't say a word. He has never seen Jack up close before, only from a distance when he picked up his laundry or went into the watch store. But both times his head was bent down, and it was difficult to see his damaged features clearly. Now, however, Jack is hovering over them, his expression transforming into one of rage as he realizes these boys have hurt Bảo.

"We didn't do anything," Buddy insists, but Jack is looking straight at Clayton, who, in his shock, hasn't dropped the third pebble still grasped in his hand. Jack sees the dirt patches on Clayton's knees, and the eyes that are struggling to take Jack's disfigurement in fully. Both of them believe the other is a monster.

He is about to lift Clayton off the ground and slug him when his instincts surprise him. Still holding Hendrix's leash in one hand as the dog snarls and barks at the two older boys, Jack reaches for Bảo.

Clayton and Buddy run. They run fast, their chests heaving as they dart over the uneven terrain, branches scratching at their faces. They reach their bicycles and frantically try to race home.

Jack lifts Bảo into his arms. The fragrance of soil and wet leaves, the scent of boyhood mixed with perspiration and fear, draws him back to the jungle in Vietnam. He carries Bảo, clutching him to his chest. Not slung over his shoulder like Chief had carried Stanley all those years earlier, but with the same honor in his heart. Jack holds Bảo high above the forest floor, a man focused on protecting his friend.

CHAPTER 67

WITH BẢO STILL IN HIS ARMS, JACK REACHES THE PAY PHONE outside the hardware store and immediately calls 911.

"I need an ambulance . . ." he pleads to the operator.

The boy is gripping his abdomen, twisting in Jack's arms.

"You're going to be okay," Jack whispers over and over again.

The little boy moans, his wet tears penetrate Jack's shirt. "Help is on the way, little man. Just stay with me and try to breathe!" A part of him is suddenly channeling Doc, using the same words he used to reassure, to calm.

He holds Bảo closer and warms him with his body heat. He reaches for the phone to make one more call.

"Bảo's been hurt!" he shouts. He quickly dials the Goldens' house and informs Tom, who has just walked in the door. Adrenaline pulses through his veins. "Meet me at the hospital as soon as you can!"

Once Bảo reaches the emergency room, the X-rays reveal just how lucky he was that Jack reached him when he did. Had he ingested one more stone, he might have suffocated. The two that he ingested will fortunately pass through his system with the help of some cod liver oil. After she's been brought to the hospital by Tom, Anh never leaves Bảo's side.

Laid out on the hospital gurney, Bảo looks tinier than she remembered him even just a few hours before. A little boy the world has finally given her, and she knows it's her duty to take care of him, protect him as though he was her own.

But several other figures are also there with her in the hospital waiting room. Tom has quietly relieved Jack, who went home immediately after the doctors said Bảo would recover. Dinh and Sister Mary Alice are also lending their support. Grace will arrive a few hours later after she has managed to console Katie and assure her that the school's grounds crew will wash off the graffiti early the next morning. "It will all fade away," she tried to comfort her eldest as she took her handkerchief and blotted her daughter's cheeks. "No one will remember this in a few days, I promise you . . ."

"A few days?" Katie shakes her head. "I think everyone's going to be talking about it for years!" She sobs.

"I know it hurts now," Grace whispers as she brushes the hair out of Katie's eyes. "And I hate to see you in pain. . . ." She leans down over the bed and kisses the top of her daughter's head, inhaling the fragrance of her shampoo, her baby-powder perfume, traces of her daughter she has only smelled this summer at a distance—are so close now it brings tears to her eyes. How wrong she's been to think her daughter no longer needed her. Her heart swells and breaks at the same time as she struggles to find the right words to assure Katie that this terrible ordeal that feels so humiliating to her now will eventually pass.

"Your grandfather believed one thing, Katie—the best way to vanquish painful memories is to move forward." She lifts her daughter's hand from where it rests on the flower quilt and brings her fingers to her lips and kisses them.

"But, Mom, everyone at school will be talking about me."

Her eyes glance at the plastic clock mounted on the wall, then an old Snoopy doll on a bookshelf, a remnant of Katie's childhood that Grace is surprised to see Katie has not yet packed away, despite her attempts this summer to reinvent herself.

"Minute by minute, you'll get past this, until one entire day passes into the next and it's all been forgotten."

Katie closes her eyes, exhaustion washing over her. "I think it was Buddy, Mom. And I didn't say anything bad to him. I only told him he was embarrassing me after he asked me to leave with him in front of all my friends."

Grace doesn't answer. She pulls the sheets closer to Katie's chin. "For tonight, let's focus on you and Bảo. I promise we'll talk about Buddy soon, but for now, I want you to try to get some sleep."

That same night, Adele will be awakened by the bright lights of a police car streaming through her bedroom. She will wrap herself in her pink chenille bathrobe, the sash tied tightly around her waist. Her fingers clawing at her heart when the officers inform her they must speak with her son.

CHAPTER 68

SCHOOL BEGAN LIKE ANOTHER CYCLE OF LIFE, A SEASON ALL ITS own. Bảo started his first week of school knowing he had at least one friend at Bellegrove Intermediate and another who, although older, gave him a pocket watch after he was released from the hospital. "It was waiting for its new owner," Jack said as he gifted him the timepiece they'd restored together. Anh started working part time at Kepler's Market and soon began saving for a down payment to rent a nearby apartment for her and Bảo.

One afternoon during those first weeks of autumn, Anh finally did what she had wanted to do since she brought Bảo home from the hospital. She wanted to personally thank Jack for how he had the saved the child she now considered her son.

She knew how deeply private he was, that he kept himself away from prying eyes, but she felt compelled to express her thankfulness to him. So, despite her self-consciousness about her English, Anh heard the encouraging words of Dinh in her head, reminding her that she needed to honor Jack in some way for his heroic act.

Anh realized it was still too early in the day for Jack to be working at the store. That he was probably tucked inside his apartment, maybe reading or watching TV. But she hoped that he'd still allow her to say some words of gratitude in person to him, so she walked to the side entrance of the old brick building and looked for the single buzzer for the apartment upstairs. She took her finger and pressed it.

***

The sound of the buzzer caught Jack off guard. He had been living above the Golden Hours for nearly five years, and he could still count the number of times someone had rang the intercom. Tom had stopped by on a few occasions during his first few weeks there, when Jack hadn't even unpacked yet, and there were a few visits from a plumber or electrician coming by to make a repair that Jack himself couldn't fix.

The voice on the other end now surprised him.

"It is me, Anh," she announced. "I have come to thank you."

Jack was still in his bedclothes. His hair uncombed. His face unshaven. The only one who had begun his morning ablutions was Hendrix, who had eaten his breakfast and now sat curled next to Jack's chair calmly licking his front paws.

The apartment reflected Jack's near-monastic way of life, so there was hardly anything now to clean up. "Just give me a minute," he spoke into the receiver quickly, reaching for his khakis draped over one of the two chairs by the small card table where he ate. "I'll let you up in a sec. . . ."

He jumped up, hurriedly brushed his teeth, and quickly combed his hair to hang over the left side of his face.

After he buzzed Anh in, Jack quickly pulled the duvet over his bed and glanced around the studio apartment. There was little else he could do in such a small amount of time except apologize about the sparseness of his existence.

He opened the door just as she was coming up the second flight of stairs. She carried in front of her a small basket of perfectly ripe apples and pears.

"I wanted to bring you gift. . . ." She offered him the fruit. "I hope I don't bother you . . . coming to your place."

He felt awkward and humbled by the earnestness of her gesture.

"You saved my boy." She touched her chest. "I must find right way to thank you."

"It was just fortunate that I took my walk a little earlier than normal that night," he said, deflecting her praise. He felt shabby standing in his worn clothes. "I suppose we all just have to be grateful for this guy," he gestured toward Hendrix, who had happily trotted to the door to greet the unexpected guest. "He's the one who wanted to head out early."

"I am grateful to you, too," she said and knelt down and patted Hendrix lightly on his back. "You save my Bảo. He safe because of you."

In that second, Jack felt a softening of his shame and the embarrassment of his scars and humble circumstances melt away.

"Do you want to come in?" He surprised himself by the offer. "I mean, I never have people over, but I could make you a cup of tea or something. . . ." He lifted the basket of fruit and his face twisted into a smile. "It's awfully nice of you to have brought me this."

"Yes." She dipped her head and followed him inside. "Thank you."

The cushions on the soft brown leather couch that had followed him from his apartment in Foxton barely sunk under Anh's delicate frame. With her hands folded elegantly in her lap, she looked around the sparse room for clues about this man who she knew so little about, other than he wore his suffering on his face. His scars, she knew, were a result from serving in the American War, his pain tethered to a place she once called her home—and she wasn't sure what she was supposed to do with that knowledge. But Anh could do nothing but accept his wounds as a terrible fact she had no power to change.

As he went to boil a kettle of water on the stove, she looked around and noticed how few possessions he had. A hanging plant with ropes of heavy green leaves dangled from the ceiling, a stack of records was neatly placed by his stereo, there was a cardboard box that look liked it had recently been rummaged through, containing some papers and a purple medal on top. But in the corner of the room, where his bed lay with the coverlet pulled hastily to the top, there was a photograph of a young man with his arm thrown around the shoulder of a girl with long brown hair.

She took the cup of steaming hot tea between her two hands and breathed in the fragrant vapor with closed eyes.

"This smells good," she said, blowing on the rim of the mug before she drank.

"It's just Lipton," he laughed. "But I like it."

She lifted her cup for another sip and smiled.

"You are kind man," Anh said. "I wish I could do more to thank you. Or thank Grace and her family."

Jack sat back in the hard dining room chair he had pulled closer to the sofa. "Ever since I moved here"—he lifted one hand and gestured around the apartment—"from the moment I started working nights downstairs . . . I've thought the same thing . . . how can I thank them for everything they've done for me?"

She nodded and her eyes wettened. "It so hard at first when we get here. To be alone. Then Bảo run away, and I feel . . ." She placed her cup down on his wooden coffee table. "I feel I fail him."

In Anh's company, Jack felt his typical steely veneer soften. Was it because they were relative strangers that they could be this open with each other? He wasn't sure, but something in him welcomed being able to speak so freely.

"You didn't fail him." Jack leaned forward and put his hands on the table. "I think you're very brave just to have even come to a new place. You study to learn a new language, to build a new life. . . ."

Anh looked down and knotted her hands. None of the things Jack described were the hardest things she had endured.

"My husband, the men they beat him. Killed him. My baby died soon later. If you not find Bảo, I lose him too." She bit her lip and tried not to let her tears fall. "You lose wife, girlfriend, too, Jack?" She pointed to the lone picture frame.

The silence that followed was thick as smoke. Jack lifted his tea to his lips and swallowed, his eyes staring into his cup. "Yes and no, I suppose," he finally answered. He hadn't spoken about Becky to anyone for years now, and yet she was still a part of his daily existence, never far from his every thought.

"She wasn't my wife, but I loved her." Jack placed the mug down and his eyes drifted toward the hanging plant. Did he dare unburden himself to this woman who was only starting to learn English, who he knew for far less time than he did Grace or Tom? Even they did not know his story fully.

"She didn't die, and I didn't lose her, exactly." He took a deep breath. Then another. "I know exactly where she is."

CHAPTER 69

HE TELLS HER SLOWLY ABOUT HOW HE'S ONLY EVER LOVED one girl. Becky with the warm, bottomless eyes, the smile that could light up a room . . .

"Back in Vietnam, I used to tell my buddy Doc that Becky was like sunshine at midnight." He swallowed hard. Saying Doc's name with hers was almost too much for him to handle without breaking down.

"I called her after my last burn treatment. But I wasn't exactly truthful with her." He lifted a finger up to his face. "As you can imagine, this isn't easy to look at. . . . It's a lot for someone to take in and not get sick to their stomach." He took another painful breath. "And spending a life with a monster . . . well, who'd ever be up for that?"

Anh put her teacup down. Her eyes didn't waver from Jack's face.

"So I made up a story. I told her I had a friend who'd had a serious injury to his face and asked if I could bring him home to live with us. But she didn't like the idea too much. Let's just say she told me she only wanted her 'handsome Jack' home." He slid back in the chair. "And I ain't too pretty now, as you can see."

Anh wrinkled her brow, trying to concentrate and comprehend Jack's every word. "Maybe I don't understand. You never let her have a try? You never let this Becky see you when you come home from war?"

"No."

"This story so sad. You never see her again?"

"I didn't say that. . . ."

Anh looked puzzled. "I don't get meaning of your words."

He looked out the window, then at Anh. His one good eye shimmered like a wet stone.

He gripped his hands together, rubbing them together to ease his nerves. And then finally Jack summoned up the courage to unburden himself and tell the whole story.

Three months after that call with Becky, Jack found himself haunted by his decision. It was one thing to spare her the horror of seeing his disfigured face, but it was quite another to close the door shut and never see her again. As much as Becky's words had hurt him, he had invented his friend with the traumatic injury to gauge her reaction. Jack would never know whether Becky's answer would have been different had she known he was speaking about himself.

One night after spending the entire day inside, his spirits lower than he could have ever imagined possible, Jack decided to get the courage to call Becky again, but the number was disconnected. He then fell into a terrible depression, often missing his appointments at the Brooke Army Medical Center. Had it not been for Nurse Starr calling him and insisting he come in, he would have abandoned his health completely. Without Becky in his life, he no longer had the will to live.

During one of his visits to check how his skin grafts were healing, Nurse Starr finally got him to reveal what was causing the changes in his behavior.

"I know none of this is easy, Jack," she sympathized as she began his medical intake. "But you've always come to your appointments in the past." She touched his hand gently to take his pulse. "Has there been something in particular that's upset you?"

He shrugged. He had no desire to tell this nurse, no matter how attractive or kind she was, what he was actually feeling.

"You can tell me anything, Jack," Nurse Starr pressed. "You know that, right?"

Jack sighed. Nurse Starr had been one of the few people during his rehabilitation that had gone beyond the call of duty. During those earliest, most painful days of his treatment, she had been the one who sat by his bedside and held his hand, because she knew he had no family, and she didn't want him to be alone. He now considered Nurse Starr a friend.

"When I was in the hospital, I didn't have a choice but to have you guys inspect every inch of this." He touched his finger to the left side of his face. "But now I wake up and think . . . why bother? There's no point . . . not even my girl wants to see this . . ."

Barbara Starr gently placed Jack's wrist on his lap and removed her stethoscope.

"This is the first time in over a year I've heard you mention a girl, Jack. You have a girlfriend?"

"I did."

She stepped back and looked at him. He was clearly suffering more than usual. He typically took great pains to cover this scar with the top part of his hair which he had grown longer since his release. But today, he looked like he hadn't even bothered to change his clothes from the day before.

"Whatever's happened, you need to give it another try," she offered gently. "One needs to find a way to keep love in our lives, Jack. Always. It's so important. Without it our hearts become as dry as paper."

Jack laughed. "That sounds awful."

"Trust me," she told him. "We all need love to survive."

That evening Barbara's words haunted him. Becky had been the only person beside his mother whom he had ever loved. He wasn't sure he would have survived his tour in Vietnam had he not had her to return to. It had always been Becky who he imagined being the one to welcome him home. Even now, he would often conjure her face from memory, her green eyes and bright smile, just so he had something beautiful to imagine before his recurring nightmares inevitably took over.

He opened the refrigerator, took out a beer and drank it quickly. Then, on impulse, he called the one person who might be able to tell him where Becky was.

He called her mother.

In the past, Mrs. Dougherty had never revealed how she felt about Jack. Though the fact that she had not come to his mother's funeral made him suspect she had never thought he was good enough for Becky.

But this time, hearing his voice on the other end of the receiver, she made her thoughts clear.

"Why the hell are you calling now, Jack?" she asked, her voice steely and cold. "Do you have any idea how much you've hurt my daughter? You call her, tell her you've returned with some injured friend you want her to find space for in her little apartment, which is barely large enough for one person, possibly two, but three . . . and then forget about it and never call her again?"

"I just . . ." He started to stammer. "I just—" He cut himself short. "I called her number, and it says it's disconnected."

"Jesus Christ, Jack." She made a click with her tongue. "You called her over a year ago. What was she supposed to do with her life? Wait around?" Her sigh revealed her deep exasperation with him. "Becky's moved away. She got a job teaching as an elementary school teacher in Foxton, New York."

There was no answer on the other end of the line. She took a deep breath and then her voice softened slightly. "Jack . . . do you want to give me your number so I can tell her you called . . . ?"

The dial tone soon rang in Mrs. Dougherty's ear. Jack had already hung up.

Jack had done few things in his life on impulse. But packing up his rented apartment and dumping what belongings he had in the old VW van he bought for a couple hundred bucks a few months before was certainly one of them. He looked on a map and estimated it would take him three days to drive from San Antonio to Foxton, New York. He wasn't thinking of how crazy he was to drop everything without any advance planning. He just knew he needed to see her one more time.

It wasn't hard to find the elementary school in the small town. All he had to do was go to a pay phone and call the operator, who told him the street address. What was harder was remaining unseen. He knew that the mere sight of him lurking around a school could attract unwanted attention.

And yet he didn't want anything from anyone, and he certainly didn't want to alert the school. All he wanted to do was see her.

So Jack parked his car in the early hours before school started, away from the main parking lot on a side street that still had a view of the entrance, and waited. One thing he knew about Becky was she was always early.

She was the fourth person to walk toward the entrance. He sensed it was her even before seeing her face in profile. Her gait, the way she placed her palm over her brown saddle bag, the carefree way she threw back her hair and laughed with another woman who was clutching a stack of papers. He just knew it was her. And the sight of her laughing, the image of her standing there with her long chestnut hair and slim physique, filled him with something that he hadn't experienced since he woke up in the burn unit of Brooke. Jack finally felt alive.

***

Anh reached for her cup of tea but found it empty. "But then what happened?"

She wasn't sure if she has grasped all the pieces in his story correctly. She wanted to know if he ever told this woman how much he loved her.

Jack opened his palms in his lap and stared at them, then lifted his eyes to Anh's. "What happened? I'd gotten what I needed. I saw she had stayed the same. That she was still as beautiful as she had been and that she was now teaching children, as she always dreamed she would. But I still had this," he said, pointing to his face. "That wasn't going to change."

Anh's face fell. "This story . . . it is too sad. . . ."

Jack lifted his head and stared directly at Anh, showing his face completely.

"I think it goes back to what that nurse told me . . . one has to find a way to keep love in your life. . . ."

Anh nodded, hanging on to his every word. "Yes, but why you leave?"

Jack bowed his head. "I didn't leave completely, Anh. I got a job at Foxton Elementary as a night janitor. . . . I worked there just so I could be as close to her as I could. I saw the classroom she had filled with joy. I saw her desk filled with all the pencils she touched and papers she had graded." He lifted his head, and a pained smile crossed his lips. "I realized that was as close to love as I was going to get."

CHAPTER 70

LOVE, THIS THING THAT AMERICANS SO ENJOYED REFERRING to, was an abstract concept to Anh. So much value was put into that word—so many expectations that she wondered how it ever managed to keep afloat.

Anh had always believed love was tied up with duty. A sense of respect and obligation to uphold those who had sworn to take care of each other. But she had learned one thing since her husband's death and that boat taking the lives of Bảo's parents. And it echoed what Jack's nurse had told him. One needed to find a way to keep love in one's life at any cost. Had she not had Bảo, Anh wondered if she would have abandoned all hope. He had given her a sense of commitment in her new life. When she imagined herself working, it was because she wanted to provide him with the best possible life. She studied her English books long into the night, after many of the others at the motherhouse had gone to sleep, saying the words quietly aloud, as though they were words in a prayer.

Dinh had been responsible for opening up her heart in other ways too. He made her laugh, made her feel like she would succeed, even though she felt herself floundering about on so many things. Love was something that inspired a sense of purpose in her, a sense of hope. She could understand how Jack could survive just on a kernel of this by working in such close proximity to Becky.

"But why you give up this job at the school?" She queried him. "Why now work in watch store?"

"I lost the janitor job five years ago," he answered. "That's around the time I met Tom. . . . He and Grace saved me in another way." He looked down and smoothed the material of his pants. "I guess I still have love in my life . . . just another kind. And when I miss Becky, sometimes I drive the twenty minutes it takes to get to Foxton and I park my car in the same spot, just as she's walking toward the entrance. And when the sunshine hits her from behind, when I see her talking with someone or laughing, it's enough. . . ." He bit his lip and straightened his shoulders. "Really, Anh, it's enough. I tell myself over and over again that it's all I need now."

CHAPTER 71

GRACE SAT NEXT TO ANH, LISTENING TO HER TRY TO REPEAT what she had learned in her conversation from Jack.

There was so much of the story that Grace still did not understand. But what she knew, not as the wife of a man who worked on watches and keeping time, but from her position as a woman who had experienced her own loss and pain, was that time did not always move in a linear path as her husband and father-in law believed. Instead, for some people, time radiated from a single epicenter, a point in time, where everything began and eventually returned. For Jack, the loss of Becky was that singular point around which everything revolved. Like the planets around the sun, his love radiated from that center. From the outside, it might appear that their love affair remained steeped in the memory of the past, not evolving the way a marriage might over time with the addition of children and the weight of age. But was it not something sacred to have one thing in your life that transcended time?

Grace's heart felt cleaved between the sadness of knowing that Jack had spent seven years living in such close proximity to Becky, never revealing himself to her in fear of rejection. The other part of her heart was awed by how deeply he felt toward her that he would have taken such steps just to be as close to her as he could.

There was not a single clock on earth that could capture the minutes or hours of a love like this. And it went back to that note Harry had taped to the wall of the workshop:

Sundials can measure the hours in the day and reservoirs every drop of water. But no one has ever invented an instrument to quantify love.

Becky does not recognize the two women who are waiting for her in the principal's office after classes have ended for the afternoon. But she finds herself silenced by their words as they explain why they've come.

She listens to the woman named Grace describe how her husband welcomed a wounded veteran into their lives, giving him a quiet and safe place to live above their family's store, as well as a chance for him to learn a trade. She begins to cry when this woman describes the disfiguring wound, the cloudy blind eye, the face that tries to smile each day despite the difficulty of scar tissue where he endured his countless skin grafts.

But it is the part of the story that the Asian woman details, about him working as a janitor at the school for two years just so he could be close to her, that makes Becky sob into her hands.

She now knows who had laid those single flowers on her desk all those years ago. The one daffodil. The solitary rose. She thought it might have been another teacher who had a crush on her, but she could never quite figure out who it could be.

Jack had been there all that time.

The two women scanned the young teacher's hand and observed no wedding band.

"We don't know what you want to do with all this information," Grace said gently. "But we thought it was important for you to know."

Becky nodded. "Thank you," she answered softly. "All these years, I wondered what had happened to Jack." She managed to get out the words, not sharing with the women that she now realized there was no friend with a facial injury when Jack called—that it was him all along.

She felt her stomach drop knowing she had caused him so much pain when he'd already suffered so much.

"I was never able to find out what happened to him, despite my efforts," she explained. "Even after that first call, I knew he was alive, but I couldn't ever locate him."

She shook her head. "And all this time, he was right here ... and then in the town next door." She reached into her purse for a tissue and dabbed her eyes. "I don't know how to feel about any of this," she confessed. "It's almost like you're raising a corpse from the dead."

Anh watched the young woman try to come to terms with the news she and Grace came to share.

"Miss," she said slowly and carefully. "This Jack. He is such a good man. He did many courageous thing. But he tell me after all this time, you're still sunshine at midnight for him." Anh smiled just saying the words. "I never heard words like this before, to have sun during darkness. But it so beautiful, right?"

Grace smiled. "It really is a beautiful thought."

"Thank you for telling me that," Becky answered, her eyes still wet with tears. She looked down at her watch. "I have to get going," she said, tapping her Timex with the thin leather band. "I'm so grateful for you telling me where Jack is."

EPILOGUE

She drives late at night through the tree-lined streets of Bellegrove, admiring the white houses with their picket fences and their neatly trimmed lawns. Windows glow with warm lanterns of light, yet she sees not a single soul, except for one lone woman sitting on a yellow porch swing outside her home. Wrapped in a pink robe, her face in her hands, she is weeping. It strikes her that even in this suburb of manicured perfection, human emotions bubble forth, that no one is immune to loneliness or grief.

Eventually, she finds the address she is looking for and parks her car on the street outside the watch store and gazes at the sign, The Golden Hours, written in old-fashioned green and bronze letters. The window is filled with clocks of various shapes and sizes. Some are tall grandfather clocks, and others are carved mantel ones displayed on wooden tables draped in red velvet cloth. A Closed sign dangles on the doorknob, but deep into the back, a single light shines like a white beacon. Becky sits and grips the steering wheel, pondering if she has enough courage to get out of her car.

On the radio, the oldies channel plays a song they used to listen to together ten years before. The melodies "I Wish It Would Rain" and "Slip Away" are like a scrapbook to another time, before the broken engagement with a man she once unsuccessfully tried to replace Jack with, or the many nights where she wondered if she might end up never finding someone who cared for her as much as her first love, Jack Grady, did when they were back in Allentown High School.

On her wrist, she still wears the watch he gave her on that afternoon when they packed up his childhood home. There was a time after that last phone call when she had stopped wearing it, banishing it to her bedroom drawer. But then, a couple of years back, she put it back on again because the gift's sentiment had been so beautifully earnest. There was something practical to her decision as well, for during her classes, she could glance down at the dial and tell the time quickly because the Roman numerals were so easy to read that she never had to let her students know she was looking at the time.

She wonders if the Jack in that workshop will ever be able to forgive her for the words she had so hastily said on the phone when he returned home injured and alone. How she hates to think that she hadn't realized the fictitious friend he spoke of had been him all along. The truth was, she realizes now, that she should have answered differently. That she should have shown an open heart to his request regardless, but she was young and only thinking of herself and her modest living situation. Since the two women had come to see her at school, she has spent hours replaying that last conversation with Jack in her mind, wishing she could turn back time and do it all over so differently.

She steps out of the car and moves quietly toward the store. She lifts her wrist and raps on the door.

She hears Jack's footsteps, the unlocking of the latch before she actually sees him. And when he stands there, his face half in darkness, and half in moonlight, she unclasps her watch and hands it to him.

"Hello. Can you help me with this?" she asks, lifting her eyes to take him in completely.

He is motionless as she steps closer; his face, a valley of red and pink flesh, is now revealed to her.

"It was given to me by a very special person some time ago." She clears her throat and wipes away her tears. "A boy named Jack. Who I've been waiting forever to welcome home."

AUTHOR'S NOTE AND ACKNOWLEDGMENTS

The Time Keepers is foremost a novel about time, memory, and healing. I have intentionally chosen to switch between past and present tense in different passages of the book in order to highlight how we mentally process pain, trauma, and love. Having interviewed several individuals who lived through the anguish of the Vietnam War, I was struck by how many of them continue to feel those painful moments in real time. It was my hope to capture this sensation—how memory can move between the past and the present—by having the language ebb and flow in the same way we experience life.

Researching this book would not have been possible without the help of so many patient and generous individuals who put their trust in me in order to tell this story. Thank you to Marie Wood, who spent hours detailing her harrowing escape from Vietnam in the early 1980s. In particular, Marie told me about a little boy who had been on her boat who partially inspired my character of Bảo. That boy tragically watched his parents drown, after his father's frantic last moments were forever fossilized in a bite mark he left on the boy's wrist. Marie also shared how, like Bảo, she was able to learn English by watching superhero cartoons on television. To my guide in Vietnam, Tran Thanh Chung, who helped truly bring Vietnam to life during my visit to that beautiful country in early 2020—fortunately, just before the pandemic made travel impossible. He shared so many memories and stories of the tumultuous years following the "American War" and the consequences his uncle's family had to go through as a result of having been on the losing side. Isabel Ngo, my professional sensitivity reader, I am tremendously grateful to you for not only your fastidious reading of my manuscript, but also your astute eye in making sure I'd written the Vietnamese passages with cultural and historical accuracy and sensitivity. It should be mentioned that because of the timeline of the novel and the period in which my characters were actually in Vietnam, the story is limited to showing the war solely from the lens of these characters' personal experiences. While I focused on the suffering of South Vietnamese families like Anh's, who were treated brutally by the new Communist regime, I am well aware that the devastation and pain from the war also affected countless lives in North Vietnam. Their stories, however, are beyond the scope of this particular novel.

Maureen Connolly, who is truly the inspiration for Grace, I am forever indebted both for your guidance about how the Sisters of Saint Joseph on Long Island brought you together with Vietnamese refugees the Archdiocese sponsored in the late 1970s and the empathy you brought in telling me your own immigrant story about coming here from Ireland. Jennifer and Jillian Keschner, it is because of both of you that this story first came into my heart. I am so grateful for all the time you spent with me, and particularly to Jillian, who served as my wonderful research assistant on the book.

But mostly to my friend Pete Mohan: this novel simply would not have been possible without you. Your dedication to the material in reliving your experiences of serving as a marine with Hotel Company, 2nd Battalion, 26th Marines, and all the hours you later spent reviewing the text to make sure literally every word and historical detail were correct were invaluable in helping me more fully understand what it was like to be a Vietnam veteran. Without your deep commitment to your fellow marines, I never would have come close to understanding what you went through both in Vietnam and upon your return home.

An additional acknowledgment must be given to your comrades in Hotel Company, Tom Lehner, Ralph Gomez, and "Doc" Michael Djiokonski. All of you shared such powerful and poignant memories of your fallen brother-in-arms, PFC Stanley Copes, and the novel is far richer because of your honesty and transparency with me. I will hold the memories of the men you mentioned, like Stanley and Chief Sandoval, in my heart forever.

I am also indebted to the help of the other Vietnam veterans for discussing their experiences with me: Dr. Nathan Blumberg, John Heil, Patrick Gillis, Bill Schwindt, Chip Sines, Michael Pergola, and Glenn Kesselman. Thank you also to the plastic surgeons of Cold Spring Harbor, who described various treatments for burn victims like my character Jack. And to Lori Ann Bibat, who also shared her knowledge working with burn victims. Thanks also to Tim Pillion, who relayed the story of his uncle, who never told his family that he had returned from Vietnam but quietly lived in the next town over from them, choosing to live in isolation because of the pain he had endured.

And a big thank you to my amazing agent, Sally Wofford-Girand, who has been my stalwart champion for over twenty years and has always fought to find each novel its perfect home; my brilliant and supportive editor, Claire Wachtel, who shares my love of the written word and fine-tuned this novel with a razor-sharp eye; and my team at Union Square & Co.: executive editor Barbara Berger, project editor Kristin Mandaglio, cover designer Jared Oriel, interior designer Kevin Ullrich, production manager Sandy Noman, publicity coordinator Nathan Siegel, and my additional publicist extraordinaire, Ann-Marie Nieves.

For my early readers, Aviva Cohen, Shaunna J. Edwards, Martin Fletcher, Charlotte and Stephen Gordon, Anh Ho, Nikki Koklanaris, Victoria Leventhal, Deborah and Jardine Libaire, Lynda Loigman, Shana Lory, Sofia Lundberg, Lindsay and Ellen Richman, Daniel Sanchez, Suzanne Sheran, Robbin Siegel, Michelle and Stephanie Sowa,

Christina Tudisco, and Allison Von Vange, I thank you all dearly; as well as Shannon Husselbeck, Charlene Edwards, and Carole Metzger, who introduced me to the veterans in their lives. This novel has reinforced my belief that stories unite us, that they help us heal and to move forward. I am grateful for every person who believed that this story needed to be told.

TOPICS AND QUESTIONS
FOR DISCUSSION

1. Grace and Tom Golden are not the typical married couple in Bellegrove. How do their backgrounds, with differing faiths, cultures, and citizenship, influence their own attitudes toward their new friendships with Jack, Anh, and Bảo? Discuss the themes of outsidership versus insidership within a small, insular community. What connects the characters of *The Time Keepers* to their neighbors, and what separates them?

2. Jack, Bảo, and Tom all have visible physical scars or injuries that make it impossible for them to hide their previous traumas, while the wounds from Anh's and Grace's painful pasts are not apparent to the naked eye. Do you think the visibility of scars affects certain characters' experiences, compared to those whose signs of trauma are internal or hidden?

3. The Golden Hours store is—in some ways—the beating heart of the novel. The store was originally founded by Tom's father, Harry Golden. How do Harry's wartime experiences, horological education, and meditations on time contribute to his own healing as well as to the healing of those who later work at the store? While Harry and Jack only meet once in the novel, what did you take away from their shared experience?

4. At the end of the novel, Grace describes time as "not always following a linear path," noting that "for some people, time radiated from a single epicenter, a point in time, where everything began and eventually returned." Discuss how Jack's enduring love for Becky defies the concept of time and how, despite its tribulations and setbacks, it remains a force that sustains him through his darkest moments.

5. Stanley Coates is one of the first people Jack meets when he arrives in Vietnam. He is described as being so innocent that he has never even drunk a bottle of beer. How is Stanley's purity and lack of worldly experience viewed by his fellow platoon members? How does his death inspire—and change—them?

6. Maternal love is an important theme that resonates throughout *The Time Keepers*. Discuss how loss is entwined in both Anh's and Grace's respective maternal experiences, and how they find healing, purpose, and connection as they navigate the challenges of motherhood. Consider the impact of the maternal role played by women who are not the actual mothers of the characters they are tending to. How does Anh transform as she takes on the role of Bảo's new guardian? How does Grace, already a mother to two girls, grow when Anh and Bảo come into her life?

7. Sensory memories have long been considered one of the most powerful tools that can connect us to our past. Jack finds himself traveling back in time when he hears a certain song on the radio, just as Bảo remembers his mother's love when he inhales the scent of mangoes. How do certain tastes, fragrances, or melodies tether us to our loved ones, both past and present? What are things in your own life that help you remember certain people and places?

8. In the author's note, Richman mentions how she shifted between past and present in the novel in order to evoke how we process memory. Discuss how the passages that were written in present tense in the novel affected how you felt as you walked in the footsteps of the characters Jack, Bảo, and Anh.

9. The author shifts perspectives on how the Vietnam War is experienced by the various characters—not only by a soldier and refugee, but also by family members who have lost a loved one. How did the shifting lenses of Jack, Bảo, Anh, and even Adele change your perspective on how you think about this devastating war?

10. Buddy and Clayton represent a dark force in the community of Bellegrove. Discuss how their home environments might have impacted their development. Do you feel Buddy and Clayton were equally evil, or was one of them more malevolent than the other?

11. *The Time Keepers* explores how unexpected friendships can often have the power to heal us. There are many different friendships that arise in this novel: Anh and Grace, Bảo and Molly, Jack and Tom, Jack and Bảo, and even Jack and Hendrix. How do these positive friendships help each character overcome their previous traumas? What connects each of these characters, and what do they learn from their newly formed bonds?